"Don't you know little girls shouldn't come to big boys' hotel rooms?"

Kell's question was a dare, but Anne Elise didn't back down. "I'm not a little girl. And you're not a boy, big or otherwise."

Kell's eyes darkened. "And therein lies a helluva lot of danger."

Anne Elise's eyes met his squarely. "Life is filled with danger."

She noticed the nearly full bottle of liquor. She took in the filled glass in his hand, the intense glint of some murky emotion in his eyes, the way his free hand was cocked at his hip, as if in defiance.

"Why are you drinking like there's no tomorrow?"

"I'm trying to put out a fire," Kell said huskily.

The admission sluiced over her like heated satin. Her voice low and breathless, she replied, "Sometimes, to put a fire out, you have to let it burn wild."

Dear Reader,

Once again, six Silhouette **Special Edition** authors present six dramatic new titles aimed at offering you moving, memorable romantic reading. Lindsay McKenna adds another piece to the puzzling, heart-tugging portrait of the noble Trayherns; Joan Hohl revives a classic couple; Linda Shaw weaves a thread of intrigue into a continental affair; Anne Lacey leads us into the "forest primeval"; and Nikki Benjamin probes one man's tortured conscience. Last, but certainly not least, award-winning Karen Keast blends agony and ecstasy into *A Tender Silence*.

What do their books have in common? Each presents men and women you can care about, root for, befriend for life. As Karen Keast puts it:

"What instantly comes to mind when someone mentions *Gone with the Wind*? Rhett and Scarlett. Characterization is the heart of any story; it's what makes you *care* what's happening. In *A Tender Silence*, I strived to portray two people struggling to survive in an imperfect world, a world that doesn't present convenient black-and-white choices. For a writer, the ultimate challenge is to create complex, unique, subtly structured individuals who are, at one and the same time, universally representative."

At Silhouette **Special Edition**, we believe that *people* are at the heart of every satisfying romantic novel, and we hope they find their way into *your* heart. Why not write and let us know?

Best wishes,

Leslie Kazanjian, Senior Editor
Silhouette Books
300 East 42nd Street
New York, N.Y. 10017

KAREN KEAST
A Tender Silence

Silhouette Special Edition

Published by Silhouette Books New York

America's Publisher of Contemporary Romance

For my special friend, Barb Vosbein,
who, along with me,
wondered what happened to Joe.

Also for M—for always and forever.

SILHOUETTE BOOKS
300 East 42nd St., New York, N.Y. 10017

ISBN: 0-373-09536-8

First Silhouette Books printing July 1989

Printed in the U.S.A.

Books by Karen Keast

Silhouette Special Edition

Once Burned . . . #435
One Lavender Evening #469
A Tender Silence #536

KAREN KEAST,

a nature-lover whose observant eye is evident in her writing, says that if she were a season she'd be autumn. The Louisiana resident admits to being a workaholic, a perfectionist and an introvert. Author of more than a dozen romances and two short stories, she likens writing a novel to running a marathon, noting that the same determination and endurance are necessary to overcome the seeming impossibility of the task and the many obstacles along the way. Still, happily married for over two decades, she is thrilled to have the opportunity to write about the "joy, pain, exhilaration and sheer mania of love" and to be able to bring two lovers together eternally through her writing.

Chapter One

The voice traveling the thousands of telephone miles between Bangkok, Thailand, and Dallas, Texas, was bourbon rough and cigarette scratchy. It also sounded as though it belonged to a man who hadn't spent a scant cent on scruples—even if they were sold a dime a dozen. This, however, Anne Elise Butler noted only marginally, for her concern was more on what the man was saying than on how he was saying it.

"Did you hear me, Mrs. Butler?" the gravelly voice asked.

"Yes," Anne Elise replied with a calm that belied the battering of her heart, "you said you had my husband's remains."

At the beginning of the conversation, when the call's purpose had become apparent, Anne Elise, her legs suddenly the consistency of pudding, had eased to the edge of the living-room sofa. It wasn't as though the call had come as a total shock; all MIA families had been warned over the years about just such black-market activities. In fact, as an active member of the National League of Families of American POWs and MIAs, she'd done her share of warning other grieving families, but she realized now that she'd never truly thought such a call would come to her. To someone else, maybe. But not to her.

She'd also realized, and with more than mild dismay, that her reaction was not what she'd thought it would be. She'd discovered that her cool, I-can-handle-the-world attitude could, indeed, be shaken. Offsetting the dismay, however, was the comforting realization that the pragmatic survivor in her was stepping forward, that undaunted individual who had first appeared seventeen years before when she'd been informed that First Lieutenant James Samuel Butler was missing in action in Vietnam and, because of that, she'd have to rear their baby daughter alone. As always, the survivor was cloaked in strength, bolstered, at the moment, by her skepticism. Even though she wanted desperately to believe it, she simply did not buy that this man, this slime who'd crawled out of some Bangkok gutter, could deliver the grim goods he was offering.

"My advice to you, Mr.—" She stared down at the name—Isaac Forbes—which she'd automatically recorded as a result of spending so much time on the telephone, either serving as the secretary of the League of Families or running her own realty company. "My advice to you, Mr. Forbes," she repeated evenly, "is to get in touch with the United States government if you have any knowledge as to the whereabouts of any MIA remains."

Isaac Forbes, who'd earlier identified himself as an American businessman working in Bangkok, laughed sharply. "Do you have any idea of the red tape—"

"Yes," Anne Elise interrupted, "but I also know, if you have a legitimate claim—" *which he didn't,* her inner voice reminded her "—you need to go through proper channels."

"Do you hear what I'm saying? I've got your husband's body. I'm willing to do a good deed here and return it to you without you having to wade up to your ankles in red-tape crap. I'm willing to do it *now.* Not some six months to a year from now. That's assuming the governments agree to do something besides disagree."

A vision of a casket draped in the bold stars and stripes of an American flag flashed in her mind's eye. She watched as the casket was nobly lowered into the ground, the way she'd dreamed countless times before, then felt the comforting cloth of the flag as some compassionate soldier pressed it into her hand. That part of her that still wanted to believe said, *Go ahead. What could it hurt to ask the question that would prove Isaac Forbes's honest intentions?*

"How much, Mr. Forbes? How much for this 'good deed' of yours?" *Please, please,* she prayed, *don't want money!*

"*I* don't want anything, Mrs. Butler..."

...*but,* she thought, her fragile hopes crashing at her feet and silently spilling across the thick cream carpet that subtly tied together the poppy-red and dark forest-green decor.

"...but you have to understand the people I'm forced to deal with are—well, let's just say they're not motivated by altruism."

Somewhere in the back of her mind, Anne Elise was surprised that this man, obviously shadier than an oak tree and coarser than its bark, even knew a word like *altruism.* The fleeting thought was swallowed up, however, by a soul-deep fatigue.

"How much, Mr. Forbes?"

"We're talking a lot of palms, Vietnamese and Thai, that'll have to be crossed—"

"How much?"

"These people could get their asses shot into the middle of next week if their governments—"

"How much, Mr. Forbes?" she insisted, not bothering to point out that those who chose to sell on the black market always ran counter to law and authority and, thereby, left themselves wide open to having "their asses shot into the middle of next week."

"Fifty thousand."

Fifty thousand. Well, at least the man wasn't a two-bit crook, Anne Elise thought, sighing and momentarily shutting her eyes. She shoved her hand, the one wearing a simple silver MIA bracelet, through fashionably tousled, shoulder-touching hair that was a rich chestnut shade of auburn. She wondered, disgustedly, if Isaac Forbes had pulled the amount out of thin air as the standard fee he would have charged any MIA family, or if he'd done his homework and knew that, while she, on a realtor's commissions supplemented with meager government assistance, couldn't afford the money, her parents could. Either way, she felt sick to her stomach at such cruel exploitation.

"As I said, if you have any information regarding my husband's remains, you should contact the government."

A silence followed, as though Isaac Forbes was plotting a new strategy. Anne Elise thought his attitude a little chilling, considering she had so adamantly refused him. Finally, he said, with the confidence of a man holding all the aces, "You think about it, Mrs. Butler. You think about it real good. And, if you change your mind, you can reach me at . . ."

He proceeded, amid long-distance static, to give her a number. Even as she was writing it down, she wondered why. She wouldn't call it—of that she was certain. And yet, she felt compelled to record it. As if it were somehow her duty.

Duty. She knew all about duty. It was what her husband had done when he'd given his life for his country. It was what she'd done by summoning, from somewhere deep inside her, the courage to go on with hers. As the wife of an MIA, it had been her duty to behave as bravely as her husband had.

"Don't take too long, Mrs. Butler," Isaac Forbes warned suddenly. "The offer won't be available forever."

Something in the tone of his voice not only rankled, but also caused another shiver of unease to slither down her spine. Anne Elise chose to focus on its rankling factor. She had just opened her mouth to inform the man that she didn't take well to intimidation when the phone crackled, then crackled again. It took her a moment to realize the line had gone dead. Her first reaction was one of anger. How dare he hang up on her! How dare he call her in the first place! But, as always, she corralled the dark, blistering emotion. Anger was nonproductive. It changed nothing. She'd been smart enough to figure that out in the first stages of coping with her husband's disappearance. Pragmatically speaking, anger took energy, energy she needed to direct toward surviving and seeing that their daughter survived.

On a long sigh, Anne Elise replaced the phone. Defying her control, however, the hand that replaced the instrument shook. She fitted one trembling hand into the other and did what she'd grown expert at doing: she just held on to herself.

"You're trembling," she heard the masculine voice say as clearly as she'd heard it nearly twenty years ago. The mem-

ory warmed her as much as the butter-colored March sun
peeking through the chintz draperies of the North Dallas
condo she and her daughter, Brooke, called home.

"You're trembling, too," she remembered telling the
blond-haired, blue-eyed man who was about to become her
husband.

They'd been standing in the elegant, manicured garden of
her parents' home right there in Dallas, in the old-money
section of the city known as Highland Park. The home—the
mansion, Jim Butler called it—had belonged to her mother's parents, both of whom had died before Anne Elise's
birth. Anne Elise had been aware, even painfully so, that her
marrying James Samuel Butler that summer afternoon was
not what her parents had wished for her. Not that it had
anything to do with James Samuel Butler. Even though he
wasn't from their social stratum, he was nonetheless hugely
liked by everyone. In fact, no one had ever disliked the
sandy-haired quarterback who'd led Texas A & M to the
winner's circle three years in a row. That he was military
oriented was a fact in his favor, at least as far as Anne Elise's
father, then a major in the United States Army, was concerned. His military aspirations even won him points with
her mother. Hadn't Sugar Terris defied her parents to marry
a man in uniform?

No, the only problem that fair summer day was that
James Samuel Butler had just graduated from college, while
the ink on Anne Elise's high-school diploma wasn't even
completely dry. Sugar Terris, by consensus the nicest, most
genteel Southern woman God ever breathed breath into,
would have been far happier if her daughter had been en-
rolling in college rather than starting a new life as the wife
of a recently commissioned second lieutenant, an officer
who was bound to end up in troubled Vietnam.

But that hot summer day, only halcyon thoughts had reigned, ruling supreme over lovers who quaked with the sweetest of anticipation. Even now, Anne Elise could see the smile curving Jim Butler's lips.

"Come here," he'd whispered, *"and we'll tremble together."*

And that, Anne Elise thought, staring down at her still-shaking hands, was the priceless thing that death had stolen from her—the sharing, the intimate camaraderie that she'd never found with anyone else.

"We're sorry to inform you, Mrs. Butler," the somber chaplain had said, *"that your husband is missing in action."*

That day, almost two years after their wedding, she'd trembled again, but this time there'd been no one to share it with, no sandy-haired, blue-eyed husband to pull her into his arms and make the world—the wicked, weary world—go away. Her parents had tried to console her, but their touches, their hugs, well-meaning as they were, weren't the same. Strangely, and maybe not so strangely, the only one who'd afforded her any solace was a baby girl. Only months old, with hair the blond of her father's, with eyes the same sky blue as his, the infant had curled her tiny fist around her mother's finger and, as if she understood they were each now alone save for the other, had hung on tightly. Oftentimes, until both, the older with eyes red and swollen, fell asleep.

A thousand times in the thousands of days that followed, Anne Elise had almost wished that her husband had been reported killed in action, rather than missing in action. Though she now accepted that he was dead, in the beginning she had held out hope. The holding out of hope in a hopeless situation had been savagely cruel, far more hurtful than death itself. Even now, there was an open-endedness to his death that bore heavily on her heart. It was like sitting through every act of a play except the last one. You could guess how the play ended, but you could never really know for sure. Nor could you know all the details that led to the ending—details that, good or bad, happy or sad, allowed you to accept what the final curtain rang down on.

It was this feeling of unfinished business that had kept her chained to memories and faded dreams. It was this unfinished business that had paved the streets of her lonely life. In recent years, her pragmatism again at the helm, she had tried to resume dating but soon realized that she herself sabotaged the dates by subtly demonstrating that friendship was all she really sought. There had been a few kisses from the bravest and most determined of the lot, one date had even pushed for more, but the encounters had left her feeling awkward and guilty and out of touch with modern mores. Had it not been for her parents and her friends, she feared she would spend all her Saturday nights alone and be the happier for it.

This same lack of closure had begun to eat at their daughter. Brooke, months shy of eighteen and graduation, had begun to ask questions about the father she'd never known, about the far-off and increasingly forgotten war that had claimed his life, as though she sensed a part of her was lost. Anne Elise understood perfectly. She'd lived with the same feeling for years. Something to bury would help them both, for with it, the past could likewise be buried. At least there was the hope it could.

Anne Elise stared down at the paper in her unsteady hands. She wanted—no, needed—to believe that Isaac Forbes could end her purgatory, but, in her heart of hearts, she knew he offered nothing more than false hope. And she'd already lived through too much of that. That hell she would not return to. Nor would she allow Brooke to walk on its miserably hot shores.

No, she'd just warn her fellow organization members that the black market had reared its ugly head and then she'd forget that people like Isaac Forbes even existed. She'd—

"What are you doing in here?"

Anne Elise glanced up sharply... and into wide, summer-blue eyes. The soon-to-be-eighteen-year-old who stood before her wore turquoise pants and an oversize apricot shirt, with matching apricot socks and white sneakers. To anyone else, she simply would have looked like a modern young woman, but to Anne Elise, she was not only her daughter, but also her best friend.

"I, uh, I just finished with a phone call," Anne Elise answered, edging the piece of paper into the folds of her khaki shirt.

"Who was it?"

"Just business." Anne Elise stood and unobtrusively pocketed the paper. Her hand was still shaking, but she willfully ignored it and spread her arm around her daughter's shoulders, which was a feat getting harder and harder to do, since Brooke, tall like her father, already eclipsed Anne Elise's five feet five inches by a full inch and a half. "You ready to go shopping?"

"Yeah. Oh, Shelley called and wants me to spend the night. She and Eric are going to the same movie David and I are, so we're gonna go together. Is that okay? I mean, about spending the night?"

"Sure," Anne Elise replied, thinking that, thankfully, none of her own friends had lined her up that night with Mr. Right. It would be a quiet Saturday, the kind that, curiously, she both liked and disliked. For a reason she couldn't explain, the silence was seeming louder these days. Or, rather, these nights.

"I want to go by Neiman-Marcus—"

Anne Elise groaned.

"No, honestly, Mom, the shoes *are* on sale—"

"Sure, and the Pope's Jewish."

Brooke, in the tradition of all her age, ignored the continuation of a subject as mundane as money. "And I want to get Nana a birthday present, and what do you think?" she asked, dragging a swath of her long hair over her shoulder, as if to assess its length. "Do I need to get my hair trimmed?"

They had arrived in the poppy-red kitchen, which sparkled with white appliances and copper pans. Dhurrie rugs, in vivid primary colors, splattered the beige flagstone floor, while cacti in large clay pots sought the sun.

The young woman proceeded to answer her own question. "I think an inch. No more than two. What do you th— Mom? Are you all right?"

Anne Elise took in her daughter's flaxen tumble of hair, the clear bright blue of her eyes, the ivory complexion made golden by the hot Texas sun, the lips that, when they smiled, smiled like another pair of lips, which was to say, they smiled all the way from the heart. Slowly, wistfully, Anne Elise's mouth curved upward.

"It's just that sometimes I'm startled by how very much you look like your father."

The comment softened the features of the young girl's face. Her hand fell away from the blond waves of her hair. "Do you think he would have liked that? I mean, that I look like him?"

"Yes. He would have liked that very much."

"You, uh, you don't think he would rather I'd been a boy, do you?"

Anne Elise shook her head. "No way. He was as proud as a peacock of his baby girl. He thought you were just about the prettiest thing he'd ever seen."

Neither woman, possibly because it was too hurtful a subject, brought up the fact that Lieutenant James Samuel Butler had never actually seen his daughter, except in a photograph. He'd never touched her, never held her, never cradled her small head in the palm of his large hand.

Brooke grinned suddenly. "Was I really a pretty baby?"

Anne Elise smiled. "You were cute as a bug. With two adorable chins."

"I was fat?"

"As a butterball."

Brooke groaned with mirth. Abruptly, however, she sobered. "You know what's the hardest part?"

Anne Elise didn't have to ask, Of what? She knew Brooke was speaking of her father's death. "What, honey?"

"There's nowhere to put flowers," the young girl-woman answered.

"No," Anne Elise replied gently, sorrowfully, but with her usual candor, "there's nowhere to put flowers."

There might have been, Anne Elise added silently, if Isaac Forbes's offer had been legitimate. But it wasn't. And the fact that it wasn't, coupled with the fact that Forbes had had the brass to call at all, sent a steamy-hot emotion purling over her. She might have called it anger if she ever indulged in that dark emotion.

But she didn't.

Because she'd learned long ago that anger was nonproductive.

She kept Isaac Forbes's phone number.

Had she asked herself why, she would have been stumped for an answer. Maybe deep in her gut she knew this and so avoided posing the question. Whatever, she placed the scrap of paper, on which was written the number, in her jewelry box, right next to the gold wedding band she'd years before stopped wearing, the wedding band that was a match to another somewhere in the world. She then tried to forget the whole incident. She was even making inroads in that direction when the package arrived at her office three days later.

The overnight express courier, tall and lanky and Texas laid-back, was the same man who appeared on her doorstep from time to time when something urgent, either realty business or MIA business, had to be dealt with quickly.

"Afternoon, Ms. Butler," he said, sauntering in on the heels of his cowboy boots and presenting her with a clipboard. "If you'd just sign right here, please, ma'am."

Anne Elise, a smile at her lips, a pen already in her hand, began to scrawl her name across the indicated line.

"This little baby's from Bangkok, Thai-land," the courier said, making the last word sound like two in his attempt to make friendly chitchat.

At the mention of Bangkok, Anne Elise's hand, and heart, went still. "Bangkok?"

"Yes, ma'am. You're not trying to sell houses there, too, are you?" he teased.

Anne Elise didn't answer. She just stared at the package . . . as though it had flown in under its own power.

If the messenger noticed Anne Elise's lack of response or the curious way she simply sat with her gaze glued to what he'd just delivered, he didn't show it. He simply tore her copy from the invoice and, handing it to her, started for the door with, "You have a nice day now, you hear?"

She heard nothing except the pounding of her heart, for intuitively she knew the package had something to do with the phone call she'd received. It was a hunch corroborated seconds later when she poured the contents of the package into her palm.

A dog tag.

No note, just a dog tag bearing her husband's name and serial number, a number indelibly etched in her heart and soul.

Hungrily, she ran her fingers over the dented metal, trying to absorb the characters, the numbers, into her fingertips. Her heart raced wildly, and she felt need well up inside her— the need to believe that Isaac Forbes did, indeed, have her husband's remains. Even as the need threatened to consume her, however, her well-honed realism forced her to make two admissions. The tag might be nothing more than a clever fake, and, even if it had been her husband's, it in no way proved that the remains she would be buying were his. Once more, she embraced caution, for it was the only sensible thing to embrace, although that night, when the sensible thing would have been to close her eyes and go to sleep, she couldn't. Instead, she remained wide awake, stroking the dog tag as though it were a lost lover.

It was through tired eyes that she saw the courier arrive the following day, with yet another quip about another baby from Thai-land. This time the package contained a worn photograph of an infant. Instantly, Anne Elise recognized it as a picture of her daughter—double chin and all. It was the first photograph she'd sent her husband of their child. Again, there was no note. Again, she forced herself to admit that the photograph proved nothing regarding the authenticity of the remains. Again, she did not sleep.

The third arrival, which came early the next morning, a cloudy Friday, shook her in a way the other two had not. Contained within the manila envelope was a letter. Frayed and tearing where it had been creased for seventeen years, the letter was one she'd written to Jim—when their love was new and tender, when their plans for the future were sadly naive, when all she feared had not yet become unalterable fact in a world of harsh reality.

This time, Isaac Forbes had attached a note, indicating that the Vietnamese who'd buried her husband had removed the personal effects from the body before interment. This letter, the photograph of the child, and the dog tag had been among those effects. That night, as thunder rolled and rain drove hard against her bedroom window, Anne Elise read and reread the letter until it was a miracle there was anything left to read. At a quarter to a dreary three o'clock, she decided that she despised Isaac Forbes for so expertly, so unforgivably, playing on her emotions. She also decided, as she reached for his telephone number, that he at last had her attention.

The next afternoon, Anne Elise sat quietly in the study of her parents' home watching her father, who was ensconced behind a huge mahogany desk, meticulously peruse the contents of the three packages that had been delivered that week. As always, General Adam Terris would neither say nor do anything to indicate his feelings until he was ready to make them known. As always, his wife, Sugar, would remain by his side and, in the tradition of the older Southern wife, let her husband take the lead. Should his feelings be other than her own, should a decision other than the one she wanted be made, she, again in the tradition of the older Southern wife, would gently manipulate, lovingly coerce him until he changed his opinion—often without his ever realizing her interference.

Then again, Adam Terris, a man who'd led men into battle, a man who, with his militarily intimidating demeanor and gruff voice, had stricken terror into the hearts of those who'd served under his command, would readily admit that he was a pushover where his wife was concerned. One look from her soft green eyes—eyes a paler green than her daughter's, but no less dramatic—and the giant of a warrior was a slave to her will. Because of the power she knew she wielded, Sugar Terris was careful never to abuse it.

The truth was—and it was a truth Anne Elise had felt from the moment she was born—her parents were deeply in love and wholly devoted to each other. If the mansion, with its high, lofty ceilings, its enormously large rooms, its servant-crafted orderliness, had the potential for coldness, that coldness was thawed by the warm love dwelling within.

Anne Elise had heard a million times how the West Point cadet, from a blue-collar background, had swept the society deb off her feet, how she had insisted on marrying him, how her parents had objected, how, in the end, they had given in. Her mother, Anne Elise knew, had never regretted marrying her father. The only thing she regretted was that her parents hadn't lived long enough to know their granddaughter, and that they hadn't lived to see Adam Terris distinguish himself so thoroughly. In the forty years of their marriage, he'd risen to the prestigious rank of general. Now retired from the military, he was getting ready to embark on a political career that would undoubtedly be just as distinguished. Rumor had it—substantial rumor—that the secretary of state would soon be appointing General Adam Terris to the position of undersecretary for political affairs, a job, which among other things, would have him involved in the making of foreign policy. All three women in his life, his wife, his daughter, and his granddaughter, beamed with pride.

Pride.

Anne Elise had been proud of her husband, too. And, in many ways, their romance had paralleled that of her parents. Except for one very important fact. They wouldn't be growing old together.

Restless, Anne Elise pulled from the plush tan leather chair and crossed to stand before the bank of windows. She could feel her mother's loving eyes caressing her back, just as she couldn't feel her father's. He would allow nothing to distract him.

The rain had ceased that morning, leaving the world, and principally the immaculately kept garden that stretched out before her, a greener place. The leaves of the oaks and elms looked newly baptized in the faith of spring, while the yellow daffodils and royal-purple tulips looked as if they'd just boldly skinny-dipped in a cool, refreshing pond.

All in all, the world looked free of all concerns.

Anne Elise knew, however, that it was not.

"You know, of course—" Anne Elise turned at her father's voice "—that all of this proves nothing. So it is Jim's dog tag, so it is a photo of Brooke, so it is a letter you'd written. It may or may not be Jim's bones."

Sugar Terris, her short auburn hair, with its single streak of gray right in front, framing her oval face, sighed. "Adam, dear, couldn't you have chosen a more delicate word?"

"Sure," the broad-shouldered, beefy, but firm-muscled, former soldier said, "but what would have been the point? Annie E. knows what happens to a body after seventeen years."

Sugar sighed again, an action that heaved the pearl choker at her throat. "And you wonder where the child gets her blunt approach to life."

"Hell, no, I never wondered! I knew from the start."

"I'm aware, sir, that this—" Anne Elise motioned toward the desk "—doesn't make an identification."

"Hell, baby," the General boomed, "even the remains that were returned legitimately couldn't be positively identified half the time!"

"I know," Anne Elise answered, remembering well the protest the National League of Families of American POWs and MIAs had lodged because of that very issue.

Several years before, under scrutinized monitoring, and after fragile negotiations with the Communist government of Vietnam, the remains of some Americans had been returned to the United States. Even under those supervised conditions, however, it was impossible, in many cases, to prove beyond a doubt that the remains were those of the men they were purported to be. Families who'd hoped to finally resolve their loved ones' deaths were, naturally, upset. It was about this time that the black market was first heard from.

"I know, also," Anne Elise added, "that, at least twice, league members have dealt with the black market and have, again at least as far as they were concerned, bought the remains of their loved ones. I know of more times, however, that positive identification re black market goods was impossible. The whole thing, approached either legitimately or illegitimately, seems to be a crapshoot."

"People deal with the black market even knowing these odds? Even after the league advised against it?" Sugar asked incredulously.

"People who are desperate do," her daughter replied.

"And are you desperate, Annie E.?" General Terris asked. His gruff voice had softened, the way it had over the years when it had read bedtime stories and when he had tended to hurt knees and hurt feelings.

Anne Elise considered before answering as honestly as she could. "I don't know, sir. I know I want an ending other than the one I have. I also want something for Brooke's sake, something therapeutic and cleansing. I want something—" Suddenly she remembered her daughter's words from the week before. "I want somewhere for her to lay flowers."

"Then you're willing to risk the odds?" her father asked.

"I'm not sure I would be solely on what you have before you." At General Terris's puzzled frown, she explained, "Forbes now says he has irrefutable proof that the remains are Jim's. He says he has a jawbone with half a dozen teeth."

"Why in hell didn't he tell you that up front?"

"I figure two possibilities. One, he's lying about the jawbone and teeth and produced them only when he sensed I was still holding back. Or, two, the man is a master at psychological manipulation and saved the best for last, knowing I couldn't refuse it after he'd laid the groundwork with that." She motioned toward the desk.

"The son of a bitch!" General Terris growled.

"A son of a bitch he may be, a son of a bitch he probably is, but he may be a son of a bitch with my husband's remains," Anne Elise pointed out pragmatically.

"And, of course," her father continued, "he won't ship the bones without the fifty thousand—"

"And I won't ship the fifty thousand without looking at the bones," Anne Elise finished.

"Then you're going?" the man asked.

"Yes, sir," she said, adding, "but I've already decided that if I can't make a positive ID, I'll back away."

Adam Terris studied his daughter with gray eyes as bold as his character. "And what if I ordered you not to go?

What if I told you the whole thing was just too damned risky and that I didn't like the feel of it?''

A small smile brushed Anne Elise's lips. "The way you ordered me not to marry him?''

Though he fought to hide it, the General's mouth twitched. "Yeah, something like that.''

"Then I'd do what I did then. I'd disobey your order.''

"That's the problem with the women in this family. They have no respect for male authority.''

Anne Elise's smile, slight though it had been, disappeared entirely. "This is something I have to do, Daddy. For me. For Brooke. Even for Jim. How would you feel not knowing where Mother was buried? Or even if she was?''

Even the thought sent a shaft of pain coursing through the brave soldier. Anne Elise saw it deep in his eyes.

"If it's the money—'' she began.

"It isn't the damned money!'' General Terris bellowed, ramming his hand through hair that was neither brown nor gray.

"It isn't the money, darling,'' Sugar said in concert with her husband, quickly rising and taking her daughter's hand. "We'd pay four times that. Part of the money is yours, anyway. And all of it will be when your father and I—''

"Put it in a trust for Brooke,'' Anne Elise said as she had a thousand times. Equally, a thousand times she'd explained that she had her job, a realty business, and that she, always blessed or cursed, depending on one's point of view, with simple tastes, didn't need money. Or, at least, hadn't needed it until the whopping sum of fifty thousand had been mentioned.

"It's not the damned money!'' General Terris said again and the way he said it settled the monetary matter. "You are not, however, going to Bangkok alone. I mean it, Anne Elise, or I will refuse you the money. And I'm not just saying it. Try me on this issue, and you'll see how serious I am."

Just how adamant he was prepared to be on the subject, Anne Elise didn't know, but it really wasn't an issue of import, since she herself didn't want to go alone. She could still remember Isaac Forbes's unsettling voice. Call it cowardice, call it caution, she didn't want to have to deal with the man by herself.

"Your father's right, darling."

"That's fine with me," Anne Elise said, her eyes on her father. "I thought you—"

General Terris shook his head. "I can't, baby. Not with this appointment so near. I need to keep a low profile, especially if I'm appointed. My involvement might be construed as government involvement. Besides, what you need to fight a son of a bitch is another son of a bitch."

"Adam," Sugar remonstrated gently.

But to no avail, for the general added, as he flipped the Rolodex on his desk, "Yes, sir, what you need is a bona fide, goddamned son of a bitch."

The Rolodex swirled, then, like one of the general's obedient soldiers, came to an abrupt halt. A card stepped crisply forward. It read: Captain Edward Keller Chaisson.

End of discussion.

Forget the twenty-five thousand dollars the general had offered him for his time and trouble.

Because it was obvious that her father thought Kell Chaisson had both the experience and personality for the mission that lay ahead, Anne Elise had asked for the man's address. She would force him to tell her no to her face. She still wondered if she'd seen a breach in her father's usual military-closed expression when she'd asked for the address. Had it been admiration for her spunk, a spunk she undoubtedly got from him? Or was he, possibly, amused that Captain Chaisson was finally going to get a taste of his own stubbornness?

She harbored no illusions, though. He'd probably say no right to her face. Rumor—she'd drained the grapevine raisin dry—said that he wasn't easily dissuaded from his opinions. Rumor also said a wide array of other interesting, actually quite fascinating, things about him. Like he was the man the government called in when the going got tough and dirty because he could get tough and dirty—but that he was quick and discreet about it. Apparently, he not only understood all the corner-dark complexities of violence, but also worshiped at its profane altar with the attention of a true devotee.

Because of their secret classification in many cases, her father had been vague about the services Kell Chaisson, now retired from the military but on retainer as a troubleshooter, provided. Anne Elise had learned, however, that, among his past jobs, he'd rescued hostages in the Middle East, picked up Soviet agents seeking to defect, laid the groundwork for a coup in a Latin American country and set up a training program for a friendly African state. Her father had also shared that Chaisson had served more tours of duty in Vietnam than three men put together, all in the

Army Special Forces, and that he'd been a POW for four and half months, after which time he'd escaped, taking two buddies with him, both of whom he'd literally carried across the border into Laos. For that, and apparently a slew of other courageous acts, he'd received more medals than a chest could comfortably hold. Even if it was a wide chest, which it purportedly was, according to the feminine gossip.

For the lace-and-frills rumors—they were always the more interesting kind—Anne Elise had gone to Jodi Ward, who had been her father's secretary when he was in the military. She had followed him into the private sector and was preparing to assist him with his political career. Jodi, in her mid-forties, divorced and with hormones in perpetual overdrive, had sighed at the mention of Kell Chaisson's name.

"What does that mean?" Anne Elise asked of the breathless sound.

"Let me just put it this way; Kell Chaisson is the kind of man every woman would love to spend one night with. Notice I said one night because only the very brave could stand more than that. He's too blatantly sensual, too intense, too... I don't know, the man always seems to be walking on some thin edge that's downright sexy, but scary, too...if you know what I mean."

"You think anything in pants is sexy," Anne Elise pointed out, her lips curling into a grin that the phone lines translated every nuance of.

"Yeah, well, laugh if you want to, but it wasn't only me. When he came into the office, every typewriter stopped and when he walked out, there was a mad dash for the water cooler and/or the rest room...if you know what I mean," she tacked on wickedly.

"I think I get the picture," Anne Elise said, actually blushing at the suggestive comment. For a modern woman, she felt she was shockingly out of touch with society's sexual openness.

"There's this junkyard-dog mean streak a mile wide in him if he's crossed. And he seems to go out of his way to get crossed. He's started brawls over everything from A to Z and back again. He's also lethal. I heard he once took down five KGB men, alone I might add, when he caught them bugging the American embassy in Washington."

"When you say 'he took them down'—"

"No, he didn't kill them, but he came close. Almost caused an international incident. The president, as in of the United States, wrote a memo suggesting that we, quote, keep Chaisson on a leash for a while, unquote. I saw the memo myself. Then there was the bar in the Philippines that he knocked one whole wall out of with about twelve bodies thrown one at a time against it. Rumor said that what started that was an improper comment made to one of the ladies of the evening. Chaisson obviously didn't like the men's disrespectful attitudes."

"Sounds gallant of Chaisson."

"Some thought it sounded as if he were looking for a reason to let off a little steam. Again. Did time in a Philippine jail for that one. Then there was the time he and half of Moammar Gadhafi's troops had this little misunderstanding—"

"My God, Jodi, you make him sound superhuman!" And exactly like what she needed. For the mission, of course.

"Let's just say, the man be bad. I've also heard he's arrogant, inconsiderate, self-centered—you know, all those things we women don't seem able to resist in a man." On the heels of that remark, Jodi Ward quickly added, "Actually it's the rumors about his humanness that are the most intriguing."

"Like what?" Anne Elise asked, captivated by the character of Kell Chaisson despite herself.

"Well...mind you, I don't know how much truth there is to any of this—"

"Just spill it."

"Well, you know that he was a POW?"

"Uh-huh."

"By the way, he was supposed to have endured all kinds of atrocities while in captivity. Anyway, when he came home, he was assigned to work with families of POWs. Well, rumor says that he got a little too involved with one of them."

"What does that mean?"

"That he fell in love with one of the wives...and she with him...but that both knew from the beginning that it couldn't work out because the husband, whom she loved, too, was coming back...and did come back...which left Kell Chaisson more than out in left field." Jodi Ward sighed. "Isn't that the most deliciously tragic story? If, of course, it's true."

Anne Elise didn't answer. She was too busy thinking that if it was true, she and this Kell Chaisson at least had one thing in common. Life hadn't been overly kind to either one of them.

"It is a documented fact," the woman went on, "that he quit the service shortly after the POWs returned home in '73—which must have relieved the government considerably, because it looks real tacky to court-martial a hero."

"Court-martial?"

"Yeah. He was facing a court-martial for punching out his commanding officer."

"Why? I mean, why did he punch him out?"

"That's where the grapevine gets real vague. No one seems to know why. Just that Chaisson decked him. Broke the man's jaw and his nose. Although he apparently never turned his back on a good fight, Chaisson's brawling seemed to escalate about this point in his life. Anyway, he shattered the man's jaw and nose and stole off into the Arkansas hills. He comes out only to do an occasional hush-hush job for the government." Jodi took a deep breath, as if inordinately pleased with her lecture. "So there you have the life and times of one Captain Chaisson, who might have been a bird colonel by now if he hadn't been fist-happy, but who is definitely the object of more than one maiden's naughty dream. Have I been of any help?"

"Yeah," Anne Elise replied, "you've told me that I'm going to see an always volatile, sometimes violent individual." And an SOB, she added silently.

"That pretty well covers it," Jodi had replied, adding one last, "That, and he's an irresistible hunk."

Anne Elise had laughed at the woman's single-mindedness...but she wasn't laughing now. The butterflies in her stomach were too real and were fluttering too wildly. On a deep sigh, she told them to shush up. Volatile or no, violent or no, she was going to confront Kell Chaisson because she needed him to accompany her to Bangkok. And as for his being an irresistible hunk...

Well, nothing could have been more irrelevant.

About forty miles outside Little Rock, Anne Elise found the object of her search. The house, at the end of a dirt trail so thin it discouraged passage, was constructed of weathered cedar and fieldstone. Modest in design, unpretentious in cost, it sat in the forested and hilly environment in such a way that it seemed a natural part of it. Indeed, one had to look closely to see it at all. It reminded Anne Elise of camouflage. As a soldier, Kell Chaisson would know all about camouflage, the purpose of which was to hide, to conceal, to disguise. Was that what the captain had done? Had he hidden himself away from the world?

It was none of her business if he had or why, Anne Elise told herself as she pushed open the car door. A bough of a lacy-leafed tree brushed against her thigh, which was clad in ivory slacks, while a fresh, forest-fragrant breeze tugged at the silk of her ivory blouse. She shivered at the chilly bite in the breeze, a bite that was all but gone from a Dallas March, but a bite very much alive several hundred miles north, when the sun was contemplating setting.

She shut the door, a sound loud in the magnificent silence that dwelled on the hillside. Her footsteps, cushioned by pine needles that had dropped over a succession of autumns, were eerily soundless. A bird, perched on a nearby branch, cocked its head as if to ask who this stranger might be.

A stranger with a mission, Anne Elise silently answered back as she inhaled the subtle scent of wood smoke wafting on the clear air.

A gently angled series of brown-and-gray stone steps led to a narrow deck of gray, roughened cedar that evidently circled the house.

Anne Elise drew her gaze back to the front door and rang the bell. She heard the muted chimes, and willed her nerves to settle down. What was the worst that could happen? He'd turn her down, right? Which he'd already done and she'd survived. So there was no need to throw a gala ball for the butterflies dancing in her stomach. At the silence the summons received, she rang the bell again, this time running her sweaty hands into the pockets of her pants. What if he was rude? What if he punched her out? What if— What if he wasn't at home? she added with a frown. No, he had to be at home. She could smell the smoke from his fire.

Instinct, coupled with desperation—she had to see the man!—drew her along the circular walkway. She quickly saw that the deck opened out into a patio, which seemed to hang suspended over a tree-studded valley. With the sun setting in pastel shades, with spring greening the world, with the mountains rising misty in the purple-and-blue distance, the view was awesome.

Awesome. The word lingered and reshaped itself into the definition of the man before her. Barefoot, eyes closed, wearing only the pants of a black sweat suit, Kell Chaisson sat folded into the lotus position associated with meditative yoga. His hands, the palms turned outward, his index fingers curled against his thumbs, rested motionlessly at his knees. His hair, coffee colored and in need of cutting, swayed slightly in the frisky breeze. A thick thatch of the same brown hair, trimmed, framed his upper lip, while a shadow of a beard, indicating he hadn't shaved all day, and maybe then some, gave him a rugged, fearsome look. From the stubble at his chin, the hair darkened to an almost sable hue as it crawled onto his chest. There, it established an interesting pattern. T-shaped, it flared above his impressive pectoral muscles in clusters of curliness before marching down the center in a tapering design that disappeared into the elasticized waistband of his sweats.

His chest. It was intriguing. To say the least. And for a number of reasons. For one, the deep and evenly bronzed color, which suggested that he'd spent hours baking in a sweltering sun. Another point of intrigue was the chest's seeming indifference to the chill of the late afternoon, a chill Anne Elise felt shudder through her. No such ripples of reaction purled across Kell Chaisson's golden skin, a fact that was somehow unnerving. The most intriguing elements of the chest, however, were the three long silver scars slashed horizontally just below his copper-colored nipples and above his hair-dusted belly. The gilded darkness of the skin only heightened their visibility.

Anne Elise frowned. They looked like knife marks. What could have possibly happened? Suddenly she remembered Jodi Ward's comment about his having endured atrocities while a prisoner of war. Surely this wasn't the result of such savagery, the civilized being in her denied. Yet, what else could they be? the logical being in her countered. Without warning she felt a little sick to her stomach.

She also felt something else that Jodi Ward had spoken of. She felt Kell Chaisson's intensity. It almost visibly emanated from him, traveling the spacious void between them in white-hot waves and engulfing her in its energy. She sensed, too, the blatant sexuality. He *was* a hunk. As a woman she could allow herself to recognize that fact without responding to it. Just as she allowed the admission of one other thing. There was something intrinsically frightening about Kell Chaisson, frightening and ... fascinating.

All rumors considered, he wasn't what she'd been expecting. She hadn't expected a son of a bitch to be fascinating.

Kell Chaisson wandered through his mind.

It was a mind capable of great imagery, both by nature and because he'd deliberately honed the ability he'd been born with. At the moment, he was traveling through a South American jungle. The jungle, though hot and steamy, though crowded with lush, crushing vegetation, nourished his senses in a pleasant way. He liked the cleansing feeling of the perspiration dampening his skin; he also liked the feeling of freedom. Unlike an enemy-infested forest in Vietnam, no one but he inhabited this forest. That fact made him feel ... safe.

He also felt pure delight at the giant rhinestone-clear raindrops that glistened on the wide banana leaves. The rain had come and gone, he watching it from the sheltering, shaded arms of a liana-draped tree trunk. It had left him with a feeling of peace. It was a feeling he liked. Just as he liked the sound of the waterfall in the distance. The clear water would be cool when he dived into the lagoon... cool, clean, calming.

And it was important that he stay calm. It was important that he be centered, that there be harmony among his physical, mental and spiritual selves. He needed to feel the positive energy flow of the universe, for with it he controlled his emotions, and his job demanded control. Without it, he sank into the dank, night-dark abyss of violence. It had been that way for longer than he cared to remember, for reasons that he'd never cared to investigate.

Calm. He let the word bathe him in its freshness, the way he let the water bathe him with its coolness as he dived into the lagoon. He felt the moist coolness enveloping his being, sluicing across his heated skin. Surfacing, he slung his head, scattering water in a wide, misty arc. It was then he heard the sound.

Violation.

Someone had entered his jungle.

His senses trained to capacity, he could smell the sweetness of a subtle perfume, could hear the softness of breathing, could feel the warmth of another body. He would have even sworn he could hear the faint stirring of hair as a sudden breeze swished it across feminine shoulders.

She had come.

Taking one last, deep meditative breath, he slowly opened his eyes—and stared directly into those of Anne Elise.

His, she thought, feeling as if she'd abruptly been plugged into an electrical socket, were the darkest brown she'd ever seen. Dark and complex. Like a river that looks smooth and calm on the surface, yet beneath runs wild with turbulent, troubled water.

Hers, he thought, were the deepest shade of green he'd ever seen. Green like his forest. Like his safe forest. Would a man feel safe lost in those eyes? A rhetorical question, it required no response.

Uncoiling his limber legs, Kell stood and immediately dwarfed Anne Elise's five feet five inches with his six-foot-seven-inch stature. She automatically tilted her gaze upward. He lowered his.

She wasn't what he'd expected, he mused, taking in the porcelain perfection of her skin, her bronze hair, the silver MIA bracelet at her wrist. She was dressed nicely, fashionably—as much as he knew to determine it—but she wasn't dressed expensively, as he'd expected someone from her background to be. Even so, though, she had class. That was as obvious as the fact that she was pretty. He was vaguely aware that he resented that prettiness, though why that should be so, he hadn't the least idea.

"You're right on time," he said, his voice low and gruff, not from emotion, but rather from natural pitch. At her startled look—he hadn't been forewarned of her visit—he added, "It's what I would have done. I'd have confronted you, too."

As he spoke, and ignoring the possibility of splinters, he turned and padded on bare feet across the cedar-planked patio to the back door, which he pulled open. He didn't offer an invitation. Anne Elise followed him, anyway. She noted two things: scars similar to those on his chest streaked across his back . . . and the door was closing in her face. She started to knock, then perversely didn't. She just caught the door before it closed entirely and slid into the house. If he could be rude, so could she.

The kitchen into which she stepped was small and clean. It was also casually cluttered, bachelor-style. Cereal boxes, like a haphazard collection of skyscrapers, sat atop the refrigerator, the door of which Kell Chaisson was at the moment opening, while dirty mugs and a Mr. Coffee indolently lazed on the cabinet. A Twinkie wrapper and the cardboard box from a TV dinner, a Hearty Man's meat loaf and potatoes, lay abandoned on the kitchen table.

He ate junk food, Anne Elise thought. Not that it looked as though it had hurt him any. There wasn't a flabby spare inch at his waist . . . or anywhere else, for that matter. This admission surprised her—not that it was true, but that she'd noted it at all. She conveniently shifted her gaze from the man to the den beyond.

The room proved a cozy reflection of the kitchen. Decorated—perhaps that was too deliberate a word—in grays and blues, both colors being repeated in the hazy mountain scene visible through the windows, the room had a comfortable, lived-in look. Newspapers were scattered around the plaid sofa and spilled onto the gray-carpeted floor. An occasional drinking glass peeked from here and there, one with a milk residue in the bottom. No green plants offered a homey warmth, although a crackling fire in the fireplace did precisely that. Against one whole wall was a sophisticated stereo sound system. At least it looked sophisticated to Anne Elise. She wondered what kind of music he listened to— rhythm and blues? soul? rock and roll? maybe country?— then wondered why she'd wondered at all.

She cut her gaze back to him.

He had just carelessly popped the top off a bottle of beer and was raising the brown glass to his lips. Leaning back into the cabinet with his hips and crossing one leg over the other at the ankle, he downed a deep swallow.

At its end, he said simply, finally, "No."

"No what?"

"No, I won't go with you."

"Why?"

"Because the whole thing is a wild-goose chase."

Though he was candid in his response, Anne Elise thought she detected a restrained anger at whoever would pull so heartless a scam.

"I'm aware that may be exactly what it is."

The bottle, again on a journey to his mouth, hesitated at the edge of his lips. His eyes, a color match to the dark to-paz glass, clearly said he hadn't expected her to admit the possibility of a deception. His eyes also said that he was impressed by her clearheadedness in the face of such an emotional issue . . . perhaps even impressed with the square of her shoulders, shoulders delicately delineated beneath the soft folds of her silken ivory blouse. He carried the bottle on to his lips and drank.

"And yet you're willing to risk—" he began.

She cut him off. "The only thing I'm risking is my time and the plane fare."

Kell pushed from the cabinet and walked toward the ta-ble—swaggered, Anne Elise thought. Such an arrogant sway of hips could be called nothing less. Turning the chair with an effortless flick of his wrist, he straddled the seat and la-zily folded his arms across the back.

"Lady, dealing with people like these, you're risking a helluva lot more than time and plane fare. Namely that pretty little ass of yours."

Anne Elise felt anger skitter down her senses. She cocked her chin upward. "Well, it's my pretty little ass, isn't it?"

"The only problem is," the man with the negligent pos-ture and beard-roughened appearance said, "it's my ass, too, if it's standing next to yours." Before she could reply that the proximity was what her father would be paying him for, and handsomely, he surprised her by asking, "When was your husband reported missing?"

She didn't flinch from what had to be a hurtful question, a fact he noted. "July of '71."

"Under what conditions?"

"His helicopter—he was a pilot—was shot down over the Cambodian border. No one seems to know exactly what happened from there—whether he was instantly killed, injured, taken prisoner...." Her voice trailed off and was softer when she said, "No one could tell me more than that."

At the mention of the phrase "taken prisoner," Kell's hand tightened on the neck of the bottle. The action was imperceptible, though, just the way he purposely made his every reaction. "Who contacted you about the remains?"

"A man named Isaac Forbes. He claims to be an American businessman living in Thailand."

"Yeah, and I'm Prince Charles and you're Lady Di," he answered sarcastically. Before she could agree with his assessment of Isaac Forbes, he added, "Just how much did our 'American businessman' want for his trouble?"

"Fifty thousand."

"Mary, Mother of Jesus, you aren't going to give—!"

"I'm not going to give him anything," Anne Elise slashed through his profane comment. "I'm making a purchase. And if the remains are those of my husband, the price will be more than reasonable."

"*If*, Ms. Butler. *If*."

"I'm well aware that the dog tag, photo and—"

He lowered the bottle. "What dog tag and photo?"

A smug look crossed Anne Elise's face. "If you hadn't been so hell-bent on turning me down, my father would have explained."

A slow smile, not at all unattractive, which was perhaps what Anne Elise disliked most, sauntered—no, swaggered; there was that damned swagger again!—across his lips. "Why, ma'am, that sounds like a reprimand," he drawled, the words dripping with Southernness.

Anne Elise felt it once more—the prickly stirrings of anger. She'd give Kell Chaisson one thing. He knew where to find the anger button that she'd heretofore kept so well hidden.

"Are you always this insufferably rude?" she asked, hating herself for even rising to take his bait, but seemingly unable to resist it.

His mouth quirked into a crooked grin. "Nah. Sometimes worse. You were just lucky enough to catch me when I was on my good behavior."

This time, forcing herself to remember why she was standing in his kitchen, she refused to be goaded. "Look, Captain Chaisson—"

"Tell me about the dog tag and photo."

Anne Elise weighed his interest and, finding it sincere, did as he'd asked. She also mentioned the letter. Finally she added, "I'm aware that this doesn't constitute identification of the remains."

"And yet you're willing to pay fifty thousand for the possibility?"

"What I'm willing to do is travel to Bangkok to make a comparison between my husband's dental records and the jawbone Isaac Forbes purportedly has."

For all that he'd trained himself not to let his emotions show, surprise flitted across Kell's face.

An if-you'd-given-us-a-chance-yesterday look claimed Anne Elise's.

"You know, of course," Kell said realistically, "that the man's probably dangling that as the means of getting you there."

Anne Elise shrugged. "If he is, then all I have to do is haul my pretty little ass out of Bangkok, isn't it?"

"Without buying the remains?"

"Without buying the remains." Encouraged by this last question, she asked more confidently than before, "Will you go with me?"

Kell didn't answer. Instead, he tipped the bottle and drained it dry.

Arrogantly tipped and drained, Anne Elise thought, as she watched the thick column of his bronzed throat convulse in swallow after swallow. She then watched as he pulled the empty bottle from his mustache-dusted lips and plunked it back onto the table. His eyes, curiously both sharp and lazy, raised to hers.

"No," he said flatly and with all the finality of a Supreme Court ruling. Unlike a Supreme Court ruling, however, he gave no explanation whatsoever.

It was this latter that Anne Elise resented the most, since she'd expected an affirmative reply. In that moment she would have died and gone to hell before she begged.

"Then I won't waste any more of your time or mine," she said, turning and starting for the door.

She was halfway there when his words wrapped around her. "This Isaac Forbes is a slimy son of a bitch."

Something in the way he said it, as if he were tossing her a crumb of an explanation, back combed her nerves. That, in combination with the other times he'd ruffled her usually smooth feathers, pushed the old anger button once more. Her eyes, if not hot, then at least decidedly warm, met his with a defiant directness.

"Funny, that's what my father said about you. Minus the slimy part."

A frown, then again it might have been a grin, slipped across Kell's lips. "The general said I was a son of a bitch?"

"He did," she answered and felt an inordinate pleasure at the revelation.

A grin. It was definitely a grin playing at his mouth, and it caused little wrinkles to crease around his suddenly mirth-filled eyes. "He always did have a keen eye for character."

"Right this moment, I'm inclined to agree with you...and with my father."

Both the smile at his lips and in his eyes broadened by just an irritating trace.

Anne Elise, however, could find no humor at all in the situation. Whipping around, she headed back toward the door.

"If you're wise," he called after her once more in a voice disgustingly calm, "you'll forget about Isaac Forbes and about Bangkok. Both'll only lead to heartache."

Anne Elise stopped. And turned. This time slowly. Her gaze immediately meshed with his. In hers dwelled determination...and something more. That something more was the honoring of her duty.

"Let me make something very clear, Captain Chaisson," she said softly, squaring her shoulders, "I'm going to Bangkok with or without you, with or without any escort, for that matter, with or without my father's financial assistance. What's mortgaging my home when my soul's been mortgaged for years? And as for heartache—frankly, captain, I wouldn't know how to live without it."

With that, she disappeared through the doorway.

It—she—wasn't his problem, Kell concluded moments later as he shoved from the chair with such force that its legs

made an angry scraping sound against the hardwood floor.
He jerked open the refrigerator door and throttled another
beer by the throat. The cap *pinged* across the cabinet counter and lay where it landed. Tipping the bottle, he drained
half the contents before coming up for air...and pro-
nouncing once more that the pretty, classy daughter of
General Terris wasn't his problem.

"Dammit, she isn't!" he swore.

For all that he wished it wasn't so, the silence still bore her
subtle imprint. Her perfume, something soft and flowery,
still lingered, as did the image of her duty-filled eyes and her
stoically squared shoulders. A feeling washed over him, a
feeling that it took a lot to inspire. In fact, it had been a long
time since he'd felt the feeling. It was called admiration.

Okay, Chaisson, so the lady's gutsy. She still isn't your
responsibility.

Granted, the devil's advocate in him agreed, but you did
come down hard on her. Why? The question was asked as
frankly as he'd earlier asked her questions concerning her
husband.

I don't want to get involved.

Why?

She's being duped.

Why?

Look, man, get off my case!

Why?

All right, all right! I don't want to return to Southeast
Asia!

Southeast Asia.

Even the thought of returning made him break out in a
cold sweat, so to counterbalance the uncomfortable emotions, Kell swigged down the remainder of the chilled beer.
He couldn't, however, stop the images, too-clear images,
from flashing through his mind. The jungle, sweltering hot,

closed in around him. Unlike his safe, imaginary jungle, this one was infested with danger, human danger. He could hear his weary footsteps, his ragged breathing, his heart pounding out the scrambled rhythm of fear. He was alone. Just he and the enemy. All the others—his men, his buddies—were dead. Blown to smithereens. Blown to the far side of hell. Blown—

He forcibly drew the gory images to a halt. Those that replaced them were just as bad, however. The chase. The capture. The cage.

The cage.

He'd been confined like a wild animal behind bars of bamboo. He could still remember the smell of his own sweat, his own dirt, his own wastes. And he could still feel the rounded, uneven slats of bamboo that comprised the cage's flooring—just another subtle form of torture so silently, so insidiously inflicted that he'd been unable to sleep in a bed for months after his escape.

The Viet Cong had known less subtle forms of torture, too. And they had introduced him to them, one by blasphemous one. The interrogations always started out the same way. He'd tell them, in his best strong voice, his name, his rank, his serial number. This he'd repeat over and over until his words would mingle with pain, wrought by whatever exquisite torture they had chosen for the day. His strong voice would give way to mumbling and stifled cries until, at last, blessed unconsciousness hugged him in its tender embrace.

And then the Viet Cong had begun to play real nasty. He could still remember the blinding glint of the knife as the sun, far too bright because he saw it so seldom, had bounced off the steel. He could remember thinking that at least it looked clean, that maybe it wasn't infection laden, that he was a fool for worrying about an infection when they were probably going to kill him. But they hadn't. And he could remember wishing they had. Just as he could remember the god-awful burning as the steel had sliced his skin. He could remember the warm, sticky feel of his blood, its sweet smell, the feeling of lightheadedness that had swarmed around him. But mostly, he could remember the taste of blood as he bit his tongue to keep from crying out. He wouldn't give the dirty bastards that much satisfaction!

And that, he thought, was why he didn't want to go back to Southeast Asia on some wild-goose chase. There were too many memories lurking in the shadows.

Liar, the devil's advocate accused. There's more to your refusal to get involved than that.

Back off, part of Kell warned, because the subject that was approaching was one he tried to avoid at all costs.

The truth is, the devil's advocate dared, the war reminds you of returning POWs, which brings back memories of a sad-eyed woman trying to explain to you how it was possible to love two men. The pain of the knife had been nothing in comparison to the pain of her words.

Kell slammed down the beer bottle and stormed out of the kitchen. The warmth of the den fire washed across his body as he passed the hearth, heading for the stereo. In seconds, the soothing notes of Debussy's *Clair de Lune*, like fingers of a gentle massage, ministered to his edginess. He sighed deeply and stepped to the wall of windows. The sun had set, leaving the gloaming to steal across the unprotected land. Kell could feel it rolling in, just as he could feel the question coming. Like the land, he was vulnerable, unprotected, at the question's mercy.

How had it happened? How had he ever gotten involved with another man's wife?

He still didn't know. He knew only that neither had intended for it to happen. In the months that had followed his escape, he'd been assigned to work with the families of POWs. Given the fact that he'd survived, the government had thought he would prove an inspiration to families praying that their loved ones would be as brave, as hearty, as courageous, as he. He had actually enjoyed the work. Until... She had been so frightened, so...alone. And, God, he knew what it was like to be alone! In the jungle, in the cage, in the deadly dark of night.

When they had realized the direction their relationship was headed in, both had fought it tooth and nail, but in the end they had become lovers simply because falling in love had left them no choice. Kell passed his hand across his face and sighed. Why were people always trying to conveniently make things black or white? Why didn't people understand that life, in its day-to-day living, couldn't be categorized in simple terms? The truth was that their loving had been as gray as a November day, but that hadn't made it wrong. Or right. It had simply made it fact.

The only thing that had been really right, all white, was her husband's return. He'd deserved to return; she'd deserved to have him return. Kell gave a half laugh. It was a situation so clear in morality that he hadn't even been able to be angry about it. And in many ways, Kell thought, her burden had been greater than his own. She'd had to reconcile two loves, while he'd only had to try to get over one. He could still vividly see her embracing, and being embraced by, her husband. He could still see the smile on her face, the pain in her eyes as she'd searched him out in the well-wishing crowd, the...the stoic square of her shoulders. The same stoic square of shoulders that he'd seen minutes before. Both women had traits in common: both had been asked to bear a heavy burden; both had done it unswervingly, gracefully; both were survivors. And in this crazy, gray world, surviving was to be admired. And rewarded?

The truth of the matter was that if he didn't escort this Anne Elise Butler to Bangkok, General Terris would only find someone else who would. Someone, no conceit intended, Kell thought, with only a quarter of his qualifications. Some military bureaucrat who'd follow every rule to the letter. And the further truth of the matter was that while the military bureaucrat was following every rule to the letter and Anne Elise Butler was running around attempting to do her duty, somebody would steal them blind and quite possibly shoot their butts off to boot!

Ah, Jesus, Kell thought wearily, disbelievingly, was he seriously considering going back to Southeast Asia?

An hour and a half later, Anne Elise sat in the Little Rock airport, awaiting the announcement of her return flight to Dallas. She was purposely willing her mind to be numb. Like famed Scarlett O'Hara, she'd worry about everything tomorrow. Right now she just wanted to go home, back to somewhere safe and secure and Kell Chaisson-free. Right now—

"Aren't you Ms. Butler?" a voice said, shaking her from her reverie.

Anne Elise glanced up into the face of the airline agent who'd checked her ticket. She nodded.

"You're being paged, ma'am. You have a phone call."

"A phone call?" she asked, rising.

"Yes, ma'am," the man returned, pointing out a nearby courtesy phone. "You can take it there."

"Thank you." Moments later, wondering who in the world the call could be from, she said, "Hello?"

A masculine voice barked out a sharp, clipped, "Be at the Dallas-Fort Worth airport at 11:00 Thursday morning.

Have the fifty thousand wired to a Bangkok bank and bring your husband's dental records. Oh, and pack light.''

Before Anne Elise could respond, she was listening to the dial tone . . . and to the relieved thudding of her heart.

Chapter Three

W hy did he change his mind?"

Anne Elise glanced over at her daughter as they waded in
and out of the throng of people flowing through DFW's
congested corridors. They were headed for the assigned gate
of Thai Airlines. Anne Elise's purse held two tickets that her
father had made arrangements for in accordance with Kell
Chaisson's wishes. Though the two men had spoken, Anne
Elise had had no further dialogue with her traveling companion—which had suited her more than fine.

"I have absolutely no idea," she answered. Despite the
fact that Kell Chaisson wasn't the most amicable person
she'd ever met, she still felt a rush of relief that she hadn't
been forced to go to Bangkok alone. Thoughts of the man
she was meeting caused her glance to raise to the overhead
clock. She was late by five minutes, a tardiness that was totally the fault of Dallas traffic . . . and her misjudgment of
it.

As she walked—ran, really—she rearranged the leather strap of the clothes bag across her shoulder. In her other hand she carried a small suitcase. She had been instructed to pack light, and that's exactly what she'd done. As an army brat and army wife, she knew how to eliminate everything but the bare essentials. She also knew not to check her luggage if it could be avoided. That way, your suitcases didn't take a vacation you didn't.

"What's he like?" Brooke asked, her longer legs easily keeping up with her mother's.

What was Kell Chaisson like? A dark image of scarred bronze skin, a scowling expression and impudent eyes swaggered, just like a familiar pair of hips, through Anne Elise's mind. "Let's just say that the good captain defies description."

"Granddad says he's a—"

"I know what your grandfather says he is, but his personality need not concern us. It's only his expertise that I care in the least about."

"Granddad says he's perfect for the job."

"Let's hope," Anne Elise answered. If disagreeable made for perfection, the man was, indeed, perfect for the job.

"How long will you be gone?"

"A few days. Maybe as little as forty-eight hours. It just depends on how fast everything goes once we get there. You're gonna stay with your grandparents, right?"

"Yeah." Brooke smiled, showing teeth made beautiful and straight by orthodontia. It had been an orthodontia that General Terris had coaxed his granddaughter through, assuring her that she did not look weird, that braces were not the end of the world, that a boy would, too, ask her to the prom. Anne Elise could still remember one lonely night when she, Anne Elise, had cried herself to sleep, remorseful that Brooke's father had been denied the chance to so reassure his daughter and that Brooke would never share those special moments with him.

Now, as she had a thousand times before, as she had over a thousand other things, Anne Elise pushed the hurtful memory aside. "What are you smiling about?"

"Nana's promised to make lasagna."

"Did you really think she wouldn't make your favorite dish?"

"Naw. I knew she would. She always does." The smile faded suddenly. "Momma, do you think there's a chance?"

Anne Elise understood perfectly the question being asked. Glancing once more at her daughter, she cautioned, "Honey, don't get your hopes up." When Brooke didn't respond, Anne Elise tacked on, "Okay?"

The young woman beside her shrugged. "Sure. It's no big deal. If it isn't my father..." She paused, then repeated, "It's no big deal."

It was a very big deal. Anne Elise could *feel* just how big a deal it was. It was tension coiled in every muscle of her daughter's body; it shone from her pretty blue eyes; it pumped through her with every beat of her young, emotion-filled heart.

Please, God, Anne Elise prayed, *let this pan out for Brooke if for no one else. And please don't let me be much later,* she thought, stepping around a slow couple. *And please let Kell Chaisson be civil. That's all I ask. Just civ—*

She saw him a gate away. Rising head and shoulders above the men around him, he leaned against a wall with his arms negligently folded across his wide chest. Jeans molded his legs in a snug embrace, while a black T-shirt—again, the thought of camouflage crossed Anne Elise's mind—spread across the thick breadth of his shoulders. The shadowy stubble of beard was gone, leaving only a brush of a mustache. His eyes, as before, appeared distinctively dark and flagrantly challenging. There was also a magnetism, as piercing as his eyes, that almost tangibly emanated from him. The moment his gaze connected with hers, that dark energy jolted through her, causing her to feel both light-headed and heavy stomached.

"That's him, isn't it?" Brooke said at her mother's elbow.

Nothing. No response. Just Anne Elise's gaze lost deep in the winter-brown eyes of Kell Chaisson.

He's the kind of man every woman would love to spend one night with...but not more...he's too blatantly sensual, too intense, too scary.

Startled that Jodi Ward's comment had chosen that moment to make itself remembered and vaguely aware that Brooke was saying something, Anne Elise turned her attention to her daughter. "What?"

"That's him, isn't it?" Brooke repeated.

Anne Elise didn't ask how Brooke had known. It seemed perfectly normal that she would, given the captain's dynamic presence.

"Yes," she answered, realizing that her eyes, against their own volition, were being drawn back to his.

Kell nudged his shoulder from the wall and, wending his way among those assembled for departure, started toward her. They met in front of the check-in booth.

"You're late," he said without preamble.

Like sweat drizzling into a scratch, the words stung. And angered. How did this man always manage to make her forget that she didn't indulge in anger?

She tipped her chin upward. "Only a few minutes."

"That's still late," he said. Giving her no time to defend herself, he ordered, "Let me have the tickets."

The command had been so imperially given, his hand was so imperially extended, that she set the luggage down and began to dig in her purse. Wordlessly, but with a look that could kill, she slapped the requested papers onto his palm. With a look no less lethal, he closed his fingers around the tickets and stepped toward the check-in booth.

Anne Elise used the time to calm her emotions. She wasn't here to spar. She was here to perhaps settle a sensitive issue in her life, and, if she had to court the devil to do that, then she would. That in mind, she forced herself to be friendly moments later when he returned. She noted that he kept the tickets rather than passing them back to her. She ignored his presumptuousness.

"Captain Chaisson, this is my daughter, Brooke. Brooke, this is Captain Chai—"

"Kell," he interrupted.

He then did something that shocked Anne Elise right down to the soles of her feet. He smiled. Well, sort of. Whatever it was called, it was sincere. Anne Elise watched as Brooke smiled back and wondered what magical spell her daughter had cast. It was obviously a magic that she herself possessed not one whit of.

"The general tells me that you graduate this year."

"Yes, sir."

"Congratulations."

"Thank you." The look Brooke turned on her mother said, "He's not so bad. You just have to know how to handle him."

As Anne Elise was still reeling from Kell's foray into civility, his smile, or whatever it was, faded and the scowl returned. Strangely, she was grateful. The scowl she was familiar with, the scowl she understood, the scowl was in no way... The word *threatening* popped to mind. Anne Elise didn't care to consider why.

"I told you to pack light," he accused, squatting down and yanking open the zipper of her suitcase.

She equally didn't care to consider the way the denim of his pants was stretched, and most suggestively, across his hips and legs, which was relatively easy to do because she was so startled by his action. "What are you doing?"

"I'm packing light," he returned, peeling down the zipper of the garment bag.

Instinctively, she bent her knees to join him "I *did* pack light I've only got two— What are you doing?"

Rummaging through her clothes, her neatly packed clothes, he obliquely answered her question. "Too hot, too hot. You'll swelter in Bangkok in this," he said, as he perused, and none too delicately, one garment after another.

Finally, he tore a pair of slacks out of the bag, following them with a short-sleeved shirt. A pair of red shorts passed his test as well, as did a white T-shirt. He also allowed her khaki skirt. All these he left heaped, heedless of wrinkles, on the floor until he could make a place for them inside the small suitcase. Which he began to do immediately by discarding some items and rearranging others.

"My God, you could do the entire Orient with what you've packed!" he bellowed.

"That's a matter of opin— Hey, that's my makeup!" she protested as he tossed a bag to the side.

"You don't need it."

"Like hell I don't!" she returned, anger once more bubbling in her veins as she jammed the bag back into the suitcase.

He considered for a moment, then said calmly, "Okay. Something else goes."

"That's my nightgown!" she cried as the next article, in soft, pale pink lawn, left its nesting place.

"You don't need a nightgown. You can sleep in the T-shirt."

"I— Oh, no, you don't. That's my underwear and I need every piece!"

People were beginning to cast surreptitious, and not so surreptitious, glances at the couple verbally slugging it out on the floor. Neither Kell nor Anne Elise seemed to notice.

Silk and lace, in ivory and nutmeg brown, spilled through Kell's long, slender fingers. Anne Elise snatched the slip, bra and panties away and returned them to the suitcase . . . with a defiant look. Kell missed the look, however, because he was busy culling a curling iron.

"I need—" she began.

"Look," he said, his patience obviously at an end, "we do things my way or count me out." The restlessness in his eyes said he meant every word he spoke.

The truth was, and Anne Elise knew it, she needed him far more than she needed a curling iron, a nightgown and sundry other articles. The further truth was, and, again, Anne Elise was consummately aware of it, the subject went far beyond luggage. He was setting the tone for the entire trip. Her reply would acknowledge or deny that tone. It annoyed, it chafed, but still she answered, "We do it your way."

His gaze delved into hers, searching for the depth of her commitment. It was while he was doing so that an airline agent made the announcement.

"Final call for passengers on flight 345 for Bangkok, now loading at gate three."

Kell drew his gaze from Anne Elise's and made a final adjustment to the small suitcase. He then zipped it shut and, pushing from the balls of his feet, rose. Anne Elise rose, too, the garment bag, now stuffed with Kell's rejects, in her hands. She passed it to Brooke.

"Take this back," she said, "and tell your grandparents I'll call."

"Okay."

With a total lack of embarrassment, Anne Elise embraced her daughter. Brooke hugged her tightly.

"Hang loose," Anne Elise said, "and try not to get your hopes too high."

"I love you."

"I love you, too, honey."

Seconds later, Anne Elise joined Kell, who had stood on the sidelines watching the exchange between mother and daughter with a curious detachment, as though he'd learned to deal with goodbyes, as though he'd learned how to cope with being the outsider, the odd man out, by not just giving a good damn.

He indicated a place in the line that was forming, indicating as well that she go in front of him. Lugging his duffle bag over his shoulder, he carried her suitcase in his right hand. In his left he carried the tickets.

They were next in line to go through the security check when Brooke called out, "Kell?"

He turned, his eyes quickly finding the young woman. Anne Elise, too, searched out her daughter.

"Take care of Mom."

Kell gave a quick, brisk nod, which strangely, at least to Anne Elise, was more reassuring than a thousand verbal responses. She suddenly felt safe with this man, this man whose warm presence she could feel behind her, this man whose body occasionally brushed against her own. He might be disagreeable, he might pique her anger, but she felt safe with him. And for someone who'd spent the past seventeen years providing safety, it felt good, for once, to be its recipient. In fact, it felt very good—better than she would have ever believed anything so simple could feel.

The Thai Airlines 747 nosed into the air.

Stewardesses and passengers alike settled in for the

twenty-two-and-a-half-hour flight to Bangkok, with stops in Seattle and Tokyo. Since they were sitting in first class, Kell and Anne Elise had been offered drinks immediately. She'd ordered a Coke, he tomato juice.

At her surprised look, which said implicitly that she'd expected him to order something stronger, he said, "I never drink when I'm on the job." He could have said that there was another thing he never did, but felt it unnecessary, even inappropriate, to go into his philosophy that alcohol, women, and a clear head didn't mix.

He thought about this later as Anne Elise crossed one stockinged leg over the other, leaving the man in him no choice but to admire the shapeliness of her calf, the delicate turn of her ankle. He would have reminded himself of his clearheaded philosophy, but it wasn't necessary. She wasn't his type; he liked earthy brunettes, not fiery redheads. Besides, even if she had been his type, she was off limits. For a variety of reasons. One, she was a client. Two, she was the general's daughter, and he'd grown real fond of wearing his ass exactly where it was, not lodged between his shoulders. Three, and most important, she belonged to another man. A dead man. And that made the belonging all the more binding.

Following drinks came lunch, a succulent filet mignon and fluffy baked potato. Exchanging only the necessary courtesies, they ate in silence. Actually Anne Elise picked more than she ate. After the trays were removed, she asked to be excused from her window seat. Kell unfastened his seat belt and stood, allowing her room to pass into the aisle. She had just cleared his seat when unexpected turbulence jostled the plane. Automatically Kell reached for her arm. Her gaze moved upward to his, his downward to hers. Neither spoke. Not even when she disengaged her arm and moved on up the aisle toward the rest room. Where he had touched her, though, continued to feel odd, strange. A short while later, she returned, scooted back into her seat and busied herself with a book she'd brought along.

Kell, on the other hand, did nothing but stretch out his legs as best he could and close his eyes. He hadn't expected first class, he mused, but then he supposed he should have. The general, after all, had made the arrangements. Albeit, they had been made to his, Kell's specifications, these first-class accommodations had been tacked on. Actually they weren't too bad. Actually a guy could grow accustomed to them, especially when the guy had once been caged and didn't cotton too well to close places, which was why he'd insisted on the aisle seat. Actually Brooke Butler must look like her father because she certainly didn't take after her mother. Not certain where this last thought had come from, he nonetheless didn't fight its presence. Rather, he loosened his imagery ability and compared blond hair to Anne Elise's chestnut red, dark skin to that of palest ivory, blue eyes to forest green. Brooke's father must also have been tall, for already the daughter topped her mother, not that her mother was petite. It was really all a matter of comparison. For example, compared to him she was petite. A man his size would dwarf her, smother her, crush—

Not liking the turn of his thoughts, he abandoned them, feeling as he did so that vague uneasiness he'd felt once before, that resentful uneasiness that said he'd feel a whole lot better if Anne Elise Butler were homely. He searched for a new image, but the one that appeared offered no more solace than the one he was trying to avoid. This was an image of a mother and daughter embracing at the airport. Such warm scenes only served to remind him how alone he was.

Annoyed with the relentless, punishing images, he popped open his eyes and barked, ''Do you have the letter?''

His voice, curiously both sharp and rusty, as if it were seldom used for normal conversation, slammed into the silence.

Anne Elise glanced up from the book she was having touble concentrating on. "What?"

"Do you have the letter?"

"Wh—"

"The letter you wrote your husband? The one you're so sure proves Forbes had your husband's remains."

Anne Elise could feel a warm, simmering fire build under her anger. "I'm not in the least certain Forbes has Jim's remains, and you know it. I've already admitted the letter means nothing. And are you ever congenial, captain?" This last she'd heard coming, had wished she could stop it, but had only been able to watch it, like an avalanche gone wild, gush down the walls of her better judgement.

"Rarely...and the name's Kell. Now, do you or don't you—"

"I have it!" she said, the fire burning hotter. She snapped the book shut and reached for her purse. Plunging her hand into it, she ignored dental records for the letter she'd carefully put in a fresh envelope. She handed it to him.

"Are you sure you wrote it?"

The fire blazed out of control. "Of course I'm sure!"

"All right, I'm just asking. And by the way, you're not exactly Miss Congeniality, yourself."

Why did he goad her? she wondered. And why did she let him? Anne Elise sighed and forced the heated emotion from her voice and body. "I'm certain I wrote the letter." Her words were clothed in a velvety softness when she added, "It's one of the last letters I wrote him. Brooke was only a few months old."

Kell's eyes raked hers—now a misty green—before he took the letter and started to read it.

With each word he read, this man who was a virtual stranger to her, Anne Elise grew more emotionally naked. The loving letter, with its intimate words, its privileged thoughts, its lover-sacred sentiments, had never been intended for any eyes other than her husband's. Would this man, this hard, harsh man, think such an outpouring of her heart foolish and silly? Would he profane the sanctity of young love?

It doesn't matter what he thinks, Anne Elise thought, returning her eyes to the book but seeing nothing on the page.

With each word he read, Kell grew more moved. Which was the ultimate testimony to the letter's power because, long ago, he had steeled his heart against emotion—certainly any warm, sweet, loving emotion. Instead, he had emptied his heart, and his soul, of feeling because emptiness, barrenness, were less painful—not pain free, but less painful than a heart and soul brimming with emotions for which there was no outlet, no one to shower them on. He now felt, however, his empty heart and soul being filled with this woman's loving words to a husband so long dead. The filling of the emptiness within him hurt, as though his heart and soul were vessels swollen from too much too soon, after so little for so long. He read the letter through, then reread it, simply because he seemed to have no choice in the matter. At last, silently, he handed the creased and battered paper back to her.

She reached for it. For the briefest of moments, each held on to it, she because it represented her past, he because it represented a past he'd never had.

Please, she prayed, her eyes begging his, *don't say anything derogatory.*

She was the kind of woman who'd love a man all the way, he thought, his gaze blended with hers. *The trip she was making proved that.* Somehow, some way, he hoped First Lieutanant James Samuel Butler knew of her devotion.

"You, uh, you need to get some rest," Kell said huskily, finally, as he turned loose of the letter. "You probably won't have much chance to rest once we reach Bangkok."

His lack of attack took her so by surprise, as did the unprecedented softness of his voice, which had sent some emotion pleasantly rippling across her, that Anne Elise could do nothing except what he bade. Without a word, she filed the letter away and quietly settled back in the seat.

Kell attempted to take his own advice. After securing two pillows from the overhead rack—he passed one to Anne Elise, who accepted it with a muted thank-you—he adjusted his seat to a reclining mode and his head on the downy cushion. He extended his long legs out before him. Anne Elise had the impression of being hemmed in, hemmed in by strength and power. She also had an impression of safety.

Safe though she felt, committed though her spirit was to resting, her body was uncooperative. She twisted, turned, fought for a position that promised sleep. None did. Her only consolation was that the man beside her seemed just as wired, just as restless. On a frustrated sigh, Anne Elise rolled her head toward the window. As clearly as she could see the bright blue sky, she could hear the long-ago voice of her husband.

"Sleeping with you is impossible. You kick like a mule."

Giggles had filled the tiny bedroom of their tiny apartment. *"I do not, James Butler."*

The blond-haired, blue-eyed man had rubbed his nose against the nose of the woman sprawled beneath him on the soft bed. *"You do, too, Annie Butler."*

Another round of giggles had sparkled throughout the room. *"Do, too. But, then, I may be making my mistake trying to sleep with you. Maybe what I should be doing is making love to you."*

With that the man's lips had closed fully over the woman's.

Anne Elise shifted in her seat, a part of her trying to dislodge the painful memory even as a part of her tried to cling to it. It was only in such scattered memories that she could remember the beauty, the glory, of being loved.

As Anne Elise twisted, the gossamer fragrance of the perfume she'd earlier dabbed at her throat and wrists flitted through the air and gently assaulted Kell's senses. The sweet, flowery scent reminded him of another woman's perfume, a smell that had lingered in his memory to haunt his days, to torment his nights.

"You smell good," he could remember saying, his nose pressed to the hollow of the woman's throat.

"It's called Possession."

He had growled. *"It's perfectly named. You do possess me."*

"Bill likes it— I'm sorry, Kell. It just slipped out. I'm sorry. I'm—"

His lips had dammed her husband's name. With a punishing, hungry kiss, he tried to possess her as surely as he was possessed by her.

Kell twisted in his seat, hoping to erase the hurtful memory. In so doing, his hand struck Anne Elise's arm, which had eased to the shared armrest in the middle of the seats.

"I'm sorry," he grumbled, he pulling his hand away, she her arm, as though each had just confronted fire.

"I'm sorry." She could hear the words echoing off his. They were her own words spoken so very long ago. *"I know I promised I wouldn't cry when your orders for Vietnam came. It's just . . . it's just . . ."*

"Ah, c'mon, Annie, don't cry. I'll be all right. I promise."

Promises were too fragile to be spoken aloud, Anne Elise thought as she listened to the mighty whir of the 747's engines. She, too, had made a promise. She'd made it as she'd watched the chaplain walk down the steps of her apartment. She'd never spoken the promise aloud, though. She hadn't needed to, for it dwelled deep inside her, so deep that it had become a part of her—like breathing, like seeing, like hearing. She had promised her husband, her missing husband, that she'd never forget him. And she never had. She never would.

The restless thoughts brought restless movement. Rearranging the pillow, she tried once more to sleep.

Kell, tired of fighting rest, sighed and forced his mind to go blank. To mock him, it filled with immediate images, bittersweet images overflowing with sight and sound.

"I love you," he heard the woman's soft voice say, saw the tears glistening in her golden-brown eyes. *"I don't know how it happened. God, I didn't mean for it to! But I love him, too, Kell. In a way. A different way. But it's still love. And I owe him so much. After what he's been through, I owe him so much."*

Kell, on another deep sigh, and another adjustment of his body in the plane seat that seemed to be fighting him, pondered the concepts of loyalty and devotion. How he hated them! Even as he admired them! The convoluted truth was that, if she hadn't been the kind of woman to hold fast to the principles of loyalty and devotion, he never would have loved her to begin with. And, because she was what, who, she was, it was destined that she part with him. He was damned if she did leave him, damned if she didn't. He was damned.

"I'm afraid, Kell," he could hear her say. *"How can I walk away from you?"*

He remembered wanting to answer her, but he was afraid he'd beg her not to go.

"I'm afraid, Kell," she'd repeated. "Hold me. Please hold me."

"Please hold me," Anne Elise could remember begging her husband. He had forbidden her to go to the airport with him. He'd said he wanted to remember her standing in the bedroom of their apartment, her eyes still hazy from making love. He also had said that he hoped he had just made her pregnant. She'd hoped it, too. She'd also hoped, prayed, that he'd hold her just one more time.

Anne Elise sighed again, acknowledging that sleep wasn't going to come just because she longed for it. Without thinking, because she knew the man beside her was likewise having trouble going to sleep, she asked impetuously, "Why did you change your mind?"

Her voice, as soft as the memories drowning him in their sticky sweetness, washed over him. He rolled his head toward her.

"Why?" she repeated, curious as to the reason he was here when it was obvious he didn't want to be.

He said nothing for so long, she thought he wasn't going to answer. His eyes, though, studied her all the while with a stark intensity. At last, he said, "Because you remind me of someone I knew a long time ago."

Who? Anne Elise wondered. The woman rumor said he'd loved? Although grateful for his help under any circumstances, she wished he'd had a different motivation. Strangely, inexplicably, she wished his reason had had something to do with herself alone.

"Thank you," she said, pushing this baffling thought aside. "For changing your mind."

His eyes darkened. When he spoke, his voice was low, gravelly. "Go to sleep."

A gentle hand and the same low, gravelly voice awakened her. Anne Elise's first reaction was surprise that she'd fallen asleep, her second the realization that the spot where he'd touched her shoulder felt warm and tingly—very much the way it had felt when he'd earlier balanced her amid the turbulence.

"We're in Seattle," he explained as the plane taxied to the terminal. "You ought to move around while you can. The flight from here to Tokyo'll be long."

She nodded, shaking away the last, disorienting vestiges of sleep and wondering if she looked as disheveled as she felt. She raked her fingers through the jumble of her hair, pulling it back from her sleep-hazy eyes. A comb and a cup of coffee. She'd sell her soul for either. Had he left her a comb? He'd bare-boned the contents of her luggage until she wasn't certain what she had. She wondered, too, if he'd slept. His hair looked mussed, attractively mussed, but his eyes appeared clear and alert. But then, this man would appear alert under any circumstances. That she'd bet the success of the mission on.

Within minutes, a stewardess announced how long they would be on the ground and that those wishing to deplane would need to secure a boarding pass. In due time and process, both Anne Elise and Kell walked through the tunnel and out into the crowded Seattle terminal.

His hand at her back, he subtly gestured the direction they'd take, then said, "I'll catch up with you." His voice was aloof, professionally detached.

"Right," she answered, watching him pass her and head toward the men's room. She turned into the ladies' room, but not before she noticed several pairs of feminine eyes surveying Kell as he walked past. He did strike an imposing figure, even a sexy one, she guessed, if you were into dark, brooding, intense types, but, like a pack of cigarettes, he needed to wear a warning label: this man is hazardous to your health.

The thought brought a snippet of a smile to her lips, the first in days. It disappeared, however, the moment she caught sight of herself in the washroom mirror. She groaned. Doing what she could with her fingers, she straightened the auburn strands, then applied a layer of copper-colored lipstick to her bare lips.

Now, if she could just find some coffee.

That was an easy thing to do. She followed her nose to the first snack bar. She had just picked up the Styrofoam cup when she heard a voice behind her.

"I'll take one of those."

Anne Elise turned and looked into the brooding eyes of Kell. His plumbed hers, then dismissed her with little show of emotion. In fact, had she not known better, she might have thought the two of them were total strangers meeting for the first time. For a reason she couldn't explain, his coolness irritated her.

"I see you don't give up caffeine while you're on a job," she quipped. "Aren't you afraid it'll jangle your razor-sharp nerves?"

He fished in the pocket of his jeans, his tight jeans, and came up with the exact change, which he plunked down on the counter. Lazily, as though she'd said nothing, he picked up the cup and took a swallow of the hot coffee.

He then said, "I don't give up caffeine for anyone or anything." He raised the cup to his lips again, but this time before he sipped at the steaming, foggy brew, that sort-of smile twisted one corner of his mouth. "Caffeine's my only vice."

It made no sense—Anne Elise was patently aware of that—but the sudden, quirky arrangement of his mouth caused her attention to focus on his mustache. It was as though she hadn't really seen it until just that second. She had never known anyone with a mustache. She found herself wondering what one felt like. Was it bristly? Soft? Did it tickle? Would it sensually define the word *vice*? This last thought was so inappropriate that Anne Elise cast it aside for the first thing that came into her head.

"Caffeine's my only vice, too."

Kell's gaze casually, but thoroughly, ran across her hair, taking in every wayward strand, strands that could just as easily have been tangled from a lover's hand as from sleep. His eyes then lowered to her freshly glossed lips.

"Why do I believe caffeine *is* your only vice?" he asked, the question as slow and deliberate as his eyes.

The question alone might have renewed her former irritation. It, in combination with his open appraisal of her, might surely have done so. In truth, however, her irritation stemmed from the sudden warm flush his appraisal had caused. She forced her eyes to meet his challengingly. "Why don't I believe it's yours?"

She would have sworn a smile nipped his lips again. "Probably because you're smart enough to know a lie when you hear it," he said. "C'mon, we wouldn't want to miss our flight."

Anne Elise heard the sarcasm in his last remark—he would have preferred missing the flight—but she refused to take the bait. Besides, his smile had again cornered her attention and had caused it to refocus on his mustache.

What did a mustache feel like? Bristly? Soft? Did it tickle? Would it sensually define the word *vice*?

Chapter Four

They were an hour out of Seattle en route to Tokyo, the blue Pacific Ocean spread wide beneath them, when Kell reached for Anne Elise's hand and read the name on the MIA bracelet she wore as a silent protest against the improper accounting of the hundreds of men missing in action. The silver bracelet was engraved with her husband's name.

"Tell me about him," Kell ordered, but not harshly. In fact, his voice bordered on gentleness without ever slipping fully into it.

Quicksilver. Kell Chaisson was the personification of quicksilver, Anne Elise thought. One moment he was brash, rude, inspiring every negative emotion she had, then, without warning—that was the killer!—he'd say or do something to hint that maybe, just maybe, there was another side to him. But then, perhaps he was just clever, drawing her in with kindness before clobbering her with his brashness, his rudeness.

No, he was serious. Something in his eyes said so. Anne Elise appreciated his openness, the way he didn't tiptoe around the subject of her husband the way some people did. She also appreciated the fact that he released her wrist. Even though he did, however, she could still feel the bold imprint of his fingers.

She shrugged. "What do you want to know?"

"Just tell me about him. Anything."

"He was…he was…" Anne Elise tried to find one word that would sum up the man who'd been her husband, the father of her child. "He was…nice. I mean, really nice. In the truest and best sense of the word. He was sensitive and caring and had a great sense of humor."

"How did you meet him?"

Anne Elise smiled. "It was fall of my senior year in high school, and a couple of girlfriends and I got invited to one of Texas A & M's football games. Jim was the quarterback, and every girl there was drooling over him. I hated football, so I didn't really pay him much attention during the game. I couldn't see him for the uniform, anyway. Well, afterward, we went to a frat party." She grinned at her youthful naiveté. "We thought we'd died and gone to heaven—us there with all those mature men versus, of course, the boys back in high school."

Kell gave her his sort-of smile.

"Well, anyway, this blond-haired, blue-eyed 'man' asked me to dance. It was only later that night that I realized who he was. It was after I'd already fallen in love with him." Anne Elise glanced into Kell's eyes to see the effect of her words, to see if he would mock her. He didn't. "I know love at first sight sounds improbable at best, but I really did fall in love that night."

"I believe you," Kell said evenly, unemotionally, giving no hint that he wouldn't have bought the story from anyone but the woman beside him. Attraction at first sight, lust at first sight, sure, but not an emotion as complicated as love. And yet, for some inexplicable reason, he didn't doubt what he'd just heard. He didn't doubt Anne Elise Butler's capacity for love. Why should he doubt her spontaneity? But why did this woman have the ability to make him believe in what heretofore he would have labeled only a romantic fairy tale?

Anne Elise thought Kell Chaisson didn't look like the kind of man who believed much of anything, and, for that reason, his simple statement pleased her. She wasn't sure why. It just did. It also rattled her a bit, as though she'd shown him a facet of herself that no one else had seen. To compensate she spoke. "Funny how fate weaves our lives together with invisible, but binding, threads."

"How so?"

"Jim wasn't even supposed to be at that party. He wasn't a member of the fraternity—any fraternity, for that matter. His roommate, who was a member, had talked him into going at the last minute."

"Yeah," Kell said, "fate can be an angel or a real bitch. Sometimes both," he added. An edge had slipped into his voice, curling the comment to a sarcastic crispness. At the same time an image had slipped into his mind. The image was that of a woman. A golden-eyed woman. A woman alone and lonely. The way he was alone and lonely. Yeah, fate had been an angel for putting her in his arms, a real bitch for taking her away.

Anne Elise heard the torment in his voice and wondered again if the rumor was true. If he had loved before, he would have loved completely. Never casually. Never for just the moment. What would it be like to be the object of such intense passion?

"So you married him," she heard Kell say in wrap-up.

Letting go of her wayward thoughts, she nodded. "Later that year. After he graduated from college and I from high school. My parents about died," she said, a twinkle in her eyes, "but they came around.

"We were married a little over a year when he got his orders for Vietnam. I discovered I was pregnant after he left. Then, when Brooke was just three months old, he..." She trailed off, unable, unwilling, to finish. After a while she sighed. "He was a nice man. Actually he was a nice kid. He died before he had a chance to be a man." A wistful look claimed her face. "That's the truly unforgivable thing about war. It kills the young."

"Yeah," Kell said, the one word rich with feeling.

So filled with emotion was his reply that Anne Elise glanced toward him... and dared to turn the conversation on him. "You were in Vietnam, too." It was a statement, not a question.

"Yeah."

"Dad said several tours." She wanted to mention his being a POW but couldn't bring herself to; she didn't think he'd want her to.

"Five," he answered, wondering why he was telling her things he rarely discussed.

"Anyone ever tell you you're masochistic?"

He saw the smile dancing at her lips and thought it looked... nice, he concluded, borrowing her word. He matched her smile with a crooked twitch of his own mouth. It was done before he thought. Done before he realized that he smiled about as rarely as he discussed his personal life. "No, but I have heard the word *insane*."

Along with a slew of other words, he thought. Words like *loner, maverick, son of a bitch*.

She saw his smile slowly fall away and asked, "Why did you keep volunteering?"

He shrugged. "Didn't have anything better to do. And I was good at fighting. When your old man's a drunk and beats up on you, you learn to fight."

Anne Elise remembered her father making the comment that Kell had graduated not from college, but from the School of Hard Knocks. He'd also said that Kell had had one of the highest graduating scores from Officer Candidate School. He hadn't mentioned anything more—maybe because he didn't know anything more; maybe because he knew Kell wouldn't have wanted his private life discussed. She wouldn't be surprised if Kell was already regretting what he himself had just said. He was certainly looking uncomfortable. It was a discomfort she wouldn't add to by saying she was sorry he'd had it rough...or that she'd heard it had gotten rougher when his lover had returned to her husband. She longed to ask if the rumor was true, but she valued her life too much to do so.

For a long while, neither spoke. Kell silently berated himself for baring his soul. Anne Elise pondered the fact that Kell, despite his harsh disposition, had been surprisingly easy to talk to. In fact, he was so easy to talk to that she heard herself saying something that she hadn't until just that moment realized was important to her. Or maybe deep within herself she'd made the realization long ago but was just now verbalizing it.

"I hope Jim died instantly in the helicopter crash." Anne Elise's eyes cut to Kell. His cut to her. "I mean, I hope he didn't suffer, or wasn't taken prisoner, or—" she shrugged "—or whatever else could have happened."

Kell had always thought it telling what people were grateful for in their lives. His father had been grateful for the price of a bottle of cheap whiskey. As a boy, he himself had been grateful when his father had been drunk enough to pass out before striking him or his mother. As a man, he'd been grateful for silence. His own silence at that moment when the pain of physical torture had racked his body, his own silence at that moment when emotional pain had racked his soul, and every fiber of his being had screamed out for him to beg the golden-eyed woman not to leave him. The woman presently sitting beside him would be grateful to learn that her husband had died instantly. Kell suddenly felt... what? He couldn't, maybe wouldn't, put a name to it, but he couldn't deny the sudden need to offer comfort.

"He probably did," he said, not at all certain he spoke the truth but hoping that he did. He hoped that James Samuel Butler hadn't suffered.

"In the beginning," Anne Elise said, "I hoped he was alive, but when it was obvious he wasn't, I began to hope he'd died instantly." She sighed. "But the mind's strange. I knew he was dead; although I grew to hope he'd died quickly, I've never gone through the paperwork of having him legally declared dead."

"Why?"

"Like I said, the mind's a strange thing. I think I felt that in so doing, I'd be killing him myself... at least symbolically."

"There's a certain metaphorical logic to that."

"I guess." Another silence wafted around them, and when she spoke again, her voice had lowered. "Sometimes his memory is so vague that it's as if he belonged to another lifetime. Sometimes I have to fight to hang on to the memories, then I'll get an image so crystal clear that it'll take my breath away. Mostly, though," she said regretfully, "his photos are almost as much those of a stranger to me as they are to our daughter." She let her gaze drift to Kell's. "That seems very sad to me."

"But normal," Kell said.

Normal. It wasn't a word Anne Elise would have ever used to describe her oh-so-brief, her oh-so-long, marriage. It was a sentiment she now expressed by saying, "It's as though nothing were final. It's always seemed that way. Which is why I want so desperately to lay him to rest—literally. I want to break the silence of the long, lonely years. I want to go on with my life."

Kell could see how a neat, tidy personality would long for closure—any closure. In truth, it was probably the kind of structure all human beings found comforting. Unfortunately it was a structure not always possible in a gray world.

"Are you serious about not buying the remains if a proper identification can't be made?" he asked.

She didn't hesitate. "Yes," she said. "I want finality, but I want a truthful one."

Kell studied her. He knew that she believed what she said, but he also knew that the issue was too emotional to be viewed that blackly, that whitely. If push came to shove, would she be able to walk away from what might be her husband's remains just because she couldn't prove their authenticity? It would take a strong woman. Anne Elise Butler, he knew, was strong, but she was also a woman with a need. A seventeen-year-old need. She needed to bury the past.

Just as he needed to protect her?

Yes. Even from herself, if that became necessary. He told himself his protection had been bought and paid for with General Terris's twenty-five thousand dollars. He told himself it was all part of the job, all part of what he'd signed on to do. He ignored the possibility that it was more. He ignored the possibility that maybe, just maybe, this woman with auburn hair and green eyes had gotten to him on some personal level.

Some things, however, could not be ignored.

That grew increasingly obvious as the in-flight movie flickered across the screen. It was a love story. A sensuous love story. A very sensuous love story that was doing very profound things to at least two of its viewers.

Kell, the earphones plugged into his ears, listened as the couple's breathing became erratic, ragged, little gasps that trailed into long, low moans. He deliberately kept his eyes averted from the woman beside him. Why, he wasn't sure. Except that suddenly he was very aware of her.

Well, why shouldn't he be aware of her? he thought with an angry defensiveness. They'd shared the same space for hours, practically living in each other's pockets. Every time she moved, her perfume drifted anew to him, and her hair, still scattered in sweet disarray, fluttered invitingly. Her crisp cotton blouse and her starched denim skirt had wilted with travel, which made it all the easier for both to hug the soft curves of her body. He hadn't gone out of his way to notice any of this; it was just that he wasn't blind, either. Or deaf. If the couple on the screen moaned one more time...

Anne Elise listened to the sounds of making love... and wished that she were just about anywhere but where she was. My goodness, when had films become so explicit? Not that this was really pornographic—in fact, it was really quite lovely—it was just that it was so... real. At least as she remembered real. Oh, my! she thought as another long, wet, thorough kiss began, this time with the camera exquisitely capturing the slow entwining of two eager tongues. Anne Elise deliberately kept her eyes on the screen and off the long-legged, thick-chested man beside her. Oh, my! she

thought again as the actor's tongue slid suggestively into the
actress's mouth. Another oh, my, this one actually forming
silently on her lips, trembled into existence as a hot restlessness slid across her own skin, skin that had almost forgotten what it was like to be caressed.

Anne Elise's "oh, my" was countered by Kell's "oh,
hell!" as the two tongues left little to the imagination.
Imagination. That was the problem, he thought. His had
always been too active. Too vivid. Too— Anne Elise Butler's mouth would be soft, lush, kissable. Not that it was any
of his business, because it wasn't. It was simply an idle observation. Want another idle observation, Chaisson? You're
getting hard. His lack of control angered him. But what
could he expect with the lethal combination of a sexy movie
and weeks of abstinence due to a government job? His condition had absolutely nothing to do with the supposition
that Anne Elise Butler's mouth would be soft, lush, and
kissable—which, of course, was just an idle observation.

Anne Elise's reaction to the kiss had left her stunned. It
had been a long while, a very long while, since she'd responded that strongly to something sensual. She supposed
her reaction was normal, though, considering the sexy
movie and her severely suppressed libido. What she couldn't
understand was why the actor's mouth so intrigued her. She
watched as it closed once more over the actress's—brushed,
actually. Brush. What would the same lips look like edged
by a mustache? She frowned. Now, why in the world would
she have thought that?

Wonder if she's had lovers? Kell frowned. Where in hell
had that question come from? And what the hell business
of his was it if she'd had four dozen lovers? No, he thought,
making it his business, anyway, she wouldn't have had four
dozen or four. While it was true that seventeen years was a
long time, it was equally true that Anne Elise Butler was a

thoroughly devoted woman. What would it feel like to have a woman that blindly devoted to him? Good. Intuitively, maybe because that depth of devotion had never been his, he knew it would feel good. Just as he knew that what the on-screen lovers were about to do would feel good. Despite the fact he knew it wouldn't help his precarious physical condition, he watched.

The love scene was discreetly, tastefully done. It was also tantalizingly effective. The slight, shadowy curve of a breast was far more provocative than the whole would have been. A masculine hand against the small of a feminine back left one breathless in a way that too much of either the man or the woman would not have. Thighs, sighs, kisses, a fade-out that sent Kell's imagination soaring. He yanked the earphones from his ears.

Startled, and more than a little guilty at being caught with her heart racing, Anne Elise jerked her head toward him.

It was only then that he realized how peculiar his action must appear. "I, uh, I've seen the movie," he growled.

She could only see his lips move—lips just beneath the brush of a dusky mustache. Disengaging one earplug, she asked, "What?"

"I've seen it." He amended the growl to a grumble, but only barely. He also reaffirmed that Anne Elise's lips would be soft, lush, kissable. Women with full lower lips and subtly curved upper lips always had mouths that were kissable. He reached for a magazine in the pouch on the back of the seat in front of him and fanned the pages across his lap—strategically fanned them to conceal the movie's effect.

Anne Elise refitted the earplug and refocused her attention on the screen. She wondered why it had taken him so long to realize he'd seen the movie before. And had he been able to tell how fast her heart was pounding?

Ten minutes later, THE END, followed by a list of credits, scrolled across the screen. Anne Elise removed the earphones. She purposely kept her eyes from the man sitting beside her, although from out of the corner of her eye, he appeared to be reading a magazine. Her heart still beat rampantly; her palms felt slick with sweat; her throat felt as dry as parchment left out in a noonday sun. She needed a drink. As she pushed the overhead button to summon the stewardess, she reminded herself that it had only been a movie.

Kell glanced toward her, a questioning look on his face.

"A dr—" She cleared her throat. "I think I'll have a drink."

"Yes, ma'am?" a stewardess asked, showing up quickly to accommodate a first-class passenger.

"Could I have some white wine, please?"

"Certainly," the friendly stewardess said, adding, as she reached for first Kell's, then Anne Elise's, earphones, "Here, let me take those."

Trying to be helpful, Anne Elise stretched toward the aisle—and Kell. Her breast grazed his arm. So slight was it, however, that she didn't even notice.

Kell did. Every cell of his body tightened. "Bourbon and water," he called out hoarsely to the stewardess who was already returning to the service area.

She turned and smiled. "Sure."

Anne Elise looked over at her traveling companion. "I thought you didn't dr—"

"I'm not in Bangkok yet," he said in a splintered tone that dared her to say more.

She didn't. Not a word through her wine and his bourbon and water. Nor did she later when Kell shut off the overhead lights—hers included—stood and, tugging at his tight jeans, grabbed two blankets from the overhead storage. He tossed one her way. The implication was clear. Not crazy about his authoritative manner, she nonetheless pulled her gaze from his tight jeans and tucked the blanket about her. She cozied back as best she could against the pillow. He dropped back into the seat beside her and did the same.

But once more, rest eluded both.

An off-chance sighting of the edge of her ivory-colored slip, which peeked from beneath her skirt, sent Kell's imagination into action with the sudden remembrance of her lacy underwear within the suitcase. The silky pieces had been a pale, pretty ivory trimmed in a rich, sultry brown. And did she really wear such scraps of fabric as the brassiere and panties?

Anne Elise, on the other hand, seemed to have nothing better to do than consider all the aspects of mustaches—viceful mustaches.

He turned.

She tossed.

He squirmed.

She wriggled.

"Will you be still?" he barked.

"Will you?" she snarled back.

A long while later, after a scheduled stop in Tokyo, they arrived in Bangkok. Both were tired and noticeably irritable. It was an irritation they seemed perfectly content to take out on each other.

"How much farther?" Anne Elise groused as they trekked through the Bangkok airport. It was just after ten p.m., and she could never in all her life remember being this tired. Which was probably the reason the airport seemed to stretch on forever. Marginally she noted the airport was very much like every other airport she'd been in—modern, clean, efficiency oriented. She also noted that it was nice to be able to breathe again. Being confined with Kell Chaisson had begun to take its toll.

His duffle bag slung over his shoulder, her suitcase in his free hand, Kell glanced over at the woman beside him. A stubble of beard once more darkened his angular face, making him look like a brawler in search of a Friday-night fight. It also, Anne Elise concluded grudgingly, made him look attractive—if one went for the savage kind of appeal.

"What's wrong, Miss Congeniality? I thought you'd be glad to walk off some of that pent-up energy."

She didn't point out that he'd been every bit as restless as she. Nor did she tell him what she'd really like to do, namely, to take his overbearing attitude and stuff it. Deep. Instead, she walked on in the direction in which he silently led.

Suddenly he asked, a frown at his lips. "You did bring your passport, didn't you?" It had been such an obvious thing that he hadn't thought to mention it.

"Of course." Her voice conveyed the insult she felt.

His frown faded. "Well, get it ready. You'll need it in a minute."

Cursory glances at passports, cursory questions posed and answered and Anne Elise and Kell were soon moving out of the building and into the night.

Anne Elise's first impression of Bangkok was that it was hot and humid, not at all unlike Southern summers.

"I'll get us a cab," Kell said, stepping toward the curb, his intent to flag down the first taxi he saw.

Before he could, however, a man approached. The man, whose skin was the color of teakwood, seemed meticulously painted in white livery, his cap regally perched upon his dark head.

"Captain Chaisson? Mrs. Butler?" he asked in slow but precise English.

Kell gave him the look he gave everything and everyone on first meeting—a glare of suspicion.

Anne Elise glanced first at the chauffeur, then at Kell, then filled in the expectant silence with, "I'm Mrs. Butler. And this is Captain Chaisson."

The man nodded in greeting. "Your father arranged for me to drive you to your hotel. This way please."

They followed in his wake until they arrived at a mile-long limousine, the color of *crème Anglaise,* which was parked quietly, elegantly by the curb. Kell's only comment was the arching of a brow. Anne Elise had no idea whether the action denoted approval or disapproval, and, as Rhett Butler had so eloquently put it, she didn't give a damn. She knew only that this man, this car, were offering her comfort, which at the moment she desperately needed. When the chauffeur opened the door for her and she slid into the air-conditioned coolness, she knew only that if this car were destined for hell, she was going along for the ride. At least partway. Obviously Kell was, too, because she felt him climb in beside her. The chauffeur hefted the luggage and started to load it in the back.

"Oh," Anne Elise cried out suddenly, "tell him to put mine up here."

Kell's brow wrinkled. "Why do you—"

"Just tell him to put it up here," she said, her voice barbed with cross-the-Pacific weariness.

Kell's frown deepened, but he opened the door and crawled back out into the heated night. "The lady—" he made the word sound less than "—would like her suitcase."

"Yes, sir," Anne Elise heard the chauffeur reply. She then peripherally saw the suitcase passed to Kell, who lifted it as though it weighed nothing. He shoved it into the back seat.

"Here," he said, crowding back in beside her.

Anne Elise smiled sweetly, too sweetly, as the suitcase landed on her lap. "The lady thanks you."

The look in his brown eyes said, "The lady's a pain in the ass."

As the car eased into the ebony night after the driver confirmed that they were indeed staying at the Hilton International near Embassy Row, Anne Elise unzipped the suitcase and began searching through it. Her fingers tunneled here and there, from one side to the other, from top to bottom.

"What are you looking for?" Kell asked finally, exasperated by her futile attempts to find something.

"I'll tell you what I'm looking for, Mr. Do-the-Orient-in-a-Paper-Sack. I'm looking for a comb and/or a brush or anything that resembles either." When it became obvious that neither was going to turn up, she slammed the lid shut and zipped it closed. "Great! Just great! You trashed them back in Dallas!" She was vaguely aware that she was glad the glass partition between the driver and passenger sections of the car was up and that the chauffeur couldn't be privy to her uncharacteristic surliness.

"Bangkok sells combs and brushes," he replied evenly.

"I had a perfectly good comb and brush."

"So take it out of my salary, ma'am," he drawled sarcastically.

"Stuff it, Chaisson!" she retorted, the petty image of a check for twenty-five thousand dollars minus the cost of a comb and brush flashing through her mind. It almost made her laugh. Almost.

She leaned her head back against the seat and watched the scenery speed by. Actually, she could see little with the nightfall and the garish glare of city lights. Behind the lights were dark streets of shuttered shops, conical-shaped shadows that she assumed by day would be revealed to be temples, and a river, a *klong*, as it was known in Thailand, that ran down the middle of the city. The Chao Phraya. She'd checked a map and knew that much. She also knew that by day the river, used as a street, swimming pool and bath, would be teeming with life. Right now, however, it was sluggishly asleep. As she longed to be.

"I'm sorry," she said at length, rolling her head toward him.

Kell slid his eyes to her. She could feel them more than she could see them. They felt hot. Like heated molasses.

"I'm just tired," she added. And suffering from jet lag and not exactly here on a stressless mission to begin with. She avoided investigating why being in such close quarters with the man beside her had done nothing to sweeten her mood.

On the other hand, Kell avoided delving too closely into the realization that her hair, instead of appearing in need of a comb and brush, looked perfect. Scattered, fetchingly tousled, but perfect. Okay. Maybe in need of a man's fingers to drag it back from her face, but nothing more.

"You're entitled," he said finally, and in that tone of voice that hinted there was a gentler side to this hard man.

Would she ever see it? she thought, suddenly sad that she might not, because she innately knew it would be something well worth viewing.

She did not see Kell's gentler side at the Hilton International Hotel.

"What do you mean we don't have adjoining rooms?" he asked the white-coated man behind the desk.

Despite a mind muddled by the long flight, Anne Elise had been admiring the rare and exotic plants gracing the lobby. Most she had no name for, but the orchids were spectacular. She knew her father had specifically chosen the

Hilton because of its botanical garden. Occupying eight-and-a-half acres of prime property, the hotel boasted everything from bougainvillea-draped balconies to water-lily pads the size of cart wheels. She'd told her father she didn't care what hotel she stayed at, but he'd insisted. Just as her traveling companion was now insisting.

"But, sir—" the frock-coated man began.

"We specified adjoining rooms."

"I have no mention of such a specification."

"Then, I'm specifying it now."

"Sir, we have a conference of Japanese—"

"Find something."

"—businessmen and we have no—"

"Find something." The cold fire of Kell's voice halted the clerk, though the smile, which seemed always in place, stayed.

"I'll check, sir," the man said, turning away.

"You do that," Kell said.

"We don't have to have adjoining rooms," Anne Elise whispered, having sidled to Kell's side during the exchange. She had clearly been embarrassed by it.

"Yes, we do."

"We don't—"

"If I'm involved in this, we do," he shot back curtly. "I have to be able to get to you." At her puzzled look, he explained. "Look, lady, we're not here just because we thought Bangkok would be a great place to visit with a stranger. We don't know what kind of people we're dealing with, or, more to the point, we probably do. I'm assuming I'm getting paid in part to get your ass back in one piece."

As always, he riled her. "Did anyone ever tell you that you have a shockingly limited vocabulary, Captain?"

He shrugged, sending broad shoulders straining against the black T-shirt. "I thought I showed remarkable diversity. I could have referred too it as your pretty little ass."

Anne Elise's face had just clouded up to thunder all over him when the clerk returned, a pained expression at his lips. "I am sorry to say, sir, that we have nothing. Only the bridal suite remains—"

"We'll take it," Kell announced, pivoting the registration book around and boldly, quickly signing their names. "Oh, and send up a rollaway bed." With that, and with the key in hand, he turned, picked up the luggage and swaggered toward the elevator. When it was obvious he was making the trip solo, he halted. "Are you coming?"

Silently, all coherent words having died moments before, she pushed from the counter. She said nothing until the elevator was making its way to the appropriate floor.

"Why not one of the other rooms if we were going to share one?"

Kell, willfully, yet unnoticeably fighting claustrophobia, glanced over at her. Her question had drawn him from his peaceful, safe jungle. It was where he went every time he was confined to a small, cagelike space. He waited until the doors slid open...and his breathing became slow, even, normal.

"The bridal suite'll be larger. At least we'll have room to walk around each other."

His logic was sound. Anne Elise couldn't fight that. Besides, at this point, a bed was a bed was a bed.

How the rollaway bed arrived before them would forever remain a mystery, but another white-coated Thai, his face thin but smiling, was just exiting the room.

"Anything else, sir?" he asked in halting English, showing absolutely no curiosity as to why a couple would want an additional bed on their honeymoon.

Kell answered him in Thai.

Anne Elise was more startled by Kell's response than by the gorgeous room, done in cream and soft pastel shades of red and orange, that she had just entered. She quickly turned back toward the doorway. Kell was just tipping the man in native currency, baht.

The butler spoke something else in his native language, glancing as he did so at Anne Elise, then, a cheery smile on his lips, he pressed his palms together beneath his chin, as if in prayer, bowed his head slightly and said, "Good night."

Kell closed the door and turned. His glance collided with Anne Elise.

"You speak the language," she said, her surprise evident.

He shrugged. "Some."

"Wh-What did he say?"

The eyes that moments before had slammed into hers now darkened until they burned with a fiery warmth. "He said he hoped we'd be happy together and that we'd have many healthy children."

His eyes, his words, blistered her. "Oh," was all she could manage to say.

Suddenly, yanking his gaze from hers, he shouldered past her. His attitude appeared to be that he shared a bridal suite with a strange woman on a routine basis. He didn't even glance around at his spacious surroundings. Curiosity had at least made her do that, taking in as she did so the canopied bed draped in rich Thai silk, the Italianate furniture, the lacquered wood tables, the bottle of champagne chilling in a silver stand, which had obviously been brought up by the butler as he'd delivered the cot. Everything in the suite had been designed for lovers.

"You take the bed," Kell said, squatting at his duffle bag, "and I'll take the rollaway. You want the bathroom first?"

The trip, the man, perhaps even the room and the butler's wish for their future, were catching up with her. She felt . . . overwhelmed, as though she'd abandoned her safe, secure world for one that wasn't quite real.

"What?" she said, uncertain what he'd asked.

"You want the bathroom first?"

"Uh, yeah," she answered, galvanizing her thoughts and forcing herself to move to the suitcase.

She removed a small case and headed for the bathroom. Flipping on the light, she saw that it was as elegantly designed for love as the bedroom, inviting couples to bathe together in the enormously large marble tub. Anne Elise ignored all the subtle invitations, which was easy to do since she was about to drop dead with fatigue. She didn't even look at the woman in the mirror as she brushed her teeth. Instead, she took the opportunity to close her eyes. Seconds later, she opened the bathroom door. She stopped, framed in the doorway of the lighted bathroom.

Kell had extinguished all the lights in the bedroom and the adjoining sitting room and now stood at the window. His pose suggested that he, ever vigilant, had been checking out their surroundings . . . or had been checking to see if they were being checked out. Anne Elise noted this, but only barely, for her attention was more fully captured by the fact that he had removed his T-shirt and was holding it in his hands. From somewhere outside shone a reddish light that sliced across his hair-dusted chest. It, coupled with the silver slashes branding his skin, created an eerie image. A sensual image.

At the sound of the bathroom door opening, Kell turned in that direction. His expression clearly indicated that he hadn't expected her to be finished so soon. What his expression didn't indicate was that his breath had been halved by the sight of the woman in the doorway, her hair tumbled about her, her soft, lush lips devoid of any artificial color, her face filled with drop-dead fatigue. A feeling of protectiveness surged through his veins.

"I'll bathe in the morning," she said, answering the question she saw on his face. "I'm just too tired tonight."

Forcing his eyes from her, not knowing what to make of the protectiveness he felt toward her, and uncomfortable with the strength of it, he growled, "Get some sleep." With that, he tossed the shirt in the direction of the duffle bag, then marched toward the bathroom.

Anne Elise, wishing his tone wasn't always so rough, stepped out of his way. She forwent wishing him a good night, which would somehow imply that everything was usual when it certainly was not. Instead, she quickly searched through the suitcase for her own T-shirt. Encouraged by the sound of the shower, she tore off her clothes, slipped into the makeshift nightgown and yanked back the covers of the bed. She then crawled into the mammoth warm womb. She had time for only one thought before sleep slugged her under the chin.

Kell Chaisson's bronzed skin would stand out dramatically against the pale marble of the bathtub.

Chapter Five

The hands caressing her were large, strong, as bronzed as the kiss of a hundred hot suns could make them. They were also gentle...and touched her everywhere the man had touched the woman in the movie—her cheek, the curve of her breast, the small of her bare back. Anne Elise moaned softly, the sound carrying a soulful entreaty for the man to continue. He did, except that suddenly the caresses grew forceful, determined, and she could feel sleep slipping, even rushing, away. She fought to hang on to the gauzy blessedness but could not. The hands were too insistent.

"Hey, Sleeping Beauty, wake up!"

Anne Elise's eyes flew open.

For a fraction of a second that seemed more like forever, she stared up into bold brown eyes. The man bending over her had shaved recently, leaving behind a smell as clean as the morning. He also wore fresh jeans and a white shirt that emphasized his bronzeness. Bronze. Was this the man she'd been dreaming about? Was this the dream man who'd touched her in such intimate places?

For a fraction of a second that seemed more like forever, Kell stared down into groggy green eyes. The woman below him looked night tousled, consummately feminine, and vulnerable. So damned vulnerable! What had she been dreaming about to make her moan the way she had? And was she wearing a panty-size scrap of lace beneath the T-shirt? This last thought made him push from her.

"Wake up," he said again, this time with a curt throatiness that hadn't been present before. "I've ordered up some coffee."

"W-what time is it?" Anne Elise asked, simultaneously raking her hand through her hair and edging her body to a semisitting position. When she saw how plainly the T-shirt molded her breasts, she clutched the cover to her.

"A few minutes till nine," he responded, crouching before the duffle bag and cramming his dirty jeans inside. The rollaway bed, linen messily sticking out in every direction, had already been folded up. Anne Elise wondered how he'd ever gotten his large frame to fit it. "I've got some things to do before we call Forbes," she heard him say and reeled in her wayward thoughts. They scattered again when he stood and she realized anew just how impressively tall he was.

"What things?" she asked, forcing the subject from his height to the business at hand.

"I need to go by the b—" A knock sounded at the door. "That's the coffee," Kell said, stepping forward.

The waiter who carried the silver urn of steaming coffee was smiling broadly. He bowed first to Kell, then to Anne Elise. The gleam in his eyes clearly said that he hoped the newlyweds had had an enjoyable night. Anne Elise turned a shade of pink. Kell seemed unmoved by both reactions.

He spoke something, which Anne Elise interpreted as thank you, then handed the waiter several bahts. The waiter responded with the same expression Kell had used, then bowed once more and disappeared out the door.

"They're certainly into bowing, aren't they?" Anne Elise said, simply to cover up her flush.

Kell didn't even look her way but rather strode to where the urn had been set on a table near the window. "It's a form of courtesy," he said, pouring a cup of coffee and holding it out to her.

From where he stood, she would have had to get out of bed to retrieve his offering. When her hesitation became obvious, Kell frowned, as though annoyed with women's inane sensibilities. Muttering something that sounded very much like a curse to Anne Elise, he crossed the room, set the cup and saucer on the bedside table—one rattled against the other—then sauntered toward the bath, where he disengaged a terry bathrobe from its hook behind the door.

"Here," he said, tossing it across the bed, "compliments of the hotel."

Anne Elise presumed she'd been too tired the night before to notice the robe.

"Thank you," she mumbled, not only for the robe, but also for the fact that Kell had retraced his steps to the coffee.

His back to her, he poured himself a cup and, ignoring the saucer, walked to the window, ostensibly to give her some privacy. She took advantage of his generosity. Throwing back the covers, she slung her bare feet to the floor and her arms into the white terry robe. It felt warm and substantive in a way that a T-shirt and a pair of panties didn't. Threading the hair back from her eyes, she reached for the cup. The coffee was hot and strong and there might be a chance that she was going to live, after all.

"What things do you have to do?" she tried again, encouraged by the caffeine coursing through her.

Kell turned toward the sound, which his highly skilled senses told him had shifted slightly. He found her standing, swallowed up in a robe that was several sizes too large. The sight shouldn't have been sexy, in fact, it should have been anything but, but the truth was that what should be wasn't always what was. He brought the cup to his lips and swallowed deeply.

"Go to the bank for one thing and get the money," he replied when the coffee had seared its way down his throat. Ignoring the fact that she still looked sexy in the oversized robe, he asked her the name of the bank she'd used. She told him. "Call them and tell them I'm gonna pick up the money. And tell them to ask me for some identification."

Anne Elise nodded as she slowly started toward him.

"Then I'm gonna meet with a dentist who was recommended—"

The cup stopped midway to her lips. "A dentist?"

"I possibly could make an identification, at least a cursory one, comparing dental records to the remains, but with something this important I don't want to rely on my judgment. At some point I'd want an expert opinion and that needs to be before the money changes hands."

Anne Elise nodded again, still making her way toward the window and him. She didn't mention that, from what she'd heard, he was more expert at knocking teeth out than making a comparative identification of them. "You have someone lined up?"

"Yeah. A Thai who's done some work for the American government before."

Which was why her father had been right about Kell Chaisson being the man for the job. He had the contacts. He had the know-how. Again, as once before, she felt safe with this man. As once before, the feeling felt good.

"I shouldn't be gone more than a couple of hours," Kell added. "When I get back, we'll call Forbes and set up a meeting. Hopefully for this afternoon."

Anne Elise nodded again, the idea of getting the confrontation over with an extremely appealing one. She was now standing beside him at the window, cursorily glancing out and sipping at the coffee. Abruptly, the cup stopped at her pursed lips. "W-What is that?"

Kell followed the direction of her gaze. His answer came in the form of a nonchalant, "It's the Nai Lert Shrine."

"Is . . . Is it what I think it is?"

The mercurial streak in his complex nature surfaced and amusement, like a night star in a velvety brown heaven, sparked in his eyes. "I guess that depends pretty much on what you think it is," he drawled.

She didn't *think*, she *knew* what it was. The array of phallic symbols was the most startling thing she'd ever seen. Most of them were made of wood and stone. There was even one on legs, mounted very much as one would a cannon. Bright ribbons—crimson, sunshine yellow, vivid orange, deep purple—adorned the phalluses. A mat had been placed on the brick pathway and, even as Anne Elise watched, a woman kneeled and placed her joined, prayerful hands in front of her bowed head.

The amusement was still there, but modified, when Kell spoke. "The shrine is believed to be inhabited by a female spirit called Tuptim. The locals take her very seriously. She's associated with prosperity and good fortune as well as fertility. Anyone—" he nodded toward the woman still kneeling before the shrine "—can make a request of her. If the request is granted, it's customary to donate another phallus to the collection."

"I see," Anne Elise said, trying to appear as nonchalant as the man beside her. "And the honeymoon suite..."

"...overlooks it," Kell finished.

"How...appropriate," Anne Elise said, her eyes shying away from his. She sipped her coffee, watched the woman rise and walk away, listened to the suddenly awkward silence. She filled it in with, "You've been here before, haven't you? I mean to Bangkok?"

The question was as needless as the one she'd posed earlier about the shrine. She already knew the answer. Kell Chaisson knew too much about Thai customs and culture. He knew the language, at least in part, and he carried currency, as though he'd had it left over from a previous visit.

All traces of amusement had vanished when he said, "On occasion."

He held the coffee cup in one hand, his fingers around the rim; his other hand he edged into the back pocket of his jeans. His tight jeans. His tight jeans that looked very much like their own phallic shrine. Appalled at the turn of her thoughts, Anne Elise welcomed the distraction of his voice.

"I used to take R&R here when I was in Nam," he explained. "I've also been back several times on government jobs." But never when I didn't have to, he could have said. Until now. Why had he let her talk him into it? Why hadn't he stuck by his first decision? When had their eyes met? It was a question both of them were asking. Just as each was asking why one or the other, or both, didn't break visual contact.

But neither did.

Anne Elise seemed helpless not to notice the way his dark hair slashed across his forehead; she couldn't help but notice, and appreciate, the curve of his lips and the way they suggestively peeked from beneath his mustache. Then there was the width of his shoulders, the taper of his waist, the skintight jeans that reminded her, even against her wishes, of the shrine beyond the window.

Kell, on the other hand, couldn't help but note the alluring madness of her early-morning hair, virginally untouched, just as she herself, though wife and mother, was symbolically virginal. He noticed, too, that her eyes were still hazed with sleep and that her lips, devoid of makeup, did look soft, lush, and kissable—though that was just an idle observation, of course. And the bathrobe... She looked little-girl lost in it, while at the same time she looked all-woman sexy in it. In fact, she looked as sexy as all get-out. Sexy as hell. Sexy as—

He gulped down the remainder of his coffee.

"Call the bank," he ordered, clunking the cup onto the table and starting for the door.

The bark in his voice started Anne Elise. And curiously bruised her feelings.

"Don't leave the room," he called, halting at the doorway.

As always, his abrasiveness rankled. "I need to buy a comb and br—"

"Don't leave the room," he interrupted. "And that's an order."

Unknowingly, she drew herself to her full height. "And what if I said I don't like orders, Captain Chaisson?"

"Then I'd say you made the trip with the wrong man." He paused for the right dramatic effect. "And that you could find your way home alone."

She knew he wasn't making an idle threat. If she didn't play ball by his rules, he'd call the game. Or force her to play it alone.

"You really are a son of a bitch, aren't you?" she said quietly.

"Yes, ma'am," he mocked. "And don't you forget it."

He returned precisely when he said he would—a little bit shy of two hours later. Anne Elise had bathed and dressed in white slacks and a red-and-white-striped shirt. She sat at the table, the empty coffeepot before her with her stomach growling in hunger.

When he opened the door, a package in his hand, his gaze raced to hers. Then sped upward to her hair, which she'd piled in a tight knot atop her head. Her hair was barely long enough to pull upward and went only with wisps whispering down in protest.

Kell frowned. He was uncertain as to the source of his displeasure. He told himself it was the result of her having clearly disobeyed him—she'd had to use a comb and brush to effect the hairstyle—though, in truth, there might have been more to his discontent. He might have been displeased with the way her hair, promising to tumble at the right man's touch, emptied his lungs of air.

"I thought I told you—" he began in a voice that could have melted iron.

"I used your comb and brush and some pins I found in the bottom of my purse." Her look dared him to criticize her for borrowing his personal items.

Far from feeling annoyed, he felt... He wasn't exactly certain what he felt. That they'd shared an intimacy? Yes. A casual intimacy, but an intimacy nonetheless.

Anne Elise had felt the same thing when she'd taken the comb and brush from the bathroom counter and drawn them through her hair. It was the same thing she was feeling now. The tilt of her chin dared him to make something of that as well.

He didn't. Rather, he closed the door behind him and started toward the unmade bed.

"I took care of everything," he said, sitting on the bed's edge. "The dentist is lined up to come whenever we call, and I've got the money in the safe downstairs."

The moment that Anne Elise realized the money wasn't in the sack he was carrying, she thought how stupid of her to have even considered that it was. One didn't walk around with fifty thousand dollars in a paper sack. She was inwardly smiling at her naiveté when Kell produced the gun from the brown bag. The smile died. Her heart stopped.

"What's that?"

He looked up at her, down at the gun, up at her again. "A gun," he said matter-of-factly, handling the bluish-gray steel as though he handled a weapon every day of his life.

Which he very possibly did, Anne Elise reflected. "Surely, you don't think—"

He glanced up from the task of loading the gun. "I'm being paid to cover every base. And a .45 automatic covers every base. Real good," he added, pulling his shirttail from his jeans and tucking the gun at the small of his back. He was obviously trying out the feel of the steel.

"I don't believe it," Anne Elise said, shaking her head. "I feel like I've walked onto the set of a B-grade movie."

"Could get worse," Kell pointed out, removing the gun and laying it on the bedside table. "It could progress into a bad B-grade movie." Without a pause, he asked, "You got Forbes's number?"

She nodded, reached for her purse and started to hand the piece of paper to Kell.

"No, you call him. I want to keep him in the dark about me as long as possible. That's assuming, of course, that he doesn't know I'm along already."

Anne Elise, her heart suddenly thrumming a fast rhythm, reached for the phone and started to dial the number.

"Tell him you want to meet this afternoon and tell him it has to be in the hotel lobby."

"What if he doesn't agree?"

"Be firm."

The phone was answered immediately. Anne Elise recognized the voice. It was still bourbon rough and cigarette scratchy. It still made her flesh crawl.

"T-this is Anne Elise Butler. I'm in Bangkok." She started to say that she was eager to meet with him, then decided that she needed to be more forceful. "I want to meet with you."

"This afternoon," Kell prompted in a whisper. He'd squatted down in front of her, his knee almost brushing hers. His nearness felt reassuring. Especially since she could feel herself beginning to tremble. Maybe it was because of the gun lying so ominously on the bedside table; maybe it was the sound of Forbes's voice; maybe it was the fact that everything was finally being put into motion.

"This afternoon!" Anne Elise hastened to add, her eyes riveted to Kell's.

"Well, now, Mrs. Butler," Forbes drawled, "I wasn't expecting you so soon. I may not be able to get everything together until tomorr—"

"This afternoon," she insisted in what she hoped was a strong voice.

There was a hesitation. "I don't kn—"

"This afternoon."

Another pause, then, "Did you bring the money?"

"Of course I brought the money," she replied, her eyes still on Kell. She wasn't sure, but she thought his irises darkened at Forbes's monetary inquiry.

"All right, then," Forbes said, "this afternoon."

"In the lobby of the Hilton International," Anne Elise specified and Kell nodded his approval.

"The Hilton?" Forbes repeated. "That's a busy place, Mrs. Butler. Don't you think you might prefer somewhere quieter, more private?"

"Actually I prefer the lobby of the Hilton."

There was another pause. "If that's what you want. Say four o'clock?"

"Four o'clock?" Anne Elise's eyes questioned the man in front of her.

Kell held up three fingers.

"No, make it three," she said, sensing that Kell wanted to gain psychological control by imposing as much of their will as possible.

She could hear Forbes resisting, though finally he gave a curt, "Three o'clock," and hung up.

Anne Elise was left listening to a powerful silence. "Three o'clock," she repeated for Kell's benefit, recradling the receiver with fingers that were now out-and-out trembling.

Kell saw that trembling and watched as one hand fitted itself into another. How many times in the all-too-many years she'd been alone had she had to be her own comforter? The answer he came up with appealed to that protective urge she seemed to trigger in him. It was an urge, however, that he once more ignored.

"You did good," he said softly, unable to deny her that much or, more to the point, unable to deny himself from offering her some sort of solace.

His praise washed sweetly over her. A shaky smile slid across her lips. "I, uh, I don't think I'm ever gonna get used to starring in B-grade movies."

"A class-A lady seldom does," Kell replied.

The compliment, coming from a man who'd done nothing but insinuate that she was a royal pain, came accompanied by the same shock that she would have experienced had she been delivered a blow to the head. His words, like a blow to the heart, stunned her, warmed her, increased the tremble of her hands.

Each just stared at the other—wordlessly.

Suddenly Anne Elise's stomach growled.

The sound broke the spell. It also ushered back Kell's usual gruff disposition.

"C'mon," he said, rising. "If I don't feed you, you're gonna die on me. And, frankly, I don't want to have to explain your demise to the general."

As Anne Elise watched Kell hide the gun within his duffle bag, she took the occasion to wonder if this man who was so ready with the scathing words, so at home with violence, so loving of his own solitary confinement from the human race, wasn't a fraud. Was it possible that in the shadow of the son of a bitch stood an honest-to-God human being?

The thought was intriguing.

Bangkok.

The village of the wild plum.

The more she saw of the city, the more Anne Elise realized it wasn't at all as she'd expected it to be. From the moment Kell, after calling the dentist and arranging for him to be present at the meeting that afternoon, had led her through the back corridors of the hotel and out the service entrance—à la a B movie—Bangkok had spoken to her in contradictions. On the one hand it was exquisitely Oriental, from the crenellated spires of the Buddhist temples to the teak ferries traveling the Chao Phraya, while on the other hand it was fascinatingly cosmopolitan with its modern hotels, its flock of internationally mixed tourists and its traffic jams that rivaled any New York or Paris could boast.

"It wasn't what I was expecting," Anne Elise admitted as they sat on the terrace of a restaurant eating lunch.

Beyond them, the river teemed with life. Rice barges, their canvas covers swollen with grain, eked out a slow passage, while little hotel ferries, their teak roofs steeply pitched, their eaves upturned like waterborne temples, carted tourists back and forth. The real speed belonged to boats about the length of a large gondola, long-tailed boats with their roaring engines and their propeller shafts slanting outward a dozen feet from their sterns. There were also floating markets, some with pots and braziers from which women served fast-food meals. At the *klong*'s edge, children swam and splashed and adults bathed, all forgiving of the filthy brown, vegetable-strewn water.

"How so?" Kell asked, bringing the glass of iced tea to his mouth. Though he was alert, his eyes constantly shifting here and there, he was more relaxed than Anne Elise had ever seen him. Certainly more relaxed than the gruff man who'd exited the hotel after offering her a compliment that he'd seemed to regret the moment it was bestowed.

"No one looks like Yul Brynner."

The lips surrounding the glass grinned. Anne Elise could tell by the flicking of the mustache. "*The King and I* is banned from local cinemas," he said.

"Why?"

"The Thai government thinks it shows the monarch in a bad light. Particularly the fact that Anna seemed to have so much influence over him. Of course," Kell continued, setting the glass back on the table, "the Thai government has also restricted the import of foreign cigarettes, and prostitution is illegal. All that's the bad news, the good, that you can rent pirated copies of *The King and I* from dozens of video shops around town, just as you can buy foreign cigarettes without even looking hard."

Anne Elise arched a brow. "And prostitution?"

"Bangkok's the brothel of Southeast Asia."

"Contradiction," she said. "I'd already decided the city was full of it."

"Mmm," Kell agreed, taking a bite of a dish called exploded catfish. Anne Elise hadn't inquired as to why it was so called. She didn't think she wanted to know. "The city really has little going for it. There're no geographic boundaries—no uptown, no downtown, the city doesn't seem to begin or end anywhere. Plus, you have financial districts right next door to residential areas, a nice house right next to a slum. For the most part, the city's ugly, dirty, and, for much of the year, chokingly hot."

Anne Elise made a motion that took in the crowded terrace. "Then why all the tourists?"

"The Thai people are hospitable. Thailand's been called the 'land of smiles.' To shout or scream is thought to be in bad taste and reveals a definite lack of *chai yen*."

"*Chai yen?*"

Kell considered. "Sort of like 'losing your cool.'"

Anne Elise nodded, her eyes coming to rest on the waiter, plump but agile, who appeared tableside with a smile on his lips. "More? I get more?"

"No, no," she said, adding, "Good. Tell him it was good."

In all, Kell had ordered a half dozen dishes, from duck to fish to shrimp, to give a palette of Thai cookery. He had explained that Thai cooking had to please the entire family, and since families more often than not included several generations, each dish was geared toward an average taste. To compensate, to appeal to the individual, sauces, curry pastes, and condiments were used in abundance. Anne Elise's favorite, and the one she'd told Kell to tell the waiter was good, was a sweet preparation of palm sugar.

Kell spoke in the language that sounded so foreign to her ears. The waiter's smile grew with each word. At last, the smile stretching from ear to ear, he bowed at her, as if in thanks. He then said something to Kell. Kell's gaze instantly rose to Anne Elise's.

"Chai," he said to the waiter. The waiter, grinning again, mumbled something and waddled away.

Anne Elise's look was expectant. It was obvious that the conversation had been about her.

Kell pushed his chair back, negligently getting more comfortable by squaring ankle to knee.

"Well?" Anne Elise said when he said nothing.

"Well, what?"

"What did he say?"

"Thais are totally uninhibited about asking personal questions."

It was not an answer to her question, and both of them knew it.

"Like what?" she was finally forced to ask.

He shrugged. "Like how much money you make."

"Is that what he asked you? How much money you make?"

Kell, his eyes on hers, said, "No." When her eyes didn't waver from his, he added, "He asked if you were my mistress."

"Mistress?"

"I guess he would have gone for wife, but he saw no ring."

Anne Elise gave a half laugh, ignoring the fluttery little feeling in her stomach. Within twenty-four hours, it had been assumed that she was both this man's wife and mistress. "God help the woman who's either," she said, battling the fluttery feeling with teasing.

Kell grinned. The fluttery feeling grew worse.

At that moment, the waiter reappeared—thankfully, Anne Elise thought. "Dessert?" he said to her, then launched into a monologue in his native tongue. At its end, Kell translated.

"He has a puddinglike dessert made with plums and mangoes—"

"Chai," Anne Elise interrupted, repeating the word to the dark-skinned Thai that she'd heard Kell use only minutes before.

The waiter nodded and walked away. Anne Elise had just begun a complaint about the hot weather and the breeze-lessness of the day when the dessert appeared before her. She looked down at it incredulously.

"But I didn't order..." She looked up at Kell. "Tell him I didn't order—"

"But you did," Kell interrupted.

"I did not—" she managed to get out before the implication struck her. "You told him I was your mistress?" When the couple at the next table glanced over, Anne Elise lowered her voice. "You told him I was your mistress?"

Kell shrugged. "It was what he wanted to hear. In fact, I doubt he would have believed me if I'd said otherwise. Besides," he said with a smile so genuine it sparkled like a forty-carat diamond, "you wouldn't want me to lose face in a country where losing face is a serious affair, would you?"

She'd never seen him tease. She'd seen him smile sarcastically; she's seen him half smile for real, but she'd never seen him tease. It was impressive, unsettling. Unsettling because it brought back a fluttery feeling to her stomach. It, and the thought of being his mistress.

"He's the kind of man every woman would like to spend one night with..."

Superimposed over this came the image of blond hair and blue eyes—the blond hair and blue eyes of her husband.

Anne Elise quickly lowered her gaze from Kell's.

"C'mon," he said, his tone suddenly rough, "eat your dessert. We've got a couple of hours to see the city before we have to return to the hotel."

It was unbelievable how much ground one could over in a fast two hours. They saw the Marble Temple, the temple of the Emerald Buddha in the Grand Palace, Wat Arun, on the banks of the Chao Phraya. They dodged traffic and tourists, prowled and poked here and there. They grew hot—hot in the afternoon sun. Interestingly, though their physical condition worsened, their moods once more lightened. Occasionally, Anne Elise felt Kell's hand at the small of her back, guiding her.

Once, as they were walking through a ratty section of the city, Kell said, "Put your purse between us." In explanation, he added, "Pickpockets are a problem here." She transferred her bag to her other shoulder. She also thought Kell moved a bit closer. But then, surely it was only natural under the circumstances?

"One more thing to see, then we'll go back," Kell said, heading them toward one final destination.

Anne Elise groaned. "My feet are killing me."

"You'll survive," he said, mercilessly leading her on and turning onto a street called Patpong Road. "This street is owned by Mr. Patpong," he said. "At night it's crawling with action. Just about any kind you want."

The street, bare by day, boasted a series of establishments whose names were at best suggestive, at worst downright crude. They presently stood in front of the Lipstick Bar.

"Sounds like you've seen it at night, Captain," Anne Elise teased. She was hot and tired and had tramped the entire town with this man, all of which prompted her to say what she might not have said otherwise.

Kell, too, was hot, his shirt splotched in sweat. Perspiration also beaded across his forehead. "Sounds like a loaded question to me," he said, grinning back.

"Sounds like a question you don't want to answer."

"Sounds like a question that could hang a man."

"Sounds like we've been out in the sun too long," Anne Elise admitted, her grin broadening.

"C'mon," Kell said, his hand at her waist, "at least you can say you've seen the notorious Patpong Road."

"And once met a man who's seen it at night."

"No comment," he replied.

They were nearly back to the hotel when Anne Elise came to the conclusion that, while Kell had seen the nightlife of Patpong Road, he hadn't paid for a bed partner. That wasn't his style. She also came to the conclusion that her curiosity was normal. Wasn't it? She willingly let her attention be distracted when she spotted the little jewelry stall.

"Wait," she said, stopping to browse.

The little cubicle, with all its merchandise seemingly up front, displayed an eclectic arrangement of jewelry. Expensive was bedded down right next to inexpensive. Buddhas sat plumply, while silver chains and gold chains and pendants of both metals gleamed and tempted. Anne Elise picked up a silver bracelet that was fashioned in four links.

"They represent the seasons," Kell explained at her elbow.

"It's pretty," Anne Elise commented, laying it back and picking up a gold necklace. The woman behind the counter smiled encouragingly, displaying a hole where two front teeth had once been.

"It's a baht chain," Kell said. "Every tourist to Thailand takes one home."

Tourist.

That was just it, Anne Elise thought, putting the chain down, smiling courteously at the woman and walking on toward the hotel. She wasn't a typical tourist. In fact, she wasn't a tourist at all. She was in Bangkok for a very grave reason, a reason she'd been able to push aside for a brief while, but a reason that was suddenly back in full force.

"I wish this afternoon were over," she said, giving voice to her feelings.

"Mai pen rai," Kell said softly.

Anne Elise glanced toward him.

"Nothing is forever," he translated.

Mai pen rai.

Anne Elise wasn't certain she agreed. She'd lived through seventeen years that had seemed like forever. Was it possible that the wait was about to end? She prayed it was . . . for herself, for Brooke. As she and Kell slipped back into the service entrance of the hotel, as they silently took the elevator upward, as he opened the door to their suite, she clung to the three strange words, hoping they possessed a magic that would end her misery.

Mai pen rai.

Chapter Six

"For God's sake, will you sit down?"

Startled, Anne Elise jerked her head toward Kell. He sat in a chair in the bridal suite, his long legs sprawled before him. He looked the epitome of a relaxed man. In fact, he looked so relaxed that Anne Elise could have easily, happily, slapped him silly.

"I have three o'clock," she said, not bothering to check her watch. There was no need. She'd checked it only seconds before. Which was all she'd done for the past half hour since they'd showered and changed into fresh clothes. That, and actually resort to praying to a spirit called Tuptim. As she'd taken a break from her pacing to stand at the window, she'd glanced down at the Nai Lert Shrine. A couple had been kneeling in prayer. Anne Elise had sent hers to join theirs, hoping that a spirit concerned with fertility might also be concerned about a heart that had ached for seventeen years. If nothing else, maybe the spirit would make the time pass more quickly. Though that seemed less the problem than convincing her companion that it was time to go.

"We'll go in a minute," he said calmly, his dark eyes displaying no emotion.

Anne Elise wanted to scream. "But he, we, said three o'clock."

"In a minute." Again, he spoke so evenly Anne Elise thought she'd go mad.

"But what if he doesn't wait?"

"He'll wait. You have something he wants. Fifty thousand somethings, as a matter of fact." At the reply obviously poised on her lips, he added with a nod of his head, "Sit down."

She did. In the chair across from him. Her feet, bound in skimpy sandals that tied at her ankles, rested very near his, which were shod in tennis shoes. She crossed one knee over the other, her leg swinging with nervous energy. When she realized what she was doing, she uncrossed her legs, recrossed them, then began to swing her leg again. Through it all, Kell's feet remained motionless, his mouth expressionlessly hidden behind the steeple of his fingers.

"For God's sake, let's go," he said at last, pulling from the chair and stooping before his duffle bag. "Before you jump out of your skin."

Anne Elise, dental records in one hand, purse in the other, was up like a shot and at the door, where she turned to wait for him. He still seemed in no hurry. Impatiently she watched as he produced the gun, leisurely checked it, then, standing, tucked it in the small of his back and pulled the tail of his shirt down over it. He glanced up, his eyes meeting hers. The visual contact held as he crossed the room.

When he was standing before her, she angling her neck painfully to keep him in view, he said, "Do what I tell you, and stay close to me."

As always, something in her rebelled. "You make it sound like a cloak-and-dagger game."

He captured her chin in his hand. The pressure he exerted was firm without being bruising. Anne Elise had the distinct feeling he had such a working knowledge of violence that he knew exactly where the line lay between the two... and that he could easily cross from one to the other.

"This is no game, lady," he drawled with an ominous evenness. "That's why you'll do what I tell you. That's why you'll stay close to me. You got that?"

When she said nothing, his fingers tightened. Gone was the man she'd teased with as they'd toured Bangkok. Gone was the man who'd paid her a grudging compliment. Gone was the shadow of a human being, replaced once more by the surly son of a bitch.

She tried to pull her chin from his grip but couldn't.

"You got that?" he repeated, each syllable the consistency of granite.

"Yes, Captain," she said, softly, sarcastically, with eyes as smolderingly dark as his.

He released her chin slowly until at last his fingers slid like silk across her face. She felt every groove of the rough pads of his fingertips. He felt the smooth alabaster of her skin. Both felt a fiery warmth that lingered... and lingered... and lingered....

"C'mon," he snapped as he yanked open the door.

The lobby was filled with people, most talking in Japanese as they prepared to board sightseeing buses already parked alongside the curb. They were obviously the Japanese businessmen, and families, the clerk had mentioned the day before.

As the elevator doors swished shut behind Anne Elise and Kell, a man, tall, distinguished, and decidedly Thai, stood and started toward them. Kell extended his hand.

"Doctor," he acknowledged, then turned to Anne Elise. "This is Dr. Kon Isrankul. The dentist who's agreed to help us. Doctor, this is Mrs. Butler."

"Mrs. Butler," the man said in flawless English. "It is a pleasure."

"The pleasure is mine," Anne Elise said. "I hope Captain Chaisson expressed my sincere thanks. I also hope he offered you monetary compensation for your expertise and kindness."

"He did both, although your thanks are all that's necessary."

"Then I thank you again," Anne Elise said.

The doctor nodded, as though signifying her act was duly noted. He also smiled, then asked seriously, "Is your party here?"

Kell's gaze fished through the sea of faces. "I don't know. I don't even know who I'm looking for, except an Amer—"

"Captain Chaisson?"

Kell whirled to face the desk clerk.

The young man, dusky skinned and dressed in the usual white coat, smiled and held up an envelope. "You have a message, sir."

Kell frowned and stepped forward. He knew who the message was from even before he asked, "Who left it?"

"I do not know, sir. I just came on duty. Some gentleman left it an hour or so ago...to be delivered to you when you came into the lobby at three o'clock."

Kell reached for the envelope and read his name printed across the front. "That at least answers the question of whether he knows you didn't come alone," he sneered to the woman who now stood beside him.

Anne Elise's heart had sunk into her stomach. "Is it from Forbes?"

Kell made no response. Instead, he ripped open the envelope, creating giant, jagged, mountainlike edges as he did. The note was simple.

I decided the lobby was no place for such a delicate meeting. We'll meet at ten in the morning in a village an hour's drive from Bangkok.

Kell unfolded the map that had been included and made a quick survey of it.

Anne Elise, who'd read the note as he had, was left to deal with the crushing weight of her disappointment. She suddenly found that it needed venting. She chose anger, which always seemed an appropriate way to deal with Kell Chaisson.

"I told you he wouldn't wait!" she accused.

Kell shifted his eyes from the map to her. Hers, once a peaceful green that had reminded him of his jungle retreat, now appeared cloudy, fraught with emotion. Typically, his gave nothing away.

"Didn't you hear the clerk say this was delivered a while back? The bastard never had any intention of meeting us here. He's just been playing head games."

"And we haven't been?" Anne Elise knew everything that Kell had said was true, but her frustration still needed expression . . . and Kell still seemed like the perfect whipping boy. She also felt like crying, but that was a weakness she wouldn't allow herself to engage in.

He didn't answer, but rather, without even asking the desk clerk for permission, dragged the phone around. "What's the slime's number?" When Anne Elise didn't respond—she seemed lost somewhere in her own world—he repeated, roughly, "What's Forbes's number?"

The harshness of the question snatched her back. "What?"

"Forbes's number. What is it?"

She dug through her purse, her fingers at last finding the slip of paper. She held it up for Kell to see. He dialed the number with sharp movements of his wrist. That done, he leaned his hip back against the counter with his usual negligence, though there was a rigid tightening to his lips that a keen observer might have noted.

Anne Elise waited quietly, impatiently, her eyes soaking in Kell's every nuance. She saw the grim slash of his mouth. He was angry. Even in the confusion of her present state of mind, she knew she never wanted to be the object of his explosive temper. What she'd already seen of it was quite enough. Whatever his reasons, to offer privacy or to steer clear of Kell, Doctor Isrankul kept his distance.

Though it seemed to take forever for the connection to be made, the phone was answered on the first ring...by a voice that was bourbon rough and cigarette scratchy.

"I've been waiting for your call, Captain Chaisson," Isaac Forbes drawled in lieu of the usual hello. If self-confidence were a fragrance, it would have cloyingly wafted through the phone line.

Kell didn't seem impressed. "I got your note telling me what you'd decided. Let me tell you what *I've* decided, Forbes," he drawled back. "I've decided to book Ms. Butler and me on the first plane out of here, which means you can take your little cat-and-mouse game and shove it up your—"

"No, wait!" Anne Elise cried.

Kell dropped his gaze to the wide-eyed woman beside him.

"What are you doing?" she asked incredulously.

"I'm putting an end to this farce."

"No. We came here to see Forbes. I don't care where we have to see him."

Kell's mouth hardened, this time drawing in his eyes, as well. He covered the receiver with the wide palm of his hand. "Are you crazy? This man is using you, ----ing—" he used a four-letter word that was crude, but most expressive "—with your emotions. He hasn't got anything; he never did have, and now he's setting you up like a turkey the night before Thanksgiving. And you're gonna help him."

"I want to meet with him," she insisted.

"Fine. Meet with him, then. But count me out."

"What's wrong, Captain? You scared?" she taunted.

"Fear's a healthy emotion. It keeps your ass sitting on top of your legs."

"I'm going with or without you."

"Fine."

"I will!"

"Great! Go!"

They stood glowering at each other, as if no one waited at the other end of the phone line, as if the Thai dentist weren't looking on, as if several hotel guests hadn't glanced up at the raised voices.

What were they doing? Anne Elise asked silently, coming to her senses. Reason. Kell Chaisson wasn't stupid. Unbelievably maddening, maybe, but not stupid. She'd try reason.

"Look," she said, "we've come this far. Both literally and figuratively. Wouldn't it make sense to at least meet with the man before coming to any conclusions?"

"We've come this far."

The words triggered similar words from Kell's past.

"I never meant for it to go this far. I never meant to fall in love with you. I never meant to hurt you, Bill,

me...anyone. Why do I have to hurt one to love another?"

The voice, which he'd heard during a thousand sleepless nights, held the same anguish as the voice presently speaking to him. Both women had been painfully bound to the past. Just as he himself was painfully bound to it. Wouldn't he do anything, risk anything, to free himself from those bonds? Would he deny the same, however risky the chance might be, to the woman who stood before him?

Anne Elise, suddenly fearing she was making no headway with reason, laid her pride aside.

"Kell, please," she begged.

It might have been her reasoning, which, despite what his better judgment told him Forbes was up to, did make a sliver of sense; it might have been the soft, pleading quality in her whispery voice; it might have been the fact that she'd called him by his first name and that the sweetness of the sound had shaken him. It might even have been the fact that where her hand clutched his arm burned as though he'd been seared with a branding iron. He glanced down at her hand. She followed his eyes and, as though astonished to see she was gripping his forearm, she quickly let go of it.

Whatever the reason, he removed his palm from the receiver and said, his gaze squarely fastened on Anne Elise's, "Be there at ten, Forbes—no more games, no more delays—or I swear I'll carry the lady kicking and screaming onto the next plane out of Bangkok."

Before Forbes could answer, Kell hung up. He was slower, however, to pull his gaze away from Anne Elise.

"Thank you," she whispered at last, feeling the need to say something under his intense stare. God, he had the most piercing eyes she'd ever seen!

He made no response. Instead, like a pair of scissors slashing a ribbon in half, he cut his eyes away. Pushing from the counter, he walked to the dentist and spoke to him quietly. The man nodded, then, smiling in Anne Elise's direction, started across the lobby and for the entrance door.

"C'mon," Kell called over his shoulder as he walked toward the elevator. One was just emptying, and he held it until Anne Elise caught up. He stepped in right behind her. And ignored the usual panic as the doors closed shut. "Pack whatever you'll need for tonight in my duffle bag," he said. "We'll leave everything else here. I'm gonna go rent a Jeep and buy a few provisions—"

"We're going tonight?" Anne Elise asked. "Why not in the morning? The drive only takes an hour."

"You still don't get it, Little Miss Pure Heart, do you?" he asked disbelievingly. "You still don't see that Forbes has set us up like a sitting duck."

"I thought we were a Thanksgiving turkey."

Kell ignored her sarcasm. "You still don't see that he has us routed on a little-traveled road to an out-in-the-middle-of-nowhere village and that he knows precisely when we'll be driving there."

Anne Elise had never had a great mind for unraveling adventure or suspense books or films, but a shadowy scenario started forming in her mind. "What about Dr. Isrankul?"

"He'll drive down in the morning. He isn't the one at risk."

"We are," she said, the shadowy scenario taking substance. "Because we have the money."

Kell grinned in mock mirth. "Bingo! The lady just won a prize."

Anne Elise ignored his sarcasm. "You don't think..." She didn't finish because the words refused to take form.

"You want to chance it?" When she said nothing, he added, "What's wrong? You finally concerned about that pretty little ass of yours?"

The opening of the elevator door negated the need for any reply. Which was good because her head was filled with images of the possible danger they were in, danger Kell had believed all along surrounded them. Suddenly that danger seemed all too real.

Kell saw the loss of her naiveté, saw how it paled her skin, and wished that he could give that innocence back to her, though it was far better that she understand what they might be facing. Otherwise, she might do something stupid.

"Where, uh, where will we stay tonight?" she asked, trying to pretend everything was all right.

He opened the hotel door and ushered her in.

"Don't worry," he said in a tone he had to fight to keep from being gentle, "I'll find us someplace."

"*This* is your idea of someplace?"

The thatched hut, windowless, its roof slanting, its door ripped off entirely and lying on the ground, curiously looked both fragile and sturdy, as though it would blow away in the first good wind, as though it had endured the primal elements countless times before and would countless times to follow. Its bark-brown color faded into the late hour, an hour made all the murkier by clouds that had seemingly fluffed into the magenta sky from nowhere. The taste of rain hung in the still, hot air.

Anne Elise had no idea where they were, only that they'd traveled for the better part of an hour, past coconut palms and orchards of jack fruit, mango, mangosteen, papaya and banana trees. She knew, too, that she was hot and tired and hungry. She was also irritable. In part, because she was hot, tired and hungry; in part, because of their reservations at the thatched-hut Hilton.

A rolled handkerchief tied around his forehead as a sweatband, Kell glanced over at his passenger. His sunglasses, which had made him look sinister and downright appealing—Anne Elise had fought against acknowledging this last, but had been forced to accept defeat—had long ago been removed. "What's wrong, Miss Astor? You got something against the simple life?"

"This is not simple. This is primitive." He had called her Miss Congeniality, Sleeping Beauty, Little Miss Pure Heart, and now Miss Astor—all in a taunting way. She wondered what her name would sound like on his lips—said naturally, softly. Even sweetly? She was certain, though, that this man would spurn anything that hinted at sweetness. Had it always been that way? Or had he once spoken sweetly to the woman rumor said he'd loved? And why was she dwelling on any of this?

"You've got a roof over your head, food to eat and water to drink. What more do you want?" he asked as he swung out of the Jeep and began gathering their provisions.

Also climbing from the Jeep, Anne Elise sidestepped the door that lay rotting on the ground and peered into the weakly lit shack. "Oh, I don't know. Maybe a floor?"

The dirt floor had been tamped down until a dull, dustless patina had been achieved. The enclosure still smelled like dirt, however, an earthiness that swelled the nostrils with its loamy fragrance.

"Hey?"

Anne Elise turned...and reflexively caught the hotel blanket Kell tossed at her.

"There's your floor," he said, reaching for a canteen and slinging the strap across his shoulder. He then grabbed a lantern and bunched a sack of groceries in the curve of his free arm. The fifty thousand dollars had been cleverly hidden in the spare tire of the Jeep.

"Gee, thanks," Anne Elise snipped. With Kell barreling down on her, urging her forward, she had no choice but to enter the hut. "What is this place, anyway?" she asked, letting the interior's comparative coolness wrap around her legs, legs bare in the red shorts she wore. Her T-shirt was drenched in perspiration, which, embarrassingly, like crescent moons, ringed the undersides of her breasts.

Thunder rumbled in the distance, teasing the hot day with relief.

"It was probably a storage shed of some kind," Kell answered, nodding toward the five or six burlap bags that had been abandoned to one side. With fibers fraying into holes, they were piled in a heap. The hut contained nothing else. Kell dumped the provisions in the middle of the shack, placed his hands on his hips and looked around. "Could be worse."

"Then again, it could be better," Anne Elise felt compelled to point out.

Kell's roaming eyes zeroed in on her. She still clasped the blanket to her chest. "Look, Duchess, it's the best I can offer for tonight. Take it or leave it."

His eyes, hard and cool, said he didn't particularly care which she chose to do. Some part of her yearned to tell him to go to hell; another part made her say, as softly as a nightingale taking to wing, "My name is Anne Elise."

He hadn't expected her reply. That was clear. His hard, cool eyes softened, heated. For a slow minute, he looked as though he might actually say her name, as though he actually *wanted* to say it.

Into the stillness, thunder grumbled, snatching the unguarded moment away.

"It's gonna rain," he said harshly, apparently angry at himself for the sheer contemplation of such folly. "I need to cover the Jeep."

And then he was gone—out the door and into the thickening evening. Anne Elise stood motionless. Curiously, she felt as if she'd been kicked in the stomach. She had no idea whether it was because he'd refused, hostilely, to say her name, or because of what she could imagine it would have sounded like had he chosen to.

Thunder rolled again, along with her stomach, and she pushed the thought of everything but food aside. Spreading out the blanket, she dropped to her knees and stretched for the paper sack. What had the good captain bought? At this stage, with lunch but a dim, lean memory, she didn't much care. Rummaging through, she found snack-type foods very similar to what she might have purchased in the States. There was a tin of potted meat, a loaf of bread, some type of cracker and even a wedge of cheddar cheese. Two bananas and two orangelike mangosteens, the latter with a thick, reddish-brown rind and the promise of sweet, white, juicy pulp, completed the offering. She started to open the box of crackers, realized how lightless the hut had grown—surely it would rain soon—and decided to turn on the lantern. In seconds, a deep, golden glow swam across the room, casting eerie shadows against the thatched walls.

Anne Elise began to lay the food out on the blanket, the tip of which overlapped onto the pile of burlap bags. As she might have anything in the way, she pushed the burlap bags aside.

The snake reared.

As though sprung full grown from her worst nightmare.

Its hood was flared, like Satan wrapping himself in an evil cloak.

Anne Elise froze, not out of any conscious design, but because fear, instant and sharp, had congealed her blood. A loud gasp sucked all the air from her lungs.

Cobra.

Some analytical part of her brain registered the fact that the snake was a cobra. Some five to six feet long. That it had yellowish to dark brown markings. That if it struck, it would hit her face or her neck or her chest because, with her on her knees, they were almost beady black eye to frightened green eye. And that if it bit her, she would die because each drop of its venom was a drop of death.

Another part of her said that it would somehow be fitting and proper that she die in Southeast Asia as her husband had. Some other part, however, realized that she didn't want to die. Not yet. And that she resented Death's jousting with her in this callous way.

Still some other distant section of her brain wanted to scream out for Kell. But he was outside. Not here. And besides, she couldn't find her voice to make even the smallest of sounds.

Sound.

The only sound in the hut's heated stillness was the subtle, though incredibly deafening, rustle of burlap as the snake swayed against the rotted fabric. That and the hideous, whiplike noise, horrible on the ear, of the lightning flicker of its forked tongue.

"Don't move!"

Another sound—low, even, but urgent.

Acting only on impulse, Anne Elise started to turn toward the savior-voice.

The savior sensed her intent and hissed, snakelike, "I said don't . . . move!"

Anne Elise, battling every primitive instinct she possessed, willed herself to remain still.

"Don't even bat an eye," Kell said quietly. Hunched down, he moved slowly—so slowly it was almost no movement at all—to Anne Elise's left. He carried the .45 automatic.

Anne Elise could see him out of the corner of her eye. The snake saw him, too, and rotated its head just a fraction. Kell halted abruptly.

"Easy," he whispered, but it was uncertain to whom he spoke—himself, the woman cowered at death's door, or the snake, whose shadow now danced a macabre ballet on the hut's wall.

Unimpressed with the suddenly motionless intruder, the cobra jerked its attention back to Anne Elise. In the lamplight, its jet-black eyes shimmered. Its tongue once more lashed out, tasting the silence.

Anne Elise tasted the salty sweat that poured from her upper lip, felt what seemed like slivers of ice sloshing around in her veins, heard a whimper that could only have come from her. She vaguely realized that her legs were beginning to cramp from the awkward, immobile position. Despite Kell's admonition to remain perfectly still, she unknowingly moved to accommodate the cramp.

The snake struck.

Anne Elise screamed and tumbled backward as the serpent lunged.

A gun fired.

Scrambling across crackers and cheese and mangosteens, Anne Elise hurled herself against Kell's chest. She almost knocked him down, but he gathered his balance, steadying himself and her by the natural act of closing his arms around her. As Anne Elise buried her face in his shoulder, she had the fleeting glimpse of the snake writhing in death coils.

She blotted everything from her mind, everything but the solid strength of one man. She was aware only of wide shoulders, a broad, sweat-dampened chest, muscle-corded thighs that protectively cradled her between them. Despite what had just happened, his heart beat with an amazing slowness—she could feel its steady rhythm pattering against her breast. On the other hand, her heartbeat skipped and raced with a wild abandon. Her breath, all too shallow, came raggedly, harshly. The sound of her own scream still echoed in her ears, along with the blaring explosion of a gun. When those noises began to recede, she heard herself whimpering tiny, incoherent utterances.

Kell heard them, too. They appealed to the possessive side of his masculine nature. It was a communication he tried to ignore. Just as he tried to ignore her trembling. Just as he tried to ignore her jagged breath warming his skin. Just as he tried to ignore the way her hands were desperately gripping fistfuls of his shirt.

But he couldn't.

Even as he told himself not to, he tightened his arms around her, enfolding her wholly within his embrace, and tucked the top of her head securely beneath his chin. All in the exquisitely expressive language of silence.

At first, Anne Elise thought she would have been content to remain where she was for the next hundred years. Slowly, however, the focus of her awareness shifted. Comforting shoulders came more to feel simply like a man's shoulders. His harboring chest, once only wide, now appeared interestingly wide, as in, Didn't she remember that the dark hair formed a T-shaped pattern? And his safe arms... When had they begun to feel so smotheringly warm? When had they begun to remind her of something that she hadn't been reminded of in a long while, namely that she was a woman?

This reminder she rejected just the way Kell had begun to reject her softness, the natural way her perspiration-moist breasts nestled against his chest, the teasing way her bare legs, legs he'd tried to avoid looking at all afternoon, fitted between his own.

Anne Elise raised her head, her eyes seeking his in explanation of a feeling she was denying existed at all. His gaze lowered to hers. She saw no explanation. In fact, had it not been ludicrous, she might have imagined the mirroring of her own questions. An eternity passed before Kell abruptly dropped his arms from her back. And pushed to his feet. Saying nothing, he shoved the gun into his waistband and moved to dispose of the snake.

"You ought to eat something," he said later, as they sat on the blanket, huddled around the lantern.

The food was scattered about them, Kell eating his share, but for all Anne Elise was consuming, the food might just as well have been on another planet. Fear had gutted her appetite. How could she possibly get anything past the lump in her throat? And assuming she could, how could she keep anything on a stomach that remembered beady black eyes all too well? She told herself that the feel of Kell's arms had nothing to do with her hollow feeling. She even half believed it.

"I, uh, I'm not hungry." She swatted at a mosquito almost as big as she.

"There're no more snakes in here," he said. The gruffness of his voice came more from the vulnerable portrait she presented, and its effect on him, than from any real anger at her refusal to eat.

"I know," she said, her tone pinched in response to his brusqueness. She spoke the truth. She did know that there weren't any more slithering guests. She'd watched Kell scour every inch of the hut, watched as he'd thrown the burlap sacks outside, watched as he'd cleaned up all evidence of the bloody fiasco. He'd even tossed out the crackers that had been crushed in her flight to reach him. Still, the memories died hard.

"Usually a snake will flee before fighting. You just had this one cornered."

"I know."

"It was probably out foraging for food. It looked like some kind of grain in those sacks."

"I know."

"Here," he said, plopping some cheese on a cracker and handing it to her. "Don't argue," he added, beating her to the punch.

She took the cracker and cheese, nibbled a bite and was surprised to find that she could swallow it. Kell then forced a half sandwich and a whole banana down her. That was followed by a swig of cool water from the canteen. Turning the canteen up, he drank. They looked at each other, then away, as though haste would negate what both were thinking. Namely, that his mouth was touching where hers had been. Lowering the canteen, he swiped the back of his hand across his mouth and held out the water to her.

"No, thank you. And I don't want anything else to eat."

In seconds, he'd cleared the blanket. Outside, the promised rain peppered the hut's shoddy roof. The big mosquito had been joined by another.

"Get some sleep," he said, leaning to turn out the lantern.

"No!" Anne Elise cried. "Don't cut it off."

Kell raked his gaze through hers. Terror, like a delicate lithograph, was etched in her emerald-green irises. He pulled his hand away from the lantern's switch, allowing the lamp to continue to illuminate the room. He stretched out on his back, lay the gun beside him and closed his eyes.

Anne Elise remained where she sat. Staring at him. Stupefied that he could just lie down and go to sleep.

In a while, he cracked open an eye. "Aren't you going to lie down?"

The question burst wide the dam.

"You're incredible, unbelievable, mind-boggling! You actually expect me to lie down and go to sleep like nothing happened? My God, I just went a round with a cobra. A cobra, Captain Chaisson! That may be part of your every-day routine, but, I assure you, it isn't mine!" She wildly raked back the hair that had tumbled from the topknot. Offended at being disturbed, the mosquitoes buzzed away. "And frankly, I don't think I have to worry about Forbes's sinister intentions. You seem quite capable yourself of getting me killed!"

At the end of her tirade, Kell asked—calmly, "Are you through?"

Her emotion had been spent, leaving her wilted and too darned tired to care anymore. "Yes."

"Then lie down."

She was left only with honesty... and with what she was sure would be Kell's mockery. "I..." she swallowed. "I'm afraid to."

There was no mockery. Instead, Kell's hand snaked out, grabbing her wrist and pulling her down beside him. Rolling to his side, he draped his arm across her waist. It was the only point of contact between their bodies and even that was nonchalantly, platonically made, as though he often slept thus with frightened women. "If anything gets you, it'll have to go through me first."

Given his attitude about the arm slung across her tummy, it was easy to adopt his attitude as her own. In fact, his rather dared her to make something more of it. She wasn't up to accepting any dare. She closed her eyes, sighed, felt her body take the first steps toward relaxing. As unbeliev-able as it was, Anne Elise began to grow drowsy. Drowsiness quickly turned into full-fledged sleep. The last thing she remembered thinking was that she felt safe. Truly safe. Safer than she'd felt in a long while. Maybe safer than she'd ever felt.

And the reason was simple.

To get to her, something would have to go through Kell Chaisson first.

Chapter Seven

Isaac Forbes, with hair the white of winter snow and eyes the blue of innocence, looked like someone's genteel grandfather. Anne Elise sensed, however, that he could be more deadly than the cobra she'd confronted the night before. Just as she sensed that the greasy-haired, ferret-eyed Thai beside him, obviously his compatriot, could also mean trouble. Big trouble. Unknowingly, she stepped closer to Kell, which, interestingly, seemed to be where she'd spent most of the night—close to Kell. Did some part of her remember the arm, platonically slung around her waist, tightening its hold? Did she remember herself scooting nearer the source of the blissfully safe feeling?

"Where are the remains?" Kell asked, his tone one of quiet authority, his eyes watching the two men's every move.

They were the first words that had been spoken since Kell and Anne Elise, accompanied by Dr. Isrankul, who'd arrived only minutes behind them, had entered the hut. This thatched hut, though similar in style to the one they'd occupied hours earlier, was in far better condition. In fact, it appeared to be inhabited, a conclusion supported by a bedroll, scattered articles of clothing, and the heavy, coarse, cabbagey smell of newly cooked food.

But why would anyone want to live here, on the fringe of a blanket of jungle, in the middle of nowhere? Anne Elise asked herself, then answered her own question. The better to carry out one's nefarious deals?

"Ah, Captain, you disappoint me," Forbes drawled. "We're not even going to exchange a proper greeting?"

Isaac Forbes, his beefy fingers entwined before him, sat sprawled behind an ordinary-looking folding card table, whose stains suggested served as a dining table. He looked as relaxed as Kell. Anne Elise knew Kell's appearance was a clever facade. She knew the gun rested at the small of his back, recognized the vigilance of his deceptively lazy eyes, remembered his forceful warning to stay close to him. She wondered if Isaac Forbes's appearance lied as falsely.

"And just what would a sleaze like you know about proper?" Kell drawled back. A leather satchel containing the money hung carelessly over his rangy shoulder.

Forbes gave a slow, mirthless grin that filled up all his cherubic face. "Anyone ever tell you you have a bad attitude?"

"Yeah," Kell answered, repeating, "Where are the remains?"

As though he'd given civility an honest try, Forbes shrugged shoulders that were as broad as Kell's. The similarity ended there, however, a fact borne out when the white-haired man lumbered to his feet. Though not fat, his waist, hidden beneath a khaki shirt tucked into khaki pants, was thick, the result of too much good living, while his thighs lacked the trim muscularity of Kell's. In his early sixties, the man also lacked Kell's youth. It was a disparity Anne Elise was willing to believe the man made up for in shrewdness.

Even as she watched from Kell's elbow, Forbes glanced over at his companion. Some silent code passed between them, for the Thai, his skin the color of roasted almonds, padded his thong-sandaled feet across the straw floor of the hut, to Kell's right.

Wiry of build with teeth tobacco stained and rotting, the Thai bent, scooped up a cardboard box that, according to the lettering on the side, had once held cans of whole kernel corn, then deposited it on the card table. He spoke low and quickly, the sounds foreign to Anne Elise, just as Forbes's reply was foreign. The dark-headed Thai nodded sharply and stepped back.

Forbes, his eyes once more on Kell, motioned toward the box.

Anne Elise lowered her gaze. The truth struck her like a sharp, stinging slap. The remains of her beloved husband—the possible remains of her beloved husband—were in a cardboard box that had once held cans of corn. And it sat unpretentiously on a rickety, stained card table in the middle of a thatched hut in the middle of Thailand. She wasn't certain what she'd expected—certainly no flag-draped casket—but surely she'd had a right to expect more than a disrespectful cardboard box.

A cardboard box, for God's sake, that had once held cans of whole kernel corn!

For the first time in a very long while—maybe since she'd been informed that her husband was missing—she felt a break with reality. Everything seemed as foreign as the language she'd heard seconds before. In that surreal moment, with emotions kicked out of kilter, she felt like laughing at that which was most serious. The watchful pragmatist in her, however, snatched the reins of reality and drew the surreal, runaway beast to a hoof-screeching halt.

As though sensing a turbulence, Kell glanced toward the woman standing at his side. His eyes made a lightning-quick survey of her. Little was needed to read the emotions written across her face, emotions she was trying so damned hard to keep under control, but then, maybe he was just getting adept at reading her.

Impatient, for her sake, to have the ordeal over with, Kell shifted his attention to Dr. Isrankul, who held the dental records in his hand. "Check the teeth. See if you can make an ID."

The dentist started forward.

"Well, now," Forbes drawled, "we've run into a little problem on that score."

Dr. Isrankul halted.

Kell's gaze, like a trap of iron, clamped on Isaac Forbes. "What do you mean 'a little problem?'" His voice shivered with a chilled calmness.

"You must understand that the people I have to deal with are not like you and me, Captain. They're not guided by honesty. They have no milk of human kindness flowing in their veins."

"What kind of little problem?" The calm had gone from chilled to icicle cold.

"They're guided only by their greed. They're—"

"You don't have the teeth, do you?" The question was sculpted from clear, sharp ice.

Forbes hesitated.

A sick feeling bubbled in Anne Elise's stomach.

"Regrettably, no," Forbes said at last.

Anne Elise's sick feeling swelled.

"You dirty bastard," Kell rasped, the accusation sounding like a dark symphony in the silence.

"You wound me, Captain."

"Don't give me any ideas," Kell said, simultaneously curling an arm around Anne Elise's waist and looking past her and toward the dentist. "Let's get out of here."

Dr. Isrankul needed no coaxing. He started for the door. Kell pushed a stunned Anne Elise behind him.

"You're being too hasty, Captain," Forbes called after him. "I have something I think will interest Mrs.—"

"Go to hell, Forbes," Kell sniped.

Dr. Isrankul had just stepped through the door when Isaac Forbes tossed something glinty gold at Anne Elise's feet. She looked down, saw the circular band nesting in the straw, and knew immediately what it was. Her heart began to race wildly.

"Wait!" she cried, balking at the pressure propelling her outside.

Kell had no choice but to bow to her wishes. As she stooped, he glanced over her and to the doctor. "Go on." At the doctor's hesitation, Kell added, "We're right behind you."

The dentist, clearly eager to leave, nodded and moved on out into the midmorning sun.

The ring, like a cherished memory, warmed her hand. Funny, she'd never thought to see it again . . . and had not really pined to do so. Now that she held it, however, the enormity of its loss overwhelmed her. It had been the symbol of so much. Of so much good. She remembered the day they'd bought the matching bands—this one was an exact replica of her own, which she'd stopped wearing when the hope of her husband's being alive had died. She remembered, too, the day they'd placed them on each other's fingers. Knowing what she'd find, Anne Elise peered inside the band. The familiar inscription greeted her: For Today. For Tomorrow. A bittersweetness flooded her soul.

"I-it's Jim's."

"Even if it is—" Kell began.

"It is!" Anne Elise interrupted, not willing to be questioned on this point.

Kell's steady gaze held hers. "It still proves nothing...and you know it."

"Surely, Mrs. Butler," Forbes said, "you're not going to turn your back on something you've wanted night and day for seventeen years. Surely you're not going to pass up the chance to bury your husband in the soil of his own country."

"He's screwing with your mind," Kell said, his gaze never once leaving Anne Elise's face—her pale face.

Her eyes roved beyond Kell's shoulder to the box sitting atop the card table. She hadn't thought she would have doubts at this point. She'd always told herself that without the proper identification, she'd just walk away, believing that she would be no worse off than before. But she now knew that wasn't true. Faced with the moment of truth, faced with the fact that she might be in possession of her husband's remains, how could she just walk away? Even if there was only the slightest chance that these remains were her husband's, wasn't she duty bound to risk it? How could she leave him in a foreign land again? How could she survive the guilt?

"You have a daughter, Mrs. Butler," Forbes coaxed. "Don't you think you owe her this much?"

Shrewd. Yes, the man was shrewd, Anne Elise admitted. He had found the way to topple her last bit of resistance; he'd found a way to shred the last fragment of her common sense.

She raised her eyes to Kell.

He heard her silent decision as clearly as if she'd shouted it.

"No!" The word, though whispered from his lips, roared. Its vibrations, like the tides of a scalding sea, lapped over her. They burned.

"But what if it's Jim?" she asked, seared by the look Kell was still leveling on her.

"And what if it isn't?"

"But I can't know that it isn't."

"And you can't know that it is."

Isaac Forbes astutely kept his silence.

"Don't you see—" she began, inexplicably desperate for him to understand.

"I see you're forgetting the promise you made."

Something in the way he said it—his presumptuousness—lit a fuse to her anger. "I don't remember ever making you a promise."

"You didn't make me one. You made one to yourself."

"That was before—"

"—you let the creep sweet-talk you."

Anne Elise's hand closed protectively around her husband's wedding band. "I want to buy the remains."

"No!"

Anne Elise proudly, defiantly, tilted her shoulders. "It's not your decision, Captain."

A black windstorm blew across the irises of his eyes, taking them from the brown of autumn leaves to the deep, cloudy brown of rage. He was angry. At the situation. At Forbes. But, most particularly, at her. She told herself it didn't matter. Strangely, however, it felt as though it did.

His eyes still on her, he stepped back, one step, then another, before he turned, his eyes now clashing with Forbes's. For a moment, the two men just stared.

Slowly, smugly, Forbes smiled. "Looks like you're outvoted, Captain."

"Looks like," Kell conceded, sauntering forward and tipping up the lid of the box. He peered inside.

"What's wrong, Captain?" Forbes sneered around a smile. "You don't trust me?"

"About like a viper."

"You ought to do something about that attitude."

"Now, why would I want to do that? I've worked real hard on this bad-ass attitude."

Kell lowered the lid and spread his hand widely, possessively, across the top of the box. Isaac Forbes splayed his hand alongside Kell's.

Abruptly Forbes's eyes froze like frosted ice. "Fifty thousand."

Each man sized up the other. Suddenly Kell's shoulders relaxed their defensive posture. "You're right, Forbes. A man ought to get paid what he's worth."

Keeping his hand on the box, ignoring the satchel slung across his left shoulder, Kell dug in the pocket of his jeans. He flicked a coin onto the table. It circled once, then rolled to its side. The copper in the penny winked.

Forbes, misunderstanding, glanced up.

"Actually," Kell drawled, "you're being overpaid. But, hey, I'm a generous kind of fellow."

Something dangerous glinted in Forbes's eyes seconds before his hand, striking faster than a coiled serpent, snaked behind his back.

Kell, however, was faster. One moment he looked as lazy as a sunny Sunday afternoon, the next, as he ripped the gun from his waistband, he was nitroglycerin blowing sky-high. The explosion, however, was silent and all the more deadly because of it.

"Don't even think it," Kell hissed, keeping the startled Thai in the corner of his eyesight.

The sound of Kell's voice sent shivers scurrying down Anne Elise's spine. That and the sight of the drawn gun. A gasp had formed, but had wedged itself in her constricted throat. It was that bad B-grade movie again, the one she just didn't seem to be able to walk off the set of.

"Take the gun out real slow," Kell commanded, "and lay it right here." He motioned with the hand on the box. "Now!"

Slowly, hate dripping from his eyes, Forbes reached behind him and plucked the gun from his pants.

Kell gave a chilling facsimile of a smile. "Great minds think alike, huh?"

"This is robbery," Forbes said, leaning and placing the gun on the box.

"Report us." Without looking behind him, Kell held out the gun to Anne Elise. She took it simply because of the authority in his silent command. The gun felt heavy, cold...unreal. "Get in the Jeep," Kell added, still not taking his gaze from the man trapped beneath the barrel of his gun...or from the man still just at the periphery of his vision. When Anne Elise hesitated, Kell repeated, "Go!"

She started backing toward the door.

Kell scooped the box under his arm. He, too, had taken a step for the door when Anne Elise cried out, "Watch out—"

Kell calmly swiveled his head toward the wiry Thai. The gun, and a part of his vision, he still kept on Isaac Forbes. "Go ahead," Kell softly encouraged the greasy-haired, ferret-eyed man, who'd just snapped the blade of a knife into existence. "Come on."

The B-grade movie had gone wild...and so had her heart, Anne Elise thought, the pounding ramming itself against her ears. Though she could see only the back of Kell's head, she could easily interpret the posture of his shoulders as defensively tense. A formidable violence had crawled into his every muscle. There was also something beckoning about his stance. And his voice. He was like a lover coaxing a woman into his bed, his only thought, his every need, to end the ache consuming him. In this case, his release would come through violence, not physical mating. She found herself frightened by the beast he could be. And intrigued. What had happened to make this man so one with the sword?

"Come on," Kell repeated, now daring the man to make a move. "Think how sweet it would be to take me down."

Anne Elise wasn't certain how much of Kell's English the man was understanding, but then the siren quality of his voice was a universal language.

Taunted, goaded, the man had little choice. He lunged...just as Kell swung the butt of the gun out, clipping the Thai's chin.

Anne Elise screamed.

The Thai moaned as blood gushed from the sudden valley in his chin. Dazed, he slumped to the floor.

Forbes made a sudden movement, but it was cut short by the refocusing of the gun at his chest. "Come on, Forbes, give me an excuse."

Forbes, his eyes cold, his lips thinned, said nothing. Nor did he move. In the least.

Slowly, Kell began to back from the room. When he bumped into Anne Elise, who seemed glued to the spot, he yelled, "Get outta here!"

She did, though how her quivering legs accepted the command sent by her brain was beyond her. The sun was hot and blinding as she raced toward the Jeep. She was just about to pull herself into the vehicle when the shot rang out. Instinctively she ducked. Then realized it was Kell shooting out the tire of Forbes's truck.

"Get in!" Kell charged, throwing the satchel and the box into the back of the Jeep and hoisting himself into the front. He tossed the gun to the seat, along with the one Anne Elise had slung there.

She barely had time to board before the Jeep was careening down the road, kicking dirt high in its hasty wake. A shot, not even audible above the roar of the motor, shattered the windshield into a weblike pattern.

Kell ducked...and dragged Anne Elise, who still sat as tall as an idiot, to the floorboard. "Will you get the hell down!"

She willingly obliged.

And wondered what a nice girl like her was doing in a nasty spot like this.

Why was he so angry? Kell asked himself. And why was he driving like a bat out of hell when it had long ago ceased to be necessary? He slowed the Jeep and looked over at Anne Elise, who, if she realized the vehicle had changed speed, gave no indication of it. As though in a trance, her copper hair whipping around her ashen face, she stared straight ahead, her salvation obviously somewhere on the ribbon of road.

They were nearing Bangkok. Unfortunately he was nowhere near an answer as to why he had gotten so angry. Especially why he'd gotten so angry with the woman beside him.

There were a lot of logical reasons for me to get angry, he defended himself as he peered through the shattered windshield.

Yeah? Name one.

Okay. I loathe seeing anyone taken advantage of, and Forbes, from the beginning, played her like a bad song.

True. But then, wouldn't it make more sense to be angry with Forbes? Why her?

Because she'd promised to walk away if a positive ID couldn't be made.

What the heck difference should that make to you? It was no skin off your nose, no money out of your bank account if Forbes had ended up with every cent of the fifty thousand. And don't give me a song and dance about your hating to see her spend that kind of money. Her parents are good for it. A dozen times over!

Maybe I'm just a caring kind of guy.

Like hell! The only thing you cared about back there was punching somebody out. You wanted it so badly you could taste it. Hell, you needed it worse than a junkie needed a fix! Hey, Chaisson, ever ask yourself why you crave violence?

No.

What's wrong? 'Fraid of the answer? Just the way you're afraid to admit that you're angry with the lady because what she did means she's still tied up in knots about the past?

Okay! I'll admit it! If she'd walked away, I think it would have been more emotionally healthy. It would have been some indication that maybe she was coming to terms with the past.

And why should her coming to terms with the past make any difference to you?

Kell balked at considering the question. He knew the answer would be too personally dangerous.

"Why are you angry with me?"

At the question that cut into the tense quietness, a question that so perfectly mirrored what was going on in his head, Kell glanced over at the woman beside him. They were the only words she'd spoken since the dramatic scene in the hut—she hadn't even uttered a sound when he'd shoved her onto the floorboard—and, if he didn't know better, he could almost believe the question was as important to her as it was to him. The reminder that it was important to him, coupled with the way she looked so vulnerable with her hair fluttering in the wind, the remembrance of how small and defenseless she'd felt in his arms the night before, and of how she'd snuggled up against him while asleep, and of how he'd let her—each and all were like gasoline to fire. He exploded.

"How could you have been so clearheaded all along and so damned stupid at the moment it counted?" As though he needed something to do to release the fire-hot emotions, he threw Forbes's gun out into a passing field. His gun he tucked back into his pants. "Why are you so determined to hang on to the past? Don't you know your husband wouldn't want you to?"

"And why are you being so callous, Kell Chaisson?" Anne Elise retaliated, her anger, idle for much too long, flaring as high as his. She fought the urge to tenderly investigate the bruise budding into black and blue across the knuckles of his right hand, the hand that had held the gun that had sent the man crumbling to the floor. Somehow, some way, Kell had received a share of his own abuse. "And how dare you presume to know what my husband would or wouldn't want me to do!"

"Great! Be a martyr!"

"It's none of your business if I am!"

"You got that right, Saint Anne of the Pining Heart!"

"Anne Elise! Dammit, my name is Anne Elise!"

Another silence crashed about them, this one thick with emotions neither understood.

Why had he lambasted her the way he had? he thought.

Why had she said such cruel things to him? she thought.

And why, each mused, did the anger feel so good even at the same time it hurt so badly?

"Where are we going?" Anne Elise asked, a frown crinkling her forehead when it became obvious they weren't returning to the Hilton.

"I'm gonna find us a hotel."

"We have a hotel."

Kell's look said that she could be incredibly obtuse.

"Forbes knows where we're staying, and I don't know whether you noticed or not, but we still have the goods and the money, and we didn't exactly leave the gentleman in the best of moods."

"You think—"

"I think we're not gonna take the chance. Whether you like it or not, I'm gonna protect—"

"—my pretty little ass," she finished sarcastically.

He smiled. It was not the real thing. "Upon my honor and with my very life."

"You have no honor, Chais—"

He jerked the car to a halt in front of a hotel that had little in common with the elegant Hilton International. Anne Elise lurched forward, spilling the unshed retort onto the dashboard.

Kell cut the motor and swung his long legs over the vehicle's side. Slinging the satchel of money across his shoulder, he picked up the box of remains and the duffle bag they'd shared. Then, without so much as a backward glance, he started toward the hotel entrance.

The hotel looked as though a giant hand had wedged it between two businesses, one a laundry, the other a small restaurant. Smells of starch and steam pressing swirled with those of fish and rice and spice. In the window of the hotel hung a vacancy sign. Below it, a plant begged for water. All in all, Anne Elise thought, it looked like another set of the same B-grade movie.

"What about the clothes?" she called after him.

"I have mine," he shouted back, still without turning around.

"What about the rest of mine at the hotel?"

"Have them sent to you in Dallas."

"But we haven't checked out!"

"Call and give 'em a credit card number!"

With that, he disappeared inside the hotel.

Anne Elise just sat, studying the spot where he'd once stood. She then looked around her. She was still holding her husband's wedding band; the windshield of the Jeep looked like a giant spider's lair; she was sweaty and dirty from plunging across a dirt floor to escape a cobra. And her husband's remains, possible remains, had just been carried inside a second-rate hotel by the most exasperating man she'd ever met.

Suddenly reality stepped back, and that surrealism she'd experienced earlier stepped forward.

Suddenly she again had that crazy urge to giggle.

Kell registered them as Mr. and Mrs. Frank Nelson. Anne Elise no longer even thought it odd that they were masquerading as a married couple, under an assumed name, and that they were walking down a narrow, uncarpeted hallway, quietly, except for the sound of their footsteps plundering the silence, to a room they would share. In fact, nothing seemed odd. Or maybe, everything did, thereby robbing the word, the feeling, of any comparative strength.

Opening the door of Room 406, Kell ushered her in. She entered and idly noted that the room was clean, if frugally decorated. A worn chair sat in the room's middle, while a double bed, with iron railings and draped with a white spread washed so many times that new was but a faded memory, stood against a wall. Zombielike, she moved to sit on the edge of the bed. She watched, distractedly, her husband's ring still clasped in her hand, as Kell deposited the box on the dresser. It was an old dresser. A small dresser. Almost as small as the box. The box that had once held cans of whole kernel corn. She should peek inside. Shouldn't she? Yes, she should. She would. In a while. It was just that she was so tired . . . so incredibly tired.

The sound of Kell's voice jostled her. He stood across from her, his jeans as dirt streaked as her white pants, speaking on the telephone. He was making arrangements for them to fly out of Bangkok. Home. Yes, she wanted to go home. Her gaze gravitated to the hand holding the black receiver. His bruised knuckles were swelling. She wanted, too, to touch those puffy knuckles, though she hadn't the foggiest idea why.

Kell hung up the phone. "In the morning at seven. We'll lay low today and tonight." He stood and dug inside his jeans pocket for a key. "I'm gonna take care of the Jeep and get us something to eat. I won't be gone long. Don't answer the door to anyone, you hear me?"

She nodded, noting that the act took more strength than she'd ever before realized it took.

He motioned toward the bathroom door. "Take a shower and try to get some rest. You look like hell."

She didn't argue. She didn't have the energy to. And, besides, she knew he was right. She must look like hell because it was exactly what she felt like.

His eyes once more raking hers, he closed the door behind him. She heard him wriggle the knob, testing the lock. And then silence. A long silence. A tender silence. The kind she'd heard over and over throughout the years.

Wearily, she pulled from the bed, crossed the room and stooped to pick up her purse. Opening the coin section of her wallet, she dropped, after one last reverent touch, her husband's wedding band inside. She then rummaged through the duffle bag. She had only one clean pair of panties and no outer garments. Both the red shorts and the white pants were filthy and everything else was at the Hilton. Not even hesitating, she selected one of Kell's clean shirts. After all, it was his bright idea to pack light in the first place, his idea to share a duffle bag the night before, his idea to abandon her other clothes. She also grabbed his brush.

Thank heaven the water was hot! Steamy hot. The kind of hot that ministered to tired muscles, the kind of hot that purified weary souls. For all of its healing capacity, however, it could not banish the feeling of unreality that still clouded about her. As she gazed into the fogged mirror, as she dragged Kell's brush through her hair, as his white shirt fell loosely about her, its texture lightly abrading the softness of her breasts, she saw a woman who she'd seen before, but it was almost as if she couldn't quite remember when or where.

She walked back into the bedroom at the exact moment Kell plowed through the door, a package in his hand. He stopped. Abruptly. As though he'd been pole-axed. His gaze, in one motion, traveled the length of her. His shirt swallowed her. The sleeves, far too long, had been rolled to midarm. The hem, sculpted, struck her just above the knees, except at the sides, where it teasingly revealed a hint of ivory thighs.

"I, uh, I didn't have anything clean. You had two clean shirts." Though the garment covered much more than her red shorts had the day before, she felt naked. Maybe that was in part because of the disarming look in Kell's eyes. Whatever, her toes curled into a honey-colored wooden floor.

Kell dragged his gaze away. When he spoke, his voice was as smoky as Southern ham, as rough as grits. "Here's something to eat," he said, tossing the sack into the chair and reaching for the buttons of his shirt. As he passed the duffle bag, he jerked out a clean pair of jeans. "I'm gonna take a shower."

Anne Elise heard the shower running, smelled the sack of food, saw the cardboard box sitting on the dresser. As though drawn by an invisible force, she stepped toward the box.

She had to look.

Though she really didn't want to look.

God, forgive me. Jim, forgive me. I really don't want to look!

She splayed her hand flat across the top of the box and listened to her heart beat out the seconds. Slowly, she raised the edge of the lid.

Bones.

A pile of bones.

For all she knew they could be of anything.

Certainly of anyone.

She'd had no choice, she thought, her eyes filled with tears. She'd never really had a choice, though she'd been too naive to know that in the beginning. If there had been even the smallest chance that this was her husband—the husband who'd smiled at her, loved her, given her his child—she had to bring him home—even if all the Kell Chaissons in the world never understood.

Kell.

Why did it matter so much that he understand?

Why had his anger hurt so badly?

Why did she suddenly feel as if unreality had finally claimed her?

She had done what she had to do, but that did not alter one unalterable fact. Nothing had changed. Her mission had netted no golden surcease of the purgatory she called home.

There was no way, ever, to prove that she was burying her husband. She still walked the path of shrouded truth...and the path went on and on and on....

Suddenly, she was tired. Oh, so very tired. Tired of doing the right thing with no reward for having done it. Tired of doing her duty. Tired of being strong. Just once—for God's sake, was once too much too ask?—couldn't someone else be the strong one?

She felt overwhelmed, empty, as though nothing were quite real anymore. Moving in a kind of haze, she lowered the lid and started for the bed. A giggle threatened, trembling on her lips for just a second, before the giggle gave way to tears. At the same time, her legs gave way. She crumpled, like a weary rag doll, to the floor by the side of the bed, her hands gripping tightly to the washed and worn spread.

She wept.

Kell heard the soft, keening sound the moment he cut off the shower. He didn't even have to consider what it was. He knew. Haphazardly drawing the towel across his skin, he shimmied his still-moist body into the jeans, not even bothering to do more than zip them. Raking his hand through his damp hair, he rushed into the bedroom. What he saw— Anne Elise curled on the floor sobbing—made his heart feel like a pound of lead.

Somewhere in the back of his mind, he thought how strange it was to feel again, anything, because, for so long, he'd denied himself that simple basic pleasure.

He tried to pick her up, but her hands clung to the spread. Prying her fingers loose, he lifted her into his arms—effortlessly, as though she weighed but a gentle whisper. He laid her on the bed, his body following hers down until he sat beside her. Her eyes, gleaming with fat tears that coursed unheeded onto her cheeks, found his.

"D-don't be . . . angry with me," she pleaded.

It was a strange thing to be saying at a moment when a thousand other things should be, and were, weighing on her. Given the emotions filling both their hearts, however, both accepted it as reasonable.

"Don't be angry," she begged again.

Her words penetrated him to the very core of his being. "Shh," he said hoarsely, wiping at a tear with the huge pad of his thumb.

"Don't be."

"No, I won't be angry. Not anymore."

"You won't?" The question was asked with an endearing childlikeness, though what she'd begun to do with her hands was far from childlike. Both hands had found his bare chest and were moving urgently across it.

"No," he said, her gentle caress knifing through him like a reckless saber.

"Tired," she whispered. "I don't want to be strong anymore. I-I'm tired of—" she raised her head from the pillow and began to nuzzle his chest with her cheek "—of being strong."

He felt her breath hot and fiery against his throat. At the wickedly wonderful feeling that slashed through him, he closed his eyes.

Anne Elise had closed hers, too. And was doing what felt natural without thinking first about it. Like a kitten, she cozied her cheek against his warm skin, his warm, damp skin. Reacting to the bead of water he'd missed, she kissed it into her mouth. Then kissed his chest again because somewhere, in her mind, in her feminine body, the pleasure of it registered. Her lips trailed to the strong, broad column of his neck, her tongue dipping into the hollow of his throat.

She kissed him, then again, then again...upward...upward as she made her way to his mouth, as she chanted, "Empty...empty...I feel so—"

"Anne Elise!" he cried, suddenly stilling her by sinking his fingers, viselike, through her hair at both temples. He held her thoroughly, even painfully, his eyes burning into hers. Hers had turned all soft and dewy. All beseeching. Her chest heaved wildly beneath his shirt. His chest, beneath her hands, beat in and out just as erratically.

"Fill me," she whispered, the words more mouthed than spoken.

Every inch of his masculine body told him that he'd like nothing more than to do what she was asking—that maybe it was what he'd wanted to do from the first moment he'd seen her. Come morning, however, he'd regret it. Just the way she'd regret having asked him. No noble gentleman would even consider complying with her wishes under these emotional circumstances. But then, he was no gentleman. Noble or otherwise. By her own accusation, by his own admission, he was a son of a bitch.

"Kell?" she breathed his name, making it sound as no woman ever had, making it sound as though it had never been spoken until just that second.

Ah, hell! he thought, wasn't that what the mornings were for? To regret what you'd done the night before? There was no answer. Only the savage silence of his mouth slamming hard against hers.

Chapter Eight

The force of his mouth, the hard wall of his bronzed, scarred chest, pressed her back into the bed. It was the most urgent journey she'd ever made. She should consider what she was doing, she thought on some hazy level, but the thought was obliterated by his lips, his powerful lips, his seductive lips, the lips that were kissing her with a strength very akin to violence.

Earlier that day, his violence had frightened her. Now it appealed to her in a primitive way she could not begin to fathom. She could only react to it with the pent-up need of far too many years.

She moaned and let her lips be molded by his sweet plunder, as though she didn't want to lose a drop of his mouth's hot nectar. In her greediness, she matched his kiss with an insistence, a desperation, as whole as his.

On a thick, guttural sound, Kell plunged his tongue forward. There was nothing of velvet and satin about his moist invasion. It was nothing short of a raging storm. His tongue didn't gently stroke, or tenderly soothe, but rather it ruthlessly swept her mouth, searching, seeking, stealing all that she had to give.

Her senses did not feel wooed or seduced. They felt battered and bruised, and it was precisely the way she wanted them to feel because this moment was not real, because she was not the woman lying beneath this darkly sensual man, because for the first time in her life feeling transcended thought. Crying out, she opened her mouth to allow the taking of still more liberties.

Kell's breath caught, then gushed out as he responded to her blatant invitation. His tongue probed more deeply, swirled with hers, over and over in an erotic mating, then flicked across the seam of her lips. He lowered his head, now giving his urgent attention to her neck, her throat, its vulnerable hollow. He blazed fire-hot kisses across her skin. She arched her neck, begging for more—yes, yes! she silently pleaded. Frantically he accommodated her until, finally, he could stand no more and, tangling his fingers in her hair, he rushed his mouth back to hers. Hers, warm and wet, was waiting.

She moaned in purest ecstasy as his lips smothered hers ... and shamelessly fanned her hands across his chest in order to maximize contact. Her palms kneaded the muscular solidity, while her fingers, more eager than she'd ever seen them, furrowed into the silky thicket of brown hair.

Kell groaned, the sound one of deep male satisfaction. As though he, too, felt compelled to touch more of her, he hastened his hand down the front of his shirt, seeking the swell of her breast. He found it. Soft and round. The nipple beaded instantly beneath his brazenness. Anne Elise, rivers of molten honey flowing through her, rivers dammed behind years of denial, whimpered and wantonly arched against his palm. At the tempting spot where her shoulder rose from the bed, Kell slipped his hand to her back and pressed her to him. Her hands fell away from his chest in order to make room for her breasts. He urged her into his flesh with a pressure that was divinely punishing, then rubbed her back and forth in accompaniment to a masculine snarl of pleasure.

Instinctively Anne Elise bent her knee, her leg hungrily hugging Kell's jean-clothed thigh. She thrust her hips upward against him. He lowered his mouth to the hollow of her throat, his hand to her buttocks. He sculpted the rich roundness of her hip, the length of her angled leg. Fire danced across her skin; madness skipped through her senses.

Then, as though he had every right, he rubbed—oh, so slowly! oh, so sensuously!—his thigh intimately against her. Once. Twice. A daring third time. She whimpered, melted, died a little at the exquisite sensations bursting to life in the pit of her stomach. Kell groaned at the fiery heat emanating from her. It was then he felt the moistness, the hot, sweet honey of her body's reaction. He raised his head, his eyes merging with hers. Hers, the color of emeralds on a foggy morning, begged, pleaded, beseeched.

Wordlessly he hooked his thumbs in the thin, lacy strips of silk that bridged her thighs. He pulled. Bringing her panties away in one swift motion that left her bare beneath his shirt. Just as wordlessly, he pushed to his knees and hauled down the zipper of his jeans. The metal hissed loudly. Boldly, even arrogantly, he shoved the jeans from his lean hips.

Anne Elise's heart stopped at the pure glory of his masculine body.

Naked, his eyes burning into hers, he lowered himself to her, his thighs easing hers apart. She let him. With a provocative slowness, with his eyes still on hers, he edged up up, up the hem of his shirt. Her heart began a wild scampering, her breath a thin shallowing. Without preliminaries, he positioned his manhood and began to enter her—slowly, caringly, but nonetheless with a sure and certain intent.

Anne Elise's breath hitched, her eyes hazed, she reached for his biceps to brace herself. His lips in a grimace at the hot, wet pleasure sliding over him, he pushed forward. She received him, his strength, his hardness, with a similar grimace, hers born of pleasure-pain. Kell eased still farther and farther, stopping once to allow her body to adjust to his. Still, he pressed on, as though the most important thing in the universe was her taking all of him. At last, deep within her, wholly within her, he stared down at her. She up at him.

Filled.

The emptiness was filled.

To overflowing.

But she had no words to tell him this.

Besides, he was a man who did not trust words.

And so, she simply laced her arms around his neck, curled her legs about his back, and pulled him down to her.

He clenched the iron railings of the bed with his white-knuckled fingers and started to roll his hips.

The fury began. It came swiftly, fiercely, like a storm shattering about the midnight hour. It was pagan and primitive and there was no pacing it, no slowing it down for enjoyment or pleasure. There was only a raw, consuming need that blazed between them. Its flames rose higher and higher, hotter and hotter. Anne Elise felt swallowed up in the heat of the beast. With each thrust of his hips, with each answering thrust she gave, she rushed more blindly toward a searing completion. Far too quickly, that completion came, shaking her body, shattering her world.

She cried out as she dug her fingernails into his well-muscled shoulders. He, just as riddled with need, groaned his release as his hands bit into the iron bars. His hips pumped against hers...again...and again...and again....

At last, there was only a breath-tattered silence as both burned in the wake of the sweet, sweet violence.

Kell rolled from her seconds, minutes, hours later. He didn't know which...and he didn't care. He cared only about taking her with him as he eased to his side. He cared only about keeping their bodies intimately joined. For a reason he couldn't explain, he hadn't had enough of her nearness yet.

Anne Elise, still reeling from the cataclysmic emotions that had claimed her, opened her eyes slowly. Kell just stared at her, as if he'd never seen her before. A ray of sunshine slanted through the window, burnishing her copper hair in richest gold. Kell reached out and brushed a wayward strand from her cheek. Her cheek. Still painted across it were the tracks of her tears. In a gesture foreign to him, he traced his knuckle down a dried runnel.

Soft.

Her cheek was soft, but that wasn't the cause of the surprise that bolted through him. It was the gentleness with which he was touching her. Gentleness. A trembling gentleness. That was something he'd long ago abandoned for harsher things, things like not giving a damn, things like callous indifference when someone walked out on you, things like violence. Why had he not known to miss this gentleness until this moment?

Unable to help himself, hungry for more of the tenderness he'd just rediscovered, he lowered his head. His lips brushed hers.

"Soft, lush, kissable," he whispered. "And that's no idle observation."

His words made no sense to Anne Elise. Nothing did. Except the sensual tickle of his mustache—so this was what a mustache felt like!—and the erotic dipping of his tongue into the corners of her mouth.

"What?" she managed to say.

"Nothing," he growled quietly as he tunneled his fingers in her hair and seriously fitted his mouth once more to hers. As he did so, he rolled to his back, taking her with him and settling her across him.

This kiss was different. Anne Elise sensed it, though she didn't know quite how to define the difference. It was still a little rough, a lot commanding, like the man himself, but it was also . . . gentle. No, that wasn't a word she'd ever use to describe Kell Chaisson. Yet, the stroking of his tongue, the fragile pressure of his lips reminded her of gentle. That is, whenever she could think at all. Which she didn't want to do. She just wanted to feel . . . just for a little longer.

"Unbutton the shirt," he whispered, his breath fanning against her mouth. She hesitated. "Or I will," he added, "and I promise to send the buttons flying."

"They're your buttons," she said, wondering where her cheekiness was coming from. Probably from the same place the surreal feeling was. It was still there, still swirling around her. Shouldn't she try to grab hold of reality? Yes. But exactly what was reality? And where was it? The only reality she knew at the moment was Kell's mouth, Kell's hands, Kell's body.

"Unbutton the shirt, Anne Elise." His mouth nibbled at hers, biting occasionally, almost violently, then tenderly kissing where he'd bitten.

"You said my name."

"I did before."

"I wasn't paying attention."

"I know."

"Say it again."

"I know."

"My name. Say my name."

"Anne Elise," he whispered, repeating, "Anne—" he ripped open the shirt. Buttons did, indeed, scatter everywhere. "—Elise," he finished around her startled gasp that brought an abrupt end to their kiss.

Her eyes flew to his. His had a lazy, I-told-you-so look.

With a maddening lack of haste, he slid his hands around the nape of her neck, then inside the collar of the shirt, where he flattened his hands against the warmth of her bare skin. Slowly he peeled the fabric from one shoulder, then the other, then down her arms. Like a cotton river, it flowed from behind her and across his thighs. He carelessly dropped the shed garment to the floor. Only then did he lower his gaze to her breasts. They were round. Pear shaped. With rosy-brown nipples that pouted even as he stared. She wore only a silver bracelet engraved with the name of her husband. For a reason that heaven alone knew, Kell wanted to tell her to take it off. But he didn't. Because he didn't have the right.

Molten-hot feelings bubbled Anne Elise's blood as she watched him watch her. But he didn't touch her. At least not where she'd expected. Or wanted him to. Instead, his hands lightly trailed up her arms, past her elbows, up, up and to the curve of her shoulders. There, he made slow, lazy circles before sliding his hands down her back—down, down, slowly down.

Thousands of sensations, as delicate as pastel field flowers blowing in a gentle spring breeze, erupted everywhere his hands touched. They tripped like whispered wind songs down the curve of her spine. The pads of his fingertips felt rough, deliciously rough, arousingly rough, and she thought that this, the feel of this man, was the only reality she wanted. She didn't want painful memories; she didn't want lonely nights; she didn't want an emptiness so profound that it hollowed out her gut. She wanted this—to feel alive. The guilt would come later; of that she had no doubt, but for now she just wanted to feel alive.

She made a sound that was half whimper, half cry as Kell's hands slid around her rib cage. His thumbs rested just at her navel. Then slowly he started his fingers upward until they bracketed her breasts. He stopped.

So did Anne Elise's heart.

Folding his hand into a fist, Kell grazed the underside of one breast with his knuckles. The action felt like a butterfly flapping its silken wings against her. She glanced down. The butterfly was black and blue, the colors of the bruise marring his flesh. Was this the same hand that, only a short while before, had violently struck a man to the ground? It hardly seemed possible. It hardly—

She moaned as the pad of his thumb stroked across her nipple. Her nipple puckering, or the fractured sound of her reaction to his touch—one or both sensually spoke to Kell as well, for deep inside her she felt him swell to life again. She bit at her bottom lip as ripples of pleasure purled through her at the point of their bodies' contact.

"Come here!" he said gruffly, impatiently.

His hands at her waist, he pulled her the length of him, his mouth fastening to her breast. The cry she'd bitten back tumbled forth. It was followed by a series of others as his mouth did the most delightfully scandalous things. His tongue licked, moistened, laved before his lips closed around her to suckle. He alternated between gentle and not so gentle until she could no longer tell which she preferred. She knew only that she didn't want him to stop. His hand played with her other breast, molding it, kneading it, knotting the nipple between his thumb and finger. He tugged with his hand, at the same time he nipped her breast with his teeth.

A shudder of pleasure roamed through her.

He felt it. Taking her hips in his palms, he rotated her against him. Another shudder shivered about him.

Responding to her reaction, he quickly rolled her to her back and, sprawled atop her, he urged his hips forward, thrusting himself deeper inside her as though claiming her. The fierce grimace of his lips only enhanced the conquering image. She gasped. And laced her hands behind his back. She felt the scars banding his skin, felt the hair of his legs mating with the smoothness of hers, felt the hot thick heat of him growing. Incredibly growing.

"Kell—"

"No. No words. Just this."

He reached behind him for her hands. Slowly he drew them the length of his chest, then mounded them over where their bodies were joined, their love-wet bodies.

"Just this," he whispered as he once more began to move inside her. Long, slow strokes that filled her hands before he slid back to fill her. Nothing in her life had ever seemed so carnally sensual, so divinely perfect. Nothing.

She moaned softly.

Without breaking the stride of his hips, he took her hands and guided them above her head and to the iron railings. Her hands, under his direction, clenched the bars. He clasped his around hers.

"Later you'll hate me," he whispered. "Later you'll hate yourself. But for right now, we're gonna give each other what we want. C'mon, Anne Elise," he commanded, her hips already seeking the paradise his offered, "give... and then take... everything you want."

What they both wanted turned out to be considerable. So considerable, so powerful, so bordering on pleasure-violence, that minutes later, when they both reached a simultaneous end, he, she, they, broke one of the iron railings they clung to.

Neither cared.

Both physically and emotionally weary, they tumbled into sleep though it was only midafternoon. The food lay forgotten. They didn't awaken until night had fallen and the only light in the room came from a nearby neon sign. It was Kell who stirred first ... and only because the hunger in his stomach would no longer allow him to sleep. Refusing to think of the pleasure that was only hours old—my God, had anything, anyone, ever made him feel so... So what? So good, so whole? He refused to complete the thought. Instead, he eased from the woman beside him, the woman whose body was as warm as a summer day, and rounded the foot of the bed. He headed for the worn chair. Cursing the crinkling sound of the sack, he slipped in his hand and pulled out a cold shrimp. He plopped it into his mouth.

"Bring me some," Anne Elise said softly. "Whatever it is."

Even in the dark, his eyes found her. She was leaning on an elbow, the sheet pulled demurely about her. Her hair was sexily wild. From his fingers. From his lovemaking. The thought started another kind of hunger. The kind that food couldn't appease.

"Shrimp," he answered thickly, though he tried to ignore the renewal of the ache. "And they're cold as hell."

"I think that's a contradiction," she said. "Bring me one, anyway."

He was naked. She could tell this as he crossed back to the bed, the sack casually held in his hand. His big hand. He eased to the bed's edge and held out the sack to her. She scooted up and leaned back against the railing. One of the iron slats was broken. She remembered vividly why it was. He remembered, too. She could see it in his neon-shrouded face. She dropped her eyes from his.

He'd been right. The shrimp were cold, as were the potatoes. She knew, too, that he was right about something else. At some point she was going to regret tonight. At some point she was going to have to deal with guilt. Was now that point in time?

"In the morning," he said. "Deal with the regret in the morning."

He'd read her mind, clearly, sharply... or maybe it was simply that they were beginning to spend too much time together. Too much intimate time.

"And are you going to regret tonight, too?" She hadn't known she was going to ask the question, but now she waited impatiently for his answer.

He hesitated, shrugged his broad shoulders, shoulders that could smother a woman in security, sensuality, then said, "Probably."

He took another shrimp, then leaned forward to feed her one. She took it, tasting more of him than the food. Unlike the shrimp, his fingers weren't cold... nor were the feelings they inspired. Somewhere deep inside, though, his answer chilled her, making her wish somehow that he wasn't going to regret what had happened between them.

Neither spoke for a while. Finally, with a motion of the bag, he silently asked if she wanted more. She shook her head. He tossed the sack to the floor, climbed back into bed, checked his watch in the spray of blue lights.

"What time is it?" Anne Elise asked.

"A little after two." He lay the watch back on the bedside table and stretched out beneath the sheet.

Embarrassed, feeling awkward now that she was beginning to grow more awake, Anne Elise started to roll to the far side of the bed. He reached for her, hauling her back against him. Their legs tangled. Her breasts flattened against his chest. His breath mingled with hers.

"We have the rest of the night," he whispered hoarsely, "and the first rule about regrets is that you make them worthwhile."

"You seem to know a lot about regrets," she said, staring up into his night-black eyes. Her body had already begun to betray her again.

"Yeah," he said, softly, roughly, as his mouth took hers.

This time they made love slowly, so slowly Anne Elise thought she'd die with pleasure. And they did things together that she'd never before done with any man. Not even with the man she'd called her husband. When the loving was over, when their bodies were wet with sweat, their breath splintering the night in the oldest of love songs, she trembled in the wake of their passion.

This time, however, there was someone to hold her.

And the someone trembled as violently as she.

With the first rays of dawn, Kell's prophecy was fulfilled.

"C'mon, let's get cracking!" he called as he rapped his knuckles against the bathroom door.

A sleepy-eyed Anne Elise, clutching the sheet to her with one hand, the clothes he'd shoved at her in the other, glanced up sharply, as though she half expected him to burst through the door. Only minutes before, he'd awakened her with a snarled, "Get up! We overslept!" Having gone from the warmth of his arms to the coolness of the black-and-white, faded-and-cracked linoleum squares of the bathroom floor, from the sexy whisper of his voice to its now-impatient roughness, she experienced a marked contrast that threw her body into a kind of shock. That and the realization of just what had happened between them, a realization growing with wakefulness. Not only had she let something happen between them, she'd initiated it! At five-thirty in the morning, dragged from a dead sleep, her life seemingly tossed in the air to land as it would, she simply didn't know how to deal with last night. So she dealt with it the way she always seemed to deal with this man. With anger.

"Give me a minute! I just woke up!"

"You haven't got a minute! The plane leaves at seven!"

"Then we should have gotten up earlier!" she said, snatching open the door and thrusting forward the dirt-stained white slacks and T-shirt. The T-shirt, which she'd worn to the village, reeked of dried perspiration. "I can't wear these," she said, her eyes refusing to meet his. The way they had from the moment he'd shaken her awake.

Already dressed in jeans and a yellow cotton shirt, the sleeves of which he'd rolled to his forearms, Kell was squatted before the duffle bag, stuffing in their personal belongings that had been scattered around the room. At present he held her lace panties and his shirt, the one now buttonless, the one he'd ripped from her in the throes of passion. He looked up at her.

The sight of her—her bare shoulders, her storm-wild hair, her kiss-bruised lips—did things to his senses that he found damned aggravating. That and the fact that she wouldn't look him straight in the eye. This last actually angered more than it aggravated. He knew his voice reflected that anger. Though to be honest, he admitted, he'd been short with her from the first moment she'd come awake—and God, she woke up so provocatively! Her eyes smoky, her lips soft-looking, her posture one of total vulnerability and innocence! Yes, he'd been short with her, and he didn't have to have a degree in psychology to figure out why. He was pulling away from her, rejecting her, before she could reject him.

"Well, that's just too bad about your clothes, Miss Astor. You're gonna have to wear them. And as for our getting up earlier, we might have been more inclined to do so if we hadn't stayed up all night."

Anne Elise blushed a beet red. Her eyes simply would not travel above the jut of his square chin.

Look at me, dammit! he thought.

"How gallant of you to remind me, Captain."

"The last thing a son of a bitch is is gallant."

No, she thought, *the last thing a son of a bitch is is tender and yet, you were tender last night. It was a tenderness that even seemed to surprise you. But it's a tenderness you obviously don't want to remember now. But then, neither do I.*

Anne Elise whirled and started back for the bathroom.

"Hey?"

She turned, her eyes still not meeting his.

"Would this help?" He indicated the buttonless shirt, which he had wadded in his hand.

She stepped back, keeping her eyes focused on the shirt. Both he and she avoided any mention as to why the buttons were missing.

"Maybe," she said, adding around a swallow, "Do you have an undershirt?"

He dug through the duffle bag and produced an ordinary white cotton undershirt. He held it out. Her eyes still downcast, she took it with a mumbled, "Thanks." She started for the bathroom.

"Anne Elise?"

The way he said her name, a growled kind of throatiness, set her pulse to racing.

"You want these?"

Her underpants. Or the scrap of lace she wore as underpants. One was her definition, the other his.

Wordlessly she took the panties and, just as wordlessly, she retraced her steps.

The fact that she still refused to look at him, the way the silk underwear had felt slipping from his fingers—the latter like cool fire burning his soul—once more lighted the fuse of his anger.

"Hurry the hell up, will ya?"

"I am hurrying!" she shot back, unduly angered herself that he apparently couldn't wait to get out of her life.

Well, she couldn't wait to get out of his, either, she thought, closing the bathroom door and quickly shedding the sheet. Ignoring the obvious love aches, she slipped her legs into her underwear and, choosing not to wear a bra, thrust her head through the neck of his undershirt. She equally ignored how the cotton felt next to her tender breasts, breasts he'd kissed so thoroughly, so cleverly, so...

She closed her eyes on a deep sigh. How could she have let any of last night happen? More to the point, how could she have been the one to start it? Which she had been. Her honesty demanded she admit no less. It was just that nothing had seemed real. And she had felt so alone. And everything had seemed so anticlimactic. As though all of her hope and been kicked squarely in the teeth. She had felt as though she were being punished for having the audacity to want to put an end to her misery and go on with her life. But in the end, nothing had changed. Everything was still at square one. She still didn't know if it was her husband she'd be burying.

The realist, the logician in her came to the forefront. How could she have let last night happen? She knew exactly. In a world that had suddenly turned unreal, Kell had seemed her only anchor to reality.

Kell.

Jim.

Anne Elise opened her eyes and stared at the woman in the mirror. Guilt seemed to surround her like a tarnished aura. How could she have betrayed Jim? No sooner had she asked the question than she realized that her betrayal wasn't entirely where the guilt was coming from. In that paradoxical way that the human psyche can be many opposing things all at the same time, she realized that she did feel guilty about betraying her husband, but the real guilt was coming from just how little guilt she did feel. Which made no sense, she thought on a groan. Nothing made sense. Except her regret. She did feel a horrible sense of regret.

God, how could she ever look Kell Chaisson in the eye again?

"Let's go!"

Anne Elise jumped and hastened into the rest of her clothes.

Minutes later, at the sound of the door opening, Kell turned. His heart skittered at how beautiful the woman standing before him looked. Beautiful in a pure kind of way. His undershirt, which she'd knotted at the hem, she wore on the outside of her slacks. Over it all she wore the shirt as a jacket. Her hair had been freshly brushed—with his brush. Still avoiding his eyes, she walked to the duffle bag and put the remainder of her things inside. She stood, still avoiding his eyes, and announced, "I'm ready."

With a quick, angry stride, he crossed to her and grabbed her chin in the vise of his fingers. He jerked her head, causing their eyes to meet.

"Dammit, look at me! You can't pretend I don't exist and that last night didn't happen. It did. Live with it!"

Even if she had been capable of pulling from his firm grasp, she couldn't have pulled from the magnetism in his dark eyes. Something in them compelled her to speak the truth. Something in them also started a tingling in places that she thought had been so completely satisfied that they'd never tingle with need again.

"Maybe I could," she breathed, "if I hadn't been the one to...to initiate..." She couldn't find the words to finish. She didn't have to.

"I'm a big boy. I know how to say no." His voice had grown huskier when he added, "The point is that neither of two consenting adults was saying no."

Another blush crept into Anne Elise's cheeks.

He saw it. He also saw her confusion. "Don't analyze it," he said. "People go to bed together for a lot of reasons."

"That's just it. I don't. I mean, I haven't since... I don't. Period. Not until...last night." The last trailed off to the feeblest of whispers.

From the beginning, it had been his guess that Anne Elise Butler had been with no man since her husband. Last night had only strengthened that belief. To have it confirmed, though, was like a hard, fast right to the solar plexus. He called himself the biggest fool of the year for even entertaining the notion that it had something to do with him personally, for he knew it didn't. It had been the circumstances. Only that. He didn't look too closely at what his motivation had been. He simply accepted as fact that he'd wanted her. Just the way her nearness was making him want her again.

"It happened. Live with it," he said gruffly, pulling his hand from her chin as though her flesh had grown too heated to touch.

Without another word, or look, they bundled up their possessions and left the room. Downstairs, Kell paid a sleepy, tousle-haired clerk with his last Thai currency.

Crossing to Anne Elise, who held the satchel of money, Kell discreetly began to search through the bills. "Give me thirty bucks," he ordered.

"How much *was* the room?" she asked, aware that what appeared to be substantial money had already crossed the clerk's hand.

"This is for the bed we broke," Kell answered.

Their eyes met—meaningfully, fire to fire, memory to memory.

"Oh," she whispered.

In a short while they were riding, silently, in the back seat of a taxi to the airport. Kell sat in one far corner, Anne Elise in the other. He was shrouded in regret. She was cloaked in it. Both were vaguely aware that what they regretted most, however, was that the other had regrets.

Chapter Nine

The stewardess was flirting with Kell.

Anne Elise picked up on it the moment the red-haired wench, with the wings spread wide above her ample bosom, smiled at him. When he semismiled back, Anne Elise had the strangest urge to personally investigate the violence that Kell knew so much about. Appalled by her reaction, she concentrated on the breakfast tray that sat before her and on the wild blue yonder that placidly sailed past the plane's window.

They had been airborne a little over an hour and a half. When she thought of the twenty-one hours left to go, she went just a little crazy. How would she ever make twenty-one hours when she was already this can't-sit-still-in-her-seat restless? Kell, on the other hand, looked as though he'd never been more settled. Of course, that was always how he appeared. No, not always. Back at the airport, she'd sensed his wariness as he, the gun still hidden at his waist, had kept

a quiet watch for Forbes. When it appeared that Forbes had
at least a modicum of common sense, and had not pursued
them, Kell had done something with the gun—the men's
room?—before boarding the plane. The money he'd kept at
his side, the box of remains he'd personally talked to the
airline about. With the delicacy the situation demanded,
they'd been stored in the plane's baggage compartment.

"Finished?"

At the sound of the woman's voice, Anne Elise looked up.
It was the smiling wench. "Are you finished with your
tray?"

"Yes," Anne Elise answered. Before she could pass it to
her, however, the stewardess bent across Kell's lap—thigh
to thigh—and scooped it up. She then smiled once more at
Kell before, likewise, retrieving his tray. Anne Elise wondered if Kell was smart enough to see through the woman's
wiles. She frowned inwardly. Maybe he was enjoying her
wiles. After all, he was an unattached, available man. The
thought sat about as comfortably as the breakfast she had
forced down.

A short while later, Kell unfastened the seat belt and rose
from the first-class aisle seat. Without a word, without a
look in Anne Elise's direction, he strode to the nearby gal-
ley. The red-haired stewardess looked more than pleased to
see him. His arm framing the doorway, he bent low and said
something, to which the stewardess gave a smile and a nod.
She then indicated for him to follow her.

Anne Elise leaned out of her seat to watch. After Kell
ducked his head, they disappeared into the plane's cockpit.

The cockpit?

Minute after slow minute passed. The only thing that kept
Anne Elise sane was the knowledge that the pilot and co-
pilot would unwittingly be chaperons. Even at that, she
breathed a sigh of relief—why should she feel such re-

lief?—when Kell finally returned and strapped himself back into the seat.

"I had them radio to Tokyo for a casket," he said in explanation. "I should have thought of it back in Bangkok, but I didn't." *I had too many other things on my mind. Things like wild, auburn hair and soft green eyes....*

"Thank you," Anne Elise said, deeply moved by his thoughtfulness. She was also deeply moved by the way a swath of his hair tumbled onto his forehead. The memory of his hair beneath her hands, the memory of his hands lost in her hair, caused her breath to flee. "Thank you," she repeated.

The reedy rush of her voice slammed Kell's heart into overdrive. It was the same voice she'd used to beg him not to stop the night before.

"You, uh, you'd better get comfortable," he muttered. "It's gonna be a long trip." *A very long trip,* he added silently.

A long, long trip, she thought.

The flight proved as lengthy as predicted. Indeed, it seemed to grow more endless by the minute. By tacit agreement, both Kell and Anne Elise tried to keep their physical and emotional distance, but, at least for Anne Elise, the trip became a blur of accidentally brushed knees, quick glances, words almost said but thought better of in that last moment before they sprang from the tongue. For Kell, a man who was no stranger to torture, the flight became a whole new journey into punishment. It was a pain he intuitively knew he could ease with the simplest of actions. What that action was he wouldn't allow himself to clearly define. He wasn't ready to face the fact that holding a certain woman in his arms was that powerful.

At some restless point after both had read every magazine on the plane, after Anne Elise had played a dozen rounds of solitaire, after Kell had tried to meditate but failed miserably, he suggested that she call her father from the plane telephone. Since she'd spoken with her father only once since leaving Dallas, she had to admit it was a good idea. Besides, she needed someone to meet her at the airport.

Both took great care to see that their bodies didn't touch when Anne Elise rose to go for the phone. Kell stood rather than risking contact. Anne Elise passed by him as though skirting a hot stove. After inserting her credit card in the telephone unit at the rear of the plane, she carried the phone back to her seat. Kell stood again for the no-touch routine.

In a short while, and to the tune of seven dollars a minute, Anne Elise heard her father's rough and blustery voice. It washed over her like warm, familiar sunshine.

"Daddy? Yeah, it's me." The connection was poor, and she had to strain to hear. "We're on our way home. I said, we're on our way home. Yes, sir." She glanced over at Kell. "When do we arrive?"

Kell told her. She repeated it to her father.

At her father's next question, her tone turned grave. "Yes, sir, I have the remains. Look, Daddy, it's a long story. No, I have the remains. I'm just not certain they're Jim's." In some distant part of her brain, she realized she was keeping her eyes averted from Kell's. Maybe because of the flare of anger she feared she'd see there again. "Daddy, I'll explain...no, sir, no positive ID...yes, sir, we still have the money...yes, sir I'm all right...no, really I am...Daddy, I'm—" She sighed in resignation, glanced over at Kell and held out the phone. "Daddy wants to talk to you."

Kell reached for the instrument. Their fingers brushed. Anne Elise's heart quickened; Kell's, too, found a new rhythm.

"Hello?" Kell said, that new rhythm making his voice choppy. "No, it didn't go as we'd planned." Nothing had gone as planned, he thought, his eyes, once they'd connected with Anne Elise's, seemingly unable to disconnect. Case in point, he'd certainly never intended to take this woman to bed. But he had. And now he heard her father asking if she was all right. "Yeah. She's all right." *In fact, she's more than all right. The way her lips melted beneath mine, the way her legs curled around me, the way her body naturally, shamelessly responded to mine was a helluva lot better than just all right.* "She's all right," he repeated on a low rumble.

After the promise to explain everything once in Dallas, Kell passed the phone back to Anne Elise. She vowed a few more times that she was all right, then broke the connection. Kell insisted on returning the phone to the rear of the plane, as though he desperately needed to walk, to pace, to get away from the woman beside him. Anne Elise, too, was grateful for the time alone. She was able to catch her breath in a way she couldn't when Kell was near.

Night overtook them, weaving its black, lacy curtain around them. For the most part, the passengers had settled down, many slumbering, at odd angles, beneath blankets provided by the airline. Even the flight attendants—the smiling wench included—had found cozy nooks to rest in until some passenger called them back into service. Contrarily, with every overhead light that went off, with every passenger that snuggled down to sleep, Anne Elise and Kell grew just that much more restless in the first-class section, which had grown quiet and shadowy.

"Will you be still?" he barked from the aisle seat he'd been sitting in for hours, for days, for—hell, it was beginning to feel like for years!

"I need a blanket," she snapped. "Do you mind?"

"Would it do me any good if I did?" he snarled, standing and tossing a blanket into her lap.

She ignored his sarcasm and spread the warm fabric over her. Seconds passed. She began to squirm again.

"Now what?" Kell asked, his voice an exercise in exasperation.

"A pillow. I need a pillow."

He lumbered to his feet and opened the overhead compartment. He threw a pillow in her direction. "Do you need anything else? A drink of water? A bedtime story?"

"Go to hell, Chaisson," she mumbled, her nerves as frazzled as her body. What she wanted was for him to hold her. Somewhere along the line, she'd at least been that honest with herself.

Hell? He couldn't go where he already was, he thought, where he'd been ever since he'd awakened that morning and known that this woman would never be in his arms again. It was an admission he surprised himself by making. He plopped back down into the seat. His thigh grazed hers.

"Sorry," they both said, each pulling tighter into his own limited space.

She tossed. He turned. She crossed her legs. He stretched his out before him. She stretched hers. He crossed an ankle to a knee.

"Do you want to change seats?" he growled suddenly.

"Yes," she growled back.

He stood, she passed into the aisle, he took the window seat, she his former seat. With a flurry of jabs, she fought to make the pillow comfortable. He slipped off his shoes.

Was that spicy smell his cologne?

Was that flowery fragrance her perfume?

Was that a five o'clock stubble forming on his face?

Was that a faint glow of lipstick or just the naturalness of her lips?

Oh, Jim, why did you have to die?

Why in hell couldn't he be impressed with the red-haired stewardess who had practically thrown herself at him? Why couldn't one red-haired woman be very much like another? Why did one have to have copper-colored hair as wild and tantalizing as an erotic daydream?

That copper-colored hair, atop a very restless head, scattered as a new position was sought. Gypsy strands, like greedy fingers, grasped the sleeve of his shirt.

"Dammit!" he exploded as he, in one action, raised the armrest between them, jammed himself in the corner and pulled her, now cradled in the juncture of his legs, back against him. "Will...you...be...still!"

In one swift second, her hand was splayed against Kell's jean-covered thigh, the pillow beneath her head tumbled to the floor and was replaced by his chest, the blanket that covered one figure was now being draped over two.

She started to protest—she needed to protest—but her body did what she was beginning to think it was impossible for it to do: it began to relax... against the hardness of Kell Chaisson... against the softness of Kell Chaisson. She closed her eyes, feeling as though she'd just made port in a surly storm.

Like steam seeping from the lid of a teapot, Kell felt the restlessness ooze from him. He angled his head back against the plane and draped his arm, which was outside the blanket, around Anne Elise's waist. Her arm ran parallel with his, so that his bruised knuckles rested next to her silver bracelet.

For a long while they rode in silence, each content to savor the nearness of the other. At length, without censoring her actions, she brushed her fingertips across the black-and-blue bruise. Kell didn't move a muscle. He simply closed his eyes and luxuriated in her touch. When he could no longer withstand the pleasure of her caress, he caught her hand in his and entwined their fingers.

Thus they sat. Through the silence. Through the dusky-darkness of the night. Perhaps it was the darkness that nudged the unexpected question forward.

"Is it true?" she heard herself ask and wondered where she was finding such audacity. But then, maybe it wasn't so much audacity as a desperate need to know.

"Is what true?" The question rumbled from his chest.

"That you fell in love with the wife of a POW?"

There was the barest tightening of muscles before the candid reply of, "Yes." Nothing. For so long that Anne Elise thought nothing more was coming. "It, uh, it wasn't sordid. At least it didn't feel that way." Why he was telling her this, when he'd never told another person, he couldn't have said, except that for some reason he felt compelled to. "It started out that I was nothing more than a bridge over her troubled water, but then..." Anne Elise could feel the shrugging of his shoulders. "I don't know what happened. I just woke up one day and... and there we were."

On the one hand Anne Elise felt his pain; on the other hand she felt her own. This latter she didn't understand. She just knew that it hurt to think of him so deeply in love with someone.

"Do you ever hear from her?"

"No." Emphatic. Followed by silence. A silence comparable to the one that had spanned the years. For both of them.

"I'm sorry," she whispered, looking back over her shoulder, thinking how lucky some woman had been to have this man's love. "I'm sor—"

Kell's mouth swooped to hers, bringing another kind of silence, this one positive, this one golden. He kissed her hard and fast and with every ounce of his being. He kissed her as though he'd been wanting to no less than a hundred years. If she'd needed him the afternoon before, he now needed her. It was a need she could feel, a tortured need, a need suddenly pressed fully, masculinely, against her. She moaned at his body's quick response, feeling that response echo deep within her. She had no idea whether he turned her in his arms or whether it was she who turned, but she found herself lying between his legs, her chest drawn along the length and breadth of his. Her mouth was giving everything that his demanded.

As his tongue sipped long, hungry drinks of her, his hands sifted through her hair, his thumbs riding the crest of her high cheeks. He anchored her tightly. His mouth still eating at hers, he sent one hand lower to the column of her soft, fragrant throat. Her pulse beat savagely against the pad of his thumb.

Nothing, however, seemed enough. For either of them.

Anne Elise sought the nape of his neck, molding her palms to its corded contours. His hands moved lower...beneath the blanket...beneath the folds of her clothing. Splaying his hands, he fanned her bare back, kneading, caressing, pressing her to him.

He felt her breasts flatten against him. She felt the hard strength of his chest cushioning her.

She moaned softly.

Dragging his mouth from hers, he trailed kisses all along her neck.

"Do you know what I want to do to you?" he asked, his voice intoxicated with drugged emotion.

"Yes."

"Do you know where I want to be?"

"Yes."

"Do you know how deep I want to be?"

"Yes."

He rushed his mouth back to hers, his tongue showing her what he'd like to be doing to her body. Slowly, however, as though remembering where they were, he began to temper the kiss. Urgency gave way to a gentleness. Insanity to sanity.

"Do you know that I'm gonna get us arrested if I don't stop?" he whispered against her lips.

She angled her head, her gaze finding his. There was a hint of laughter in his dark irises.

"Yes, I know," she said with an answering smile.

The smiles faded. He pulled her down, settling her against him. The hands that still rested beneath her clothing slid farther up her back until he smothered her in his solid embrace. Sexual gave way to soulful as he tucked her head beneath his chin.

"Go to sleep," he whispered. He bent his knee, angled his hips—all to get as comfortable as he could. On a sigh, she sprawled lazily against him.

In minutes, defying the hours of restlessness, defying the past, they both fell asleep.

The flight arrived in Dallas on schedule.

Anne Elise and Kell deplaned in silence, a silence that had grown in magnitude the closer their destination loomed. As they walked through the tunnel toward the waiting room, Kell, the satchel thrown over one shoulder, the duffle bag the other, guided her with a hand at the small of her back. Once, when an eager passenger cut in front of her, Kell steadied her by throwing his arm around her waist and pulling her back against him. She glanced up, he down. She started to say something, but didn't.

What did one say at a moment like this?

Look, thanks a bunch for accompanying me to Bangkok. I appreciate more than I can say your watching out for

my pretty little ass. Bye now and have a nice life and if
you're ever in Dallas, look me up. Oh, and by the way,
thanks for taking me to bed.

No, nothing seemed quite appropriate. Yet she longed to
say goodbye. She just didn't know how.

"Momma? Hey, Momma?"

At the familiar voice, Anne Elise abandoned her troubling train of thought and began to search the crowd. At the
sight of her waving daughter, she smiled and waved back.
Home. She was home. At least that much felt right and
good.

"Hi, baby," Anne Elise said, hugging Brooke tightly.

Brooke squeezed back, then found her mother's gaze.
Anne Elise saw caution written across her daughter's face.
Apparently the general had warned his granddaughter that
things had not gone as hoped, though to what extent they
had not everyone had yet to find out. That included Anne
Elise's mother, who waited patiently at her granddaughter's side.

"Did you take good care of my mother?" Brooke asked
the man still standing behind Anne Elise. The duffle bag was
still thrown over one broad shoulder, the satchel the other.
His laid-back posture, his stubbly jaw, made him look like
a drifter who had just blown into town.

"I gave it my best shot," Kell answered around a tightening in his gut. The tightening had begun the moment the
plane had touched down. He wasn't crazy about goodbyes.
In fact, he loathed them.

"Did you bring my father back?" Brooke pointedly asked
Kell.

Anne Elise looked over her shoulder. Kell's eyes were
steady, even, truthful. "I don't know," he replied, pulling
no punches and leaving an unsettled silence to follow his

words. "I do think there's reason to hope, though," he added.

A warm, fuzzy feeling skittered through Anne Elise. He'd been adamantly opposed to bringing the remains back because there had been no positive identification, yet he was willing to give this young woman the gift of hope. Anne Elise's eyes willed Kell's to hers. When his obeyed, she silently thanked him.

"Annie E.?" came the starched, blustery voice of her father. "Are you all right?"

"Yes, sir," she replied, wondering if she was, why she felt so empty inside now that everything was over. The truth was, though, that she'd felt empty before. The only time in seventeen years that that emptiness had been filled was the time she'd spent in the arms of the man standing beside her.

"Chaisson," the general thundered, "what in hell happened over there?"

"Things didn't go as we'd expected," Kell drawled.

"There were no teeth," Anne Elise interjected.

Her father frowned. "I thought you were gonna pass on the deal, then?"

"He had Jim's wedding ring." Her eyes pleaded for her father to understand. "I couldn't take the chance, Daddy. If there was even the slightest chance the remains were his, I had to bring Jim home."

The crusty old soldier studied his daughter. His only gesture of understanding—but then none other was necessary—was the placement of his hand on her shoulder. His eyes lifted from Anne Elise to Kell.

"Any problems?"

"None I couldn't handle." With a snap of his wrist, Kell whipped the satchel off his shoulder. "Under the circumstances, I thought fifty thousand a bit overpriced. By about fifty thousand dollars."

General Terris eyed the bruises splattered on Kell's knuckles. It was obvious he was wondering if Kell had received the injury while "handling the problems." The older man reached for the money.

"Oh," Kell said, as though he'd just thought of it, "that's fifty thousand minus thirty bucks. Incidentals," he added, his gaze raking Anne Elise's.

A pale blush crept into her cheeks. She hastily glanced away. Not so Kell. His eyes lingered, just as did the memories of the broken slat of a bed.

Suddenly a red-coated airport attendant, walkie-talkie in hand, appeared from nowhere. "Ms. Butler? What arrangement have you made for the casket?"

Anne Elise looked startled by the question. Kell had taken such efficient care of everything since leaving for Bangkok that she'd forgotten that it was she who had to make these final arrangements. "Actually I've made no plans. I, uh, I guess—"

"I'll take care of everything," General Terris answered, stepping off to one side with the man.

Almost at the same instant, another couple, the age of the Terrises, walked up.

"Sorry," the white-haired man said, "but we couldn't find a parking space."

"Nancy, William," Anne Elise acknowledged, surprised, yet not surprised, to see that her parents-in-law had driven in from Amarillo.

"Hi, Grandmom," Brooke said, moving into her other grandmother's arms.

"Well, tell us everything," William prodded.

Amid hugs and kisses, Anne Elise repeated the story.

Kell watched as she was swallowed up by love. As always, he felt like the outsider looking in. As always, it was he who didn't belong. As always, it was he who'd be going his way alone. As he had moments before, he let his eyes roam over the red-haired woman before him. This time he seemed to be storing new memories, memories, like sepia-edged photographs, that he'd pull out later and look at. Suddenly, silently, the duffle bag still hitched across his shoulder, he took one last look, then moved off into the flow of pedestrian traffic. He didn't look back.

"Darling, you need to rest," Sugar said.

"Your mother's right," her mother-in-law agreed.

"I'm fine," Anne Elise protested. "Really, I am. William, Nancy, I want you to meet..." She turned...to find Kell gone.

A strange panic seized her, followed by an inexplicable loneliness. Desperately she searched the crowd. In the far, far distance, his shoulders bobbing above the sea of people, she saw him.

Was he staying the night in Dallas? Was he flying immediately back to Arkansas? Would she ever see him again? She didn't know. She just knew that he'd never said goodbye.

Chapter Ten

The next week, in a private, solemn ceremony, with the casket draped in the American flag, Anne Elise buried the remains. Unfortunately, she could not bury the fact that she would never know for certain if they were her husband's. A situation that had always seemed open-ended now appeared to sit at the edge of a mile-wide chasm, because forever was gone the hope of fully resolving the issue. Anne Elise suspected, however, that Brooke had chosen to believe the remains were those of her father. It was a suspicion confirmed when the young woman, acting on her own, carried a spray of flowers to the grave site. That night, the two women had cried together, though Anne Elise was uncertain as to the source of her tears—frustration, certainly, guilt, quite possibly. There had also been an unidentifiable emotion when she'd placed her husband's ring next to her own in the jewelry box. It was a hot, scalding feeling not unlike anger. But then, wasn't that an emotion she didn't waste her energy on?

Later that week, Anne Elise's clothes arrived—both those forwarded from the Hilton International in Bangkok and those sent from an address in Arkansas. The latter interested her most. These were the few personal belongings she'd stored in the duffle bag. Hastily she'd searched the package for a note. There was none. The fact that Kell had touched what she was now touching did strange things to her senses. She tried to explain her reaction but couldn't. No more than she could truly explain what had happened between them.

Oh, she had rationalized it from every angle she could find, and, psychologically, their going to bed together had been sound. She had been acting under the stimulus of a trauma, a powerful trauma, caused both by the danger they'd shared and the anticlimactic ending to the mission, and she had simply sought solace in the arms of a stranger. It wasn't the first time it had happened to a member of the human race. It wouldn't be the last. Yes, it was all psychologically sound. The only thing she couldn't rationalize was why, now, supposedly after the trauma had calmed, Kell's having touched the same articles of clothing she was touching should do such strange things to her senses.

And why couldn't she get the man out of her mind? And why did she feel that she was sending a part of herself when she mailed his clothes, without a note, back to him?

Monday of the following week, as per schedule, as the group's current secretary, Anne Elise attended a meeting of the National League of Families of American POWs and MIAs. She shared her recent experience. The organization, seeking new officers, queried her as to whether she'd chair the national organization. She told them that she'd give it some thought. Though she didn't really know how she could consider it, for each and every thought seemed to be focused on a man named Kell Chaisson, a man as bound to the past as she.

Did he ever think about her?

Would she ever see him again?

Did she really want to?

Exactly two weeks to the day since their arrival back in Dallas from Bangkok, Kell, dressed in the pants of a black sweat suit, his legs folded into a lotus position, sat on his breeze-caressed patio. He was wandering through his mind. The jungle, his sanctuary of peace, was hot and humid, its sultriness seeping into him like a steam bath. He welcomed the relaxation this meditation promised. He needed to relax...desperately. His body was wound tighter than a coiled watch spring. And had been ever since Bangkok. For the first time in years, the mind capable of great imagery was having a helluva hard time meditating. Or, more to the point, it was having a helluva hard time meditating on what he wanted it to.

Images of lush vegetation had given way far too often to images of a lush feminine body. The smell of a rain-drenched forest gave way to the sweet, flowery smell of perfume. The sun striping the canopy of trees with its copper rays could in no way compete with the sunny, copper tresses of one particular woman.

But maybe today he could put her out of his mind. Maybe today, for just a little while, he could lose himself in something besides heated memories. The forest beckoned to him, and he willingly walked into its green sheltering embrace.

Hot.

Sweaty hot.

Like the sound of a whispered breath against his neck.

Anne Elise's breath.

No woman had ever felt beneath him the way she did. He had struggled against that admission, but finally, in the mist of one sleepless night, he'd had to accept it. He'd loved Susan; there'd been a chemistry between them, but nothing as profound as the physical and emotional chemistry that sparked between him and Anne Elise Butler. What was between them didn't just spark. It exploded. Blowing him into a million pieces. A million pieces that she could then magically put back together again. With a touch. With a look. With the calling of his name.

Whole.

She made him feel whole.

Yet, she herself wasn't whole.

Part of her still belonged to First Lieutenant James Samuel Butler.

Dammit, his mind was wandering! Think green. Think jungle. Think hot and steamy. Think peace. Think—

The phone rang, its shrillness trampling out onto the patio via an open kitchen window. Kell cursed as he pulled to his feet. The fact that he'd noticed the phone at all was testimony to how ineffective the meditation was.

"Yeah?" he growled like an angry lion into the receiver.

"Chaisson?" a full, big-bodied voice bellowed back. "This is General Terris."

Kell's stomach tightened. Not because of who was calling, but because of who the general reminded him of. Namely his daughter. Unknowingly Kell ran his hand across his bare, sweat-sheened chest in an imitation of a gesture he couldn't get out of his senses.

"Yeah, general, what can I do for you? Besides returning to Bangkok?" This last was slathered with sarcasm. Sarcasm seemed very appealing these days. That and the urge to do something violent.

"You can explain why I'm looking at a check for twenty-five thousand dollars."

"Simple. I returned it."

"Why?"

"Didn't like the color of the ink you used."

"Can the sarcastic bullshit, Chaisson, and give me a straight answer."

"Things didn't turn out as we'd expected."

It was no explanation, and Kell knew it. But what was he going to say? *Look, I laid your daughter, and that kinda changes things? That and the way I can't get her out of my mind?*

"Your fee wasn't contingent on how anything turned out," General Terris said. "You did the job you were hired for. And damned well, my daughter tells me."

And did she tell you that my body exactly fits hers? Or, maybe, it's her body that exactly fits mine. Kell nudged the phone between his ear and his shoulder and opened the refrigerator. Dragging out a beer, he popped the top.

"I don't want the money, general," he said, putting the bottle to his lips and letting the cool, malty liquid slide down his suddenly dry throat.

"We need to at least talk—"

"I don't want the money."

"Look, I've just been appointed under secretary for political affairs—"

"Congratulations," Kell interrupted.

"That's not the point."

"What is?"

"They're throwing a big celebration bash next Thursday night in D.C. Come on up and we'll have time to talk then."

"Sorry, General, I'm not real big on bashes." He took another swig of the beer.

"Dammit, Chaisson, I'm trying to say thanks."

"None are necessary."

Kell heard the scrambling of the phone, then a soft, familiar, "Kell?"

The sound of Anne Elise's voice clipped him at the back of the knees. If it hadn't been for the kitchen cabinet, he wouldn't have sworn that he'd have been able to remain standing. That notwithstanding, he wasn't certain his heart was going to keep on beating. He set down the bottle of beer. And wondered if she had any idea how many times he'd searched through the returned clothes, looking for a note... and how disappointed he'd been when he'd found none.

"Kell?" she repeated.

"Yeah," he said, his voice as thick as an early-morning Arkansas fog.

"It, uh, it would please Daddy if you'd come to the party."

"And what about you? Would it please you, too?" Kell asked, stunned at what he was hearing himself ask. Jesus Christ, Chaisson, why don't you just stand in front of an itchy-fingered firing squad? The only satisfaction he got was hearing the frank question cut Anne Elise's breath in two.

A silence followed, during which both clearly wondered what her answer would be.

Finally, firmly, she said, "Yes. Yes, it would."

It was Kell's turn to have his breath halved. Any would-be response got lost in the simple act of trying to breathe.

When he said nothing, Anne Elise dared further. "Will you at least think about it?"

"Yeah," he managed to say.

There was another scrambling of the phone. "Chaisson? Get your butt to D.C. And that's a goddamned order!"

The next thing Kell knew he was listening to a dial tone...and wondering if cold common sense had any power over silk and lace.

Cold common sense had never stood a chance.

This Kell admitted as he stepped into the hotel ballroom that had been reserved for the reception honoring General Terris's appointment as under secretary. The plush room was alive with people, mostly politicians, who were smiling, shaking hands and liberally patting backs. The rest of the people Kell pegged as either reporters or Secret Service agents assigned to guard the notables present. Kell recognized the vice president and his family and the widow of a former president. Everyone was dressed to the nines. Even the Secret Service agents scanning the crowd for potential troublemakers.

Troublemaker.

He'd been called that a time or two himself. He'd probably be called it a time or two more. The truth was that sometimes it felt good to make a little trouble. He'd never looked too closely at why. It was just that sometimes edgy emotions boiled over to get the best of him. That was when only his fist in someone's face would neutralize the pent-up feelings. No, that wasn't exactly true. He could remember the recent touch of a woman who made him feel a gentleness he'd forgotten, a soothing kind of gentleness that eased his restlessness. As though desperately needing a glimpse of that tender emotion again, he urgently searched the crowd for that woman.

He spotted her in the middle of the room.

At the sight of her, his heart turned over in his chest. He was certain he'd never seen anything, anyone, quite so beautiful. A black dress, which from his male perspective he could describe only as clingy and sexy, molded her body to

just above her knees. It slanted over one shoulder, leaving
the other enticingly bare. Decorated in gold-and-bronze se-
quins, the dress glittered almost as much as the auburn hair,
swept atop her head, did in the light from the crystal chan-
delier. Black stockings silkened her legs, while black satin
heels made her tower to the height of a man's naughtiest
fantasy. Kell's reaction was typically male. Though he appreciated the outer trappings, he wondered what she had on
beneath them. At the lacy image that came to mind, he tried
to cool down the heat that seared him.

He reined in his wayward thoughts and made himself notice something besides how she was dressed. Like the fact
that she was surrounded by a half dozen or so women. As
though prisoners shackled to the past, they all wore silver
bracelets. A staunch supporter of the organization they obviously represented, he longed, however, to yank one of the
bracelets from the wearer's wrist. In fact, the urge was so
strong that he felt a dark emotion bubbling in the caldron
of his soul. It was the kind of dark, boiling emotion that
demanded release—as in fist-to-the-face release, as in let's-
make-a-little-trouble release. No, in this instance, he preferred another kind of release. No less dynamic, no less ca-
thartic.

*Wonder what the Secret Service agents would do if I threw
the lovely lady to the floor and made love to her until she
made those soft little pleading sounds?*

Before or after they envied the hell out of you?

Either. Both.

Lock you up, throw away the key and call you a troublemaker.

The troublemaker scooped a glass of champagne from a
passing tray, swallowed down a good half of the fizzing
contents and vehemently wished he had something stronger.
He started toward the lady in black.

"I'd love to see you at the helm," one of the ladies was saying to Anne Elise.

"I've had no experience being at the helm," she countered absently, her mind dealing with far more pressing matters. Would he come? What would she do if he didn't? What would she do if he did?

"You don't have to have experience," another woman was saying. "All you need to lead the organization is enthusiasm. And that you have."

"I appreciate your encouragement, really I do, but I'm going to have to think about accepting that kind of responsibility. I need time—" She stopped as Jodi Ward, dressed in a multicolored gown that made her look like a happy harlequin, sidled to her side.

"Hunk at one o'clock," she whispered before gaily flitting on.

Anne Elise's gaze flew upward, then leveled on the tuxedo-clad man approaching her. Her breath screeched to a halt. Her head swirled with a crazy, light-headed dizziness. The tux fit him to perfection, with the long black pants hugging his legs, his thighs, in all the right and masculinely relevant places. The white-pleated shirt, stiffly starched, drew attention to a chest capable of drawing a lot of attention on its own. Anne Elise remembered vividly the feel of it beneath her caressing palms. She also remembered—as in couldn't even come close to forgetting—how almost savagely this man made love. His savage image only seemed enhanced by the ultracivilized clothes he wore.

"Would you excuse me, please?" she said, stepping around the covey of women. She adjusted the thin strap of her black evening bag over her shoulder with fingers that trembled.

The savage-looking man and the lady in black stopped in front of each other. Silence tumbled after silence, just as heartbeats, like sea waves against sea walls, crashed one against the other.

"Hi," she finally managed to say.

He answered with a long, tall, slow-drawled, "Hi."

Another silence followed, a silence during which each absorbed the sight of the other.

"I, uh, I see you found the champagne," she said, not knowing what to say and grasping for the first thing she could think of.

"Yeah," he answered, taking a lazy swallow.

Anne Elise's eyes lowered to his lips, lips just above a mustache, a mustache that could tickle and tease and drive a woman crazy. Kell would have much preferred the taste of her lips to the bubbly wine.

"How, uh, how have you been?" she asked.

"All right, I guess," he replied, thinking that he'd never told a bolder lie. "How 'bout you?"

She shrugged. "All right, I guess."

The slight raising of her bare shoulder drew his attention. Was her skin still as soft as spring rain?

"You look good," he said, silently adding, *Good enough to devour*.

"So do you," she replied, thinking that how he looked fell more into the category of great.

"I hate tuxedos," he said, rimming his finger around the tight collar. A gray bow tie, which exactly matched a gray cummerbund, rested at his throat.

She smiled. "I can say unequivocally that they don't hate you."

He grinned—not much, but just enough to be devastating to any woman watching. Including Anne Elise. "Well, they damned sure feel like they do."

Her smile broadened, then died, swallowed alive by an-honest-to-God moment of seriousness. "I wasn't sure you'd come."

"If you'll recall, the general gave me an order...a god-damned order."

"And is that the only reason you came? Because Daddy ordered you to?"

Game.

They had suddenly begun to play a very dangerous, very hot game. A heart game. A body game. A game that could involve the forfeiture of one's very soul.

"No." The word was spoken low, so low it was barely audible in the noisy room. It was all Anne Elise heard. That and the roar of her heart.

What was happening between them? she thought. And why didn't she stop the craziness here and now? Because there was no way she could, she admitted. And, more to the point, she didn't want to stop it. She just wanted to be consumed by the fire in his eyes.

Not yanking her into his arms indicated the greatest restraint Kell had ever shown. It might be a battle he was going to lose, anyway, if she didn't quit looking at him the way she was. Like a woman who needed to be bedded...badly.

"Anne Elise? Is that you?" an elderly man—a Texas senator—asked.

And thus began the first of many party interruptions.

It seemed that everyone wanted to talk to Anne Elise. Etiquette demanded she talk back. After introducing Kell over and over and over, invariably the two of them would be split into separate conversations. At those times, each pair of eyes kept seeking out the other. Each always saw the same thing: hungry eyes looking back.

"Chaisson," General Terris bellowed, "good to see you!"

Anne Elise heard her father's booming voice and looked up. She saw the two men shaking hands. Kell's hand then slid into a pants pocket in a way that was sexually casual. She longed to edge away from the dull conversation going on around her but couldn't without being rude.

What were they talking about?

Even as she thought it, Kell's eyes found hers.

Her.

They were talking about her.

"I'm insistent on the money—" General Terris began, only to be cut off.

"I'm insistent about it, too, sir," Kell said, his eyes holding hers. God, if she didn't stop looking at him like that!

"But—"

"No," he said, literally forcing his eyes from hers. "This one was on me."

The general studied the man before him. Kell wondered just how transparent he was. "Then there's nothing for me to say except thank you," the general said at length.

Kell said nothing. He simply gave a clipped nod as a gesture of acceptance.

"Adam!" a voice beside the general roared. "I thought you were going to retire to pasture."

General Terris laughed. "You can't retire a soldier. Mr. Vice President, I'd like you to meet Captain Chaisson—"

Kell said all the right things, though his attention was elsewhere. When propriety allowed, he slipped away to stand alone. His eyes unerringly found Anne Elise. She was once more talking to a woman with a silver bracelet. A man with a silver bracelet soon joined them, followed by another braceleted woman...then another...then another....

Suddenly his world seemed to be shaded in silver. That angered him. The basis of the anger was simple and complex. He was frightened by just how much he wanted this woman. Having her beneath him—making love to him, whispering his name—seemed more important than breathing another breath of air. He didn't doubt that she, too, needed him. He'd seen the evidence of it in Bangkok. He'd seen it tonight on her face, but—and here was the kicker—was she capable of wanting him the way he needed to be wanted? He was tired of being odd man out, tired of it being him who lost out to some other guy. He wouldn't share another woman. Particularly not with a dead man.

Anger and fear coalesced into panic, pushing the common sense that had lost out to silk and lace to the forefront.

Setting the unfinished champagne down on the nearest table, Kell stalked from the room. As was his habit, he never looked back. The hotel bar beckoned like a fast-talking prostitute. Kell was buying anything she was selling.

"Whiskey on the rocks," he ordered, slinging his hip onto the bar stool and yanking at the bow tie until it dangled impotently. He wrestled open the first button of the shirt and sucked in the first good breath of air he'd had in hours.

In the dimly lit room, someone played the blues on a lonely saxophone. Kell had the urge to bend the sax into a new and totally unique design. Instead, he reached for the glass the bartender set before him. On impulse, when the bartender started to removed the bottle, Kell snatched at it, too, grabbing it by the neck as if it were a rope and he a drowning man.

"I'll take the whole thing," Kell said, sliding from the stool and digging in his pocket for his room key. "Charge it to 867."

"You got it, man," the bartender, whose quiet, easy manner said he'd seen it all, replied, "but you need to sign—"

"Forge it—Kell 'Sucker' Chaisson." With that, he stormed from the bar.

The couple in the elevator exchanged furtive looks when the scowling stranger, a nearly full bottle of whisky in one hand, a drink in the other, came aboard. The fact that he leaned against the padded wall with an I-don't-give-a-damn posture, while his eyes, broody and dark, begged someone, anyone, to come go a round with him, did nothing to alleviate the couple's fears. Together, they moved closer to the door. It was all they could do to keep from sighing with relief when the elevator stopped at their floor. Kell, downing a generous swallow of the drink, continued on. At the claustrophobic feeling that always came to him in a tight space, he downed the rest of what the glass held. He bared his teeth at the whiskey's bite.

Seconds later, he jiggled the key in the lock and slung open the hotel-room door. He switched on a single lamp under the premise that a man couldn't be moody in too much light. And he wanted to be moody. Or drunk. Or a satisfying combination of both. Toe to heel, he slipped out of his shoes at the same instant he clunked down the bottle. Switching the glass from one hand to the other, as if he refused to part with it regardless of the fact it was empty, he shed the tux jacket and threw it at the bed. It grazed it, then flowed to the floor. Kell didn't give it a second's worth of attention. Unfastening two more buttons of the shirt, now bringing the slit to midchest, he grabbed the bottle, tipped it, filled the glass, then settled back in a chair with his feet propped on the bed.

He had just brought the glass to his lips for some serious drinking when a knock sounded on the door. He muttered something black and vile. Then decided to ignore the interruption, hoping whoever it was would just go away. He took a long swig of the drink. The knock came again. Whoever it was wasn't going away. Kell muttered something blacker and viler. A quick, angry stride took him to the door... which he jerked open.

"Yeah, what in hell—?"

His gaze collided with that of Anne Elise.

Her eyes instantly, thoroughly, surveyed him. She took in the filled glass in his hand, the intense glint of some murky emotion in his eyes, the way his free hand was cocked at his hip, as if in defiance. The woman in her noticed also the dark hair peeking from the wide gap of his shirt. The woman in her liked what she saw.

Once the shock had worn away, his eyes were not idle, either. They took in the wisps of hair that were beginning to fall beguilingly at her temples and at the nape of her neck, her bare shoulder, black-stockinged legs that seemed to go on forever despite the fact that she wasn't all that tall. His eyes hazed in masculine appreciation.

"Don't you know that little girls shouldn't come to big boys' hotel rooms?" he drawled. The question itself was a dare, the tone in which it was asked a blatancy *extraordinaire*.

Anne Elise didn't back down. Not even as much as an inch. "I'm not a little girl. And you're not a boy, big or otherwise."

Kell's eyes darkened. "And therein lies a helluva lot of danger."

Anne Elise's gaze never budged from his. "Life is filled with danger."

He brought the glass to his lips. "I'll drink to that."

"May I come in?"

For a moment his answer seemed in question. Finally he shrugged and stepped back. "Whatever you want, Mrs. Butler."

The return to formality hurt, but Anne Elise sensed it was his way of psychologically distancing himself from her. Pretending not to notice, she entered the room...the dimly lit room. She let her purse slide from her shoulder to the chair. She immediately noticed the nearly full bottle of liquor.

"You have a bad habit, Captain," she said, trying his distancing technique.

He laughed harshly, a sound that mingled with the door's closing. "Lady, I've got enough bad habits to string 'em to hell and back. Which particular one did you have in mind?"

"This is twice now that you've left without saying goodbye."

"I don't do goodbyes," he said harshly, adding without skipping a beat, "What are you doing here?"

Games. They were back to playing those games, because both knew why she was there. The pounding of her heart told her; the thickening of his blood told him. Neither was quite ready to admit it yet, however. They needed to play the game, the man-woman game, just a little longer.

"Daddy said you turned down the money."

"Why are you here?" he persisted.

"I, uh, I wanted to thank you," she said. It was the excuse she'd given herself as she'd discreetly found out his room number. It had seemed like an excuse then; it seemed like a bigger one now. It was, however, the only excuse she had, so she clung to it. "I mean, for going with me to Bangkok," she added, trailing her fingers along the back of the chair. "And for doing it for nothing. You should have taken the money, though. You earned it."

"Why are you here?" he repeated, ignoring all she'd just said.

She pinned him with her stare. "Why didn't you take the money?"

Setting down the glass, he stepped closer, now looming directly before her. She had to angle her head backward. "Why...are...you...here?"

"Why are you drinking like there's no tomorrow?"

His heart beat like the crash of cymbals.

Her heart thumped as though a wild beast had been trapped in her chest.

The game playing was almost over.

"I'm trying to put out a fire," Kell said huskily, the admission sluicing over her like heated satin.

Anne Elise, her voice low and breathless, replied, "Sometimes to put a fire out, you have to let it burn wild."

His heartbeat moved into a final, frenzied crescendo.

The wild beast in her chest suddenly screamed to be free.

The game playing was over.

On a deep-seated groan, Kell pulled her to him.

Chapter Eleven

His lips sought hers as if he were a prisoner seeking freedom—freedom from days of longing, freedom from nights of torture, freedom from endless hours of wanting her body next to his. His fierce embrace half lifted her off the floor, giving her arms the perfect excuse, if any had been needed, to find his shoulders and cling tightly.

He tasted of whiskey and passion. It was impossible to tell which of the two was more potent, more inebriating. Both swirled in Anne Elise's head as though she'd been drinking for hours. She was not so drunk, however, that she couldn't feel the steel strength of his manhood urging itself into her softness, his hand slipping to her hip to press her into him and rub her back and forth against him, his other hand, cool from the icy drink he'd been holding, splaying wide across her bare shoulder. The contradiction of cold to hot, the cold of his fingers, the hot of desire spilling over and through her, was deliciously heady.

Anne Elise gasped softly. Kell used the moment to thrust his tongue deep inside her mouth, stroking, teasing, until the gasp turned into a trembling whimper. Her hands, as if seeking support from the dizzying sensations accosting her, slipped within the folds of his shirt. The feel of his hair-covered chest, the object of a thousand dreams, made her greedy for more and more of him. Her hands slid over hair and nipples and a rippling rib cage.

Kell sucked in his breath. Tearing his mouth from hers, he stared down at her. Both his mouth and hers were wet, parted, beginning to swell from the urgency of their kisses. His look said, "Lady, if you're leaving, you'd better do it now."

Was she leaving?

Her mind had been a confused jumble every since they'd returned to Dallas. She was torn between the past and the present, torn between a blond-haired man she'd loved and a dark-haired, dark-spirited man whom she refused to categorize her feelings for. She knew only that she couldn't get him out of her mind. And that she wanted, needed, to be in his arms.

Was she leaving?

Only if rivers ceased to flow downstream. Only if birds ceased to sing. Only if her legs suddenly grew a lot stronger.

At the desire he saw in her eyes, Kell groaned and reached for the zipper of her dress. There was no subtlety in the way he hastily rasped it open. Gone, too, was all finesse as he dragged the fabric over her one shoulder. The sequined dress fell to the floor, heaping at her feet and winking like a wicked invitation.

At the sight that greeted him, the sight of her body tantalizingly encased in nothing but her silky underwear, Kell's heart stopped entirely, then burst into a rhythm that threatened consciousness. The way that black lace was seriously threatening his sanity.

. He groaned... and uttered something so provocatively erotic that Anne Elise closed her eyes against the torrent of fiery images that blazed through her mind. Yes, yes, she wanted him to do all of that to her! And a thousand things more! Somewhere in the back of her mind, she wondered just when she'd become so shameless.

Kell was wondering how in the name of all that was holy could he kiss her, touch her, everywhere he wanted to at the same time. And if he didn't kiss all of her, touch all of her, soon, he was going to die. 'Course he was going to die if he did. Hell, he was just gonna die! In a flurry of heat, his mouth kissed the ivory of her shoulders, the swell of her breasts rising above the black strapless bustier. Through the fabric, his mouth sought a nipple. His tongue flicked it to hardness. He then bit, primitively, paganly, at the tight bead.

Anne Elise moaned and sagged against him.

Because his hands were busy elsewhere, at her sculpted waist, at the thighs that rode bare beneath the thin straps of the garters and the beginning of her silken hose, he used his nose and cheek to nuzzle aside the fabric confining her breast. One breast plumped to instant freedom. Just as instantly, he took it into his mouth, tonguing, tugging, teasing her until she felt faint.

"Kell!" she whimpered, feeling her legs give way beneath her.

He scooped her into his arms and carried her to the bed. There, he laid her down. Brazenly, his eyes on her, he stripped off his clothing—the shirt, which he practically ripped from his shoulders, his pants which he raked from his legs, his socks, the briefs molding his manhood.

His erect manhood.

Warm, wet feelings erupted inside her.

Stretching alongside her, his mouth claimed hers as his hands searched the softness of her body. When his hands began to quest for ways to remove the lacy garments, Anne Elise, her tongue playing with his, led his hand to the garter. With fingers she could feel trembling, he released one, then another, followed by two more. Desperately, with no concern for a stocking's fragility, he rolled the black hose from her legs. With the same haste, he tugged the bikini panties, a splash of ebony lace, from her hips. At the soft auburn curls he found, at the shaft of desire that shot through him, he made a low guttural sound . . . and did what he'd hoped to wait to do until he had her completely naked. He slid between her legs and surged into her.

She cried out.

He grimaced as she swallowed him whole.

His hips began an immediate rhythm. As he maintained it, he fought to unhook the bustier, little by little, as her body shifted with the swaying motion. Finally, her breasts, her belly, lay bare to him, and he moved over her, lifting her legs and drawing them around him. He thrust deeper inside her.

"I've been going crazy for this!" he growled, his mouth once more at hers.

Crazy.

It was the only word to describe their lovemaking. Anne Elise, more wanton than she would ever have believed that she could be, met his every thrust with one just as eager. This, too, was what she'd been going crazy for—the feel of him sliding into her, the feel of him almost pulling out before sliding deep again, the heat and heaviness of his body trapping her beneath it.

"I need . . ." she whispered, praying for a quick release from feelings far too painful, far too strong, far too wild.

"What?" he whispered into her mouth. "What do you need?"

Breathless, straining to bring an end, she whispered back, "You . . . you . . . God, I need you!"

He increased the tempo, wanting now only what she sought—to end the exquisite torment racking his body.

Suddenly, like a diamond exploding into a thousand splinters of jeweled light, her release came, raining down until it dewed her forehead and slicked her body. Nothing had ever felt like it before. It was like dying; it was like being born; it was like traveling a sacred road on a divine journey. And when she felt Kell taking the same journey, his body exploding with the same intensity as hers, shattering into the same diamond gems, she felt as if she'd suddenly, safely, arrived at journey's end.

Kell's body sprawled heavily atop hers. He knew he was crushing her, yet he couldn't make himself pull from her. Not yet. Instead, he pressed himself deeper into her, this time not seeking the sensual, but the spiritual. He needed to be one with this woman—one in a whole and profound way.

Anne Elise drew him close. He was heavy, but she needed the heavy feel of him. She needed the heavy reality of him. She felt the scars scoring his back and longed to ask about them. But she wouldn't. Not now. Because she wasn't certain she could deal with what he might say. The thought of him in pain, any pain, sickened her heart.

At length, and because he knew he must, Kell eased from the sanctuary of her body and to his side. His eyes found hers. Hers were soft, giving and hazed with the same peace he felt. Beneath the veneer of peace, however, he saw confusion. It, too, was an emotion he could identify with.

"What's happening between us?" she whispered.

If he'd learned anything about this woman, he'd learned that she could be as blunt as he. "I don't know," he said honestly. "What do you think is happening?"

"I don't know. I'm having trouble thinking at all. And when I can, all I think about is you."

The admission squeezed Kell's chest. It was what he wanted to hear. He just didn't want to hear the pain in her voice. "And that worries you...because you think you should be thinking about your husband."

He had a way of cutting to the heart of things, Anne Elise thought. It was a directness she could appreciate even at the same time she wished it didn't force her to admit things she didn't want to admit.

"Yes," she said simply.

"Well, let me give you two Kell Chaisson observations of life. One, if guilt were money, we'd all be rich. And two—" he kissed the fingertips that were toying with his mustache, an act that he wasn't even certain she knew she was performing "—don't ever think when you can feel."

At that, his mouth lowered to hers. With the gentleness that was so uncharacteristic, he kissed her long and sweet. As he did, he tried to tunnel his fingers through her hair, but met with failure since it was fastened atop her head.

"Does this have to stay up?" he asked impatiently.

"Not if you want it down."

He began searching for and pulling out pins. "I want it down." He scattered the pins to the floor and buried his fingers to the knuckles. "I want it down; I want you under me—" he rolled her to her back "—and I want your mouth next to mine."

She moaned as he kissed her again, hotly, magically, making need once more coil in her belly.

"Sex," she breathed. "Maybe there's nothing more than sex between us." This she said as he nibbled and bit at her mouth, as she bit and nibbled at his. His tongue probed and tasted and mated hungrily, provocatively with hers.

"Maybe," he said, shifting and penetrating her soft body once more with the vital hardness of his. Feminine to masculine. Need to need. Insatiable to insatiable.

As he began to move, as she again began to die a little, both had the thought that maybe what was between them was more than mere sex, for surely mere sex could at some point be slaked. What was between them, however, seemed to know no limits, no bounds. At the implications of such a thought, Kell called himself a fool, while Anne Elise felt a wash of guilt. Both then prudently relinquished troubling thought to exquisite feeling.

A long while later, he propped against the headboard, she propped against his chest, Kell fingered the silver bracelet at her wrist. He'd been touching it for several, silent minutes. His touch looked casual enough. No one would have suspected the tension building inside him. It had begun when passion had cooled enough for him to spot the bracelet.

"The league has asked me to lead them for the coming year," Anne Elise said. She'd sensed a change in him, a change in just the past few minutes. It worried her that maybe he was feeling the guilt he'd spoken of earlier. Did he feel he was betraying the woman of long ago?

At her announcement, Kell's fingers stilled.

"Are you?"

She glanced over her shoulder. If it hadn't been so illogical, she might have thought he looked grim, even angry. "I don't know. I haven't decided."

Kell felt the anger, like a rushing wind, escalate suddenly. "Did it ever occur to you to just give the past a rest?"

His attitude, in addition to what she'd just been thinking about his guilt, built a fire under her own anger. It was an anger that never seemed far away when she was with him. "Like you have?" she snapped.

A darkness passed across his eyes, making him look like the dangerous creature he could be. "At least I don't go around chaining myself to it," he said, holding up her wrist.

"How dare—"

"I dare because it's the truth. You're hiding in the shadows of yesterday to keep from facing today."

"You...you...you insufferable..."

"Son of a bitch?"

"Yes, you imperious, pompous, insufferable son of a bitch!"

With that, she threw back the sheet and started from the bed. He grabbed her around the waist.

"Where are you going?"

"Back to my room."

"The hell you are!"

"The hell I'm not!"

He hauled her, naked, her hair atumble, back onto the bed. Kicking, pushing, she tried to free herself. He simply pinned her beneath him with a strength so superior she couldn't even hope to contend with it. Though she felt compelled to keep trying.

"Dammit, be still!" he growled, catching a flying hand. "I said be still! Dammit, Anne Elise!" he said, throwing his hairy leg across her squirming form. "Be still!"

She had no choice but to be still since he had immobilized her with his bare body, a body that was threatening to crush the breath from her. Breathing hard, her face flushed with exertion, she stared up at him, daring him with a silent look to say more.

"I'm sorry," he said softly. More softly than she'd ever heard him say anything. "I had no right to say what I did."

When she said nothing, he repeated, "Did you hear me? I said I was sorry."

Every fight-tense muscle of her body wilted. Kell's followed suit.

"I'm sorry, too," she whispered, adding on a sigh, "Why do we hurt each other when we've both already been hurt so badly? Fighting seems the only thing we're good at."

Kell lowered his forehead to hers. "Actually fighting's what we're second best at."

Anne Elise felt his mustache crook into one of those priceless smiles that were so rare she thought they should be placed under lock and key. She was helpless not to respond to it. In seconds both had gone from fighting to smiling.

"Stay the night with me," Kell said, pulling back to find her eyes.

"And what if someone calls my room?"

"They'll think you're a sound sleeper."

"I can't, Kell," she whispered.

"Why?"

"Brooke's gonna call at midnight. She stayed in Dallas. She had something at school she couldn't miss."

"You could call her from here."

Anne Elise shook her head. "Mother and Daddy might call...I know it's crazy—a woman in her thirties answering to her parents—but they're overprotective. Mother'll surely call."

"I'll make you a compromise, then." At her silent inquiry, he explained. "Stay over a few days in D.C. We'll even make a peace pact. No arguing allowed."

The thought of a few days alone with this man did unnatural things to her senses. Their not fighting was an added enticement. "Could we do the town? I've never had time to play tourist in Washington."

"Yeah, we could do the town, but I'd rather do you."

She grinned.

He grinned.

She reached out to touch his smile. "And would you grin a lot?"

"I'll be a regular Cheshire cat," he said, lowering his mouth to hers, "if you'll promise to be the cream."

She moaned.

He moaned.

They then began to explore once more what their fighting was forced to take a second place to.

From the smiles on the tourists' faces to the hundreds of shades of new green to the cherry blossoms lining the Tidal Basin with their infinite clusters of delicate pink and cloud-like white, Washington, D.C., was aglow with springtime. Anne Elise was simply aglow with Kell's company. There had never been any doubt about her staying over for a few days. When a naked man, whose body defined sensuality at all its explicit levels, asked you to stay, you jolly well stayed. Especially when your body no longer seemed to belong to you, but to the naked man. True to his word, no fighting was allowed. In fact, the idea was never even entertained. How could it have been when smiles were more plentiful than sunshine and a whole lot warmer? This side of Kell, this relaxed, carefree side, was a total surprise, a total delight. Anne Elise had the feeling Kell was as surprised with his new disposition as she was.

And as delighted?

Well, the man did smile a lot.

They did every touristy thing that time and energy allowed. They toured the Smithsonian until their feet ached, visited the Washington Monument and the Lincoln Memorial, and traipsed through 1600 Pennsylvania Avenue. At each, they stole caresses and kisses that were far more memorable than what they were viewing—all due respect to national history. At night they made love, over and over, before falling asleep in each other's arms. Anne Elise had forgotten how pleasurable it could be awakening with someone beside you. Kell had forgotten what the absence of loneliness felt like. Neither forgot, however, that their three-day interlude had been stolen from time. They would return to their separate and private lives as they'd left them, each with a past he could not deny.

For Anne Elise, she wondered what Kell felt for her. That he wanted her, she had no doubt. That she could tell every time his mouth met hers, every time their eyes brushed, every time their bodies became intimate, but what did he feel for her? What did she feel for him? Moreover, what was she free to feel for him?

For Kell, he simply wondered how much longer he could play second best.

Neither, however, vocalized the questions, for each was afraid of answers that might shatter the fragile, crystalline idyll.

"How many of those things are you gonna eat?" Kell asked on the last afternoon of their stay. They were seated at an outdoor restaurant that specialized in fast, very fast, food. Anne Elise was just downing her second hot dog. Both had been piled high with chili and gooey cheese.

She glanced over at the man now sprawled out in the white wrought-iron chair. Dark sunglasses shaded his eyes. They were eyes she knew were laughing because his mouth was having a hard time restraining itself from the same activity.

"You should talk. You wolfed down four."

"Yeah, but I'm a growing boy."

Anne Elise popped the last bite of the hot dog in her mouth, then swiped the napkin across her lips. "I'm a growing girl."

"Trust me, lady, you're no girl," he drawled, the accusation dawdling somewhere around licentious.

"Trust me, mister, you're no boy."

He semigrinned, not at all like a boy, and started leaning forward. "Come to think of it, though, you're about as messy as a little girl."

She frowned, noting that he was still closing in on her.

When his mouth was very near her own, as his hand cupped her chin, he whispered, "Chili. You missed some chili." Before she knew what was happening, his tongue had darted out and claimed the offending speck.

Sensations far spicier than chili con carne scampered through her. Those sensations intensified as his lips brushed against hers.

"Kell!" she remonstrated, looking up to see if anyone was watching them. No one was. At least not at the moment. Probably because they were seated at a far table.

"Hmm?" he mumbled, his lips nibbling at hers.

"What are you doing?" Her breath had grown reedy, restless.

"Kissing you," he said, taking her mouth fully in a wide slant and giving her a taste of his tongue. Despite herself, she swayed toward him. "Let's go back to the hotel," he whispered.

"It's only midafternoon."

"Let's go back to the hotel."

"That's decadent...."

His tongue sipped at the corners of her mouth.

"...indecent..."

The same tongue slid across the parted seam of her lips.

"...sinful."

The tongue probed again.

"Let's go back to the hotel," she groaned and started to stand. He grabbed her wrist and drew her back down.

At her sudden look of inquiry, he said, "Give me a minute." He then grinned, like a fourteen-karat male. "I told you I was a growing boy."

He delighted in the lovely shade of pink she turned. It was a color she maintained all the way back to the hotel.

"Will you stop looking at me like that?"

"Like what?" he asked nonchalantly, his shoulder leaning against the elevator. He had removed his sunglasses, his eyes now boring hotly, wolfishly, into hers.

"Like you're going to jump me the first chance you get." Though she appeared to be complaining, she was reveling in his silent, seductive promises. Her body was already beginning to respond in heavy and moist ways.

"Why should I look at you any other way? That's exactly what I'm gonna do."

Her body took a quantum responsive leap.

"Do you think you could wait until we get to the room?" she asked breathlessly, a sexy smile playing at her lips.

"Lady, I'm not promising anything."

The elevator doors slid open. Anne Elise and Kell stepped out. Silently, two hearts beginning to pound, they walked toward the room. Kell inserted the key, pushed open the door and wordlessly indicated for her to precede him. She did. She'd taken only a couple of steps, however, when he grabbed her wrist, whirled her around and pinned her against the door. He crushed her mouth with his.

The kiss was wild, wet, and oh, so welcome. As their lips mated, he ran his hands beneath the hem of her skirt and palmed her panty-clad hips. Her skin felt soft, incredibly soft, softer than the satin of her skimpy underwear. So soft that he sighed.

"I was right," he breathed. "You do have a pretty little ass."

Her hands similarly, aggressively moved over his taut, lean hips, hips hidden beneath a tempting layer of tight denim.

"So do you," she whispered, feeling him grow hard against her stomach.

As though he could wait no longer, he threw her caveman-style over his shoulder. The rear end he'd just lavished with praise hiked into the air as her head lowered to his trim waistline. She cried out in surprise, then giggled. He dumped her into the middle of the mattress and fell across her. Both were grinning hugely.

"Wanna break a bed?" he asked.

She giggled again, and then the giggling stopped— abruptly. It was replaced by a bevy of deep-throated moans.

Anne Elise woke slowly. The sun was shouting its last faded hurrah, waiting patiently for twilight to gauze the sky in gray. In the shadowy dusk, she stretched, like a well-content cat, and searched for the warmth of the man she intuitively knew would be beside her—the way he'd been beside her each time she'd awakened for three days, an act a woman could grow dangerously addicted to. Her hand slid over and over, up and down, connecting with . . . nothing. Nothing except a cold sheet. Anne Elise's eyes flew open, while a surge of panic gushed over her.

She sat up. Peering into the swelling darkness. Probing the deafening silence. In the distance, she heard the spray of the shower. She slowly let out the breath she'd unknowingly been holding and threw her legs over the side of the bed. Crossing the room, she quietly opened the bathroom door.

Behind the frosted panes of glass that converted the bathtub into a shower, Anne Elise saw Kell's blurred image. She also saw that water was raining onto the floor because he'd failed to close the back half of the stall. She registered the fact as strange, though nothing more. Her mind was already filled with thoughts of the naked man who stood only feet away. She walked toward the tub.

At the unexpected sound of someone joining him, Kell looked up sharply. It was the woman he couldn't get out of his mind, the woman who'd so suffused his body and soul, that the idea of parting with her within the next few hours was sheer torture. So painful had it become that he hadn't been able to sleep, so he'd just watched her sleep. But that had only worsened the pain until, finally, driven to seek some peace, he'd crawled into the shower and prayed that hot water would wash away at least some of the mounting desperation he felt.

At the sight of Anne Elise, her body bare, her hair tousled, her eyes soft with a satisfied look, the pain only grew worse. Anne Elise knew the same clutching feeling of pain, for as her eyes took in the man before her, his wet hair, his wet torso, his wet, hair-roughened legs, she wondered how she was ever going to go back to a daily routine that didn't include him. For now, though, she could ease the pain by simply moving to his side.

She closed the shower door behind her.

"Don't!" he called out abruptly, harshly.

At the urgency in the one word, at the panic that streaked across his eyes, her hand stilled. Her expression said clearly that she didn't understand what unpardonable act she'd committed.

At her startled look, and struggling to make his voice normal amid the fear clotting his throat, he said, "Don't close the door. I'm ... I'm claustrophobic.'' The admission seemed to embarrass him.

Anne Elise noted this, as well as the anxiety still swimming in his eyes. She shoved the back half of the door open as far as it would go. He rewarded her by exhaling a deep breath. He still seemed embarrassed, however. He also evidently felt some explanation necessary.

"When I was a POW, the Viet Cong ... they kept me in a—'' she could see him swallow "—in a cage.''

The words sleeted through Anne Elise like an Antarctic blizzard, turning everything inside her ice-cold, dead-cold. What he disclosed was heinous enough, but she knew it was only the tip of the iceberg when it came to the torture he'd had to endure. Her eyes lowered to the scars on his chest, cruel ribbons of silver that had been carved into his body by sadistic hands. She could not begin to imagine the pain, nor was she brave enough to even try.

She stepped toward him. The steamy needles of the shower struck her, instantly moistening her hair, her shoulders, her firm, rosy-tipped breasts. She seemed not to notice. She seemed to care even less. All of her attention was centered on the man before her. Gently she lay her palm across his stubbly, seductively scratchy cheek. Runnels of water rushed across her fingers. Raising on tiptoe, she feathered her lips to his—tenderly, healingly.

Kell stood perfectly still. With closed eyes, he simply let himself be kissed. When she'd finished with his lips, she ducked her head, her mouth finding the first of the three scars that slashed his chest. She slow-kissed each, her lips lingering, her lips quivering. At the beauty of her tender touch, Kell's skin rippled with reaction, just as his heart pounded out a leaded beat. Finally, stripped to raw emotion, he groaned, and, threading his fingers through her now-drenched hair, he raised her face to his. Water sluiced across her cheeks, making them appear as dew kissed as a mountain morning. That, however, was not the moisture that claimed Kell's attention. It was that shining from her eyes.

"Don't!" he said raggedly. "Don't cry!"

But it was already too late. Teardrops ran onto her cheeks, mingling with the moistness already there.

"Don't!" he repeated, roughly yanking her into his arms and squeezing her so tightly he knew he must be hurting her, but unable to stop himself. "It was a long time ago."

Anne Elise crossed her arms across his back, knowing that forever would not be long enough for him to forget what unspeakable things had happened to him, nor would it ever be long enough for her to forgive those who'd done them to him. She cried softly, wholly, vaguely aware of the full feeling in her chest. She was uncertain what to name the heart feeling. She knew only that its power was tremendous.

Kell, protectively tucking her head beneath his chin, held her as though his very life depended on the embrace. He, too, was overwhelmed with the feelings bombarding him. He knew only that the kisses of one woman had miraculously vanquished his pain—both that inflicted by a knife and by another woman's goodbye.

Chapter Twelve

They returned home, Kell to Arkansas, Anne Elise to Texas. She was struck by how different Dallas suddenly seemed...until she realized that it was she who was different and not the city. Different. She *was* different. In too many ways to count, in ways too subtle to define. The only thing that wasn't different was the fact that she still felt caught somewhere between yesterday and today. Kell had accused her of hiding in the shadows of yesterday, and maybe it was true that she was, but the shadows were home, the place where she'd lived for so long that she wasn't certain she could change her address. Besides, no matter how illogical it was, no matter how many times she told herself she was only guiltily flaying herself, she couldn't help but feel if she did one other something, whatever that nebulous something might be, she could write a definite ending to a story that seemed to have no ending.

Had she buried her husband?

One moment she would prime herself to believe she had, the next her well-defined sense of duty demanded she question again. That and the memories of a young love, memories that were always pure and perfect. Had the situation been reversed, wouldn't Jim have moved heaven and earth to bring her body home? And to have been certain that he had? The demon within her whispered that her husband could have somehow done something that she couldn't have. He could have succeeded where she'd failed. Surely there was one other something she could do to make certain that she'd brought him home. Surely her duty required her to do that one other something. Surely she was going to go crazy if she didn't get off this insidious merry-go-round.

And surely, certainly, without a doubt, she was going to go crazy if Kell didn't call.

They'd been back for three days, and though she told herself that Kell had said nothing about calling—in fact, he'd said nothing at all when they'd parted in the DFW airport; he'd simply kissed her—her heart went wild every time the phone rang at the office or at home.

On the fifth day, or rather the fifth night, a rainy Friday that she was spending at home alone since Brooke was staying over with a friend, the phone rang at precisely 9:00. Wearing her daughter's nightshirt which proclaimed White Snake's Killer, a high compliment in teenage lingo, Anne Elise sat propped in bed reading. Her heart burst into a staccato beat at the sound of the phone. She told herself to act her age . . . at least half of it.

"Hello?"

For a long heartbeat, there was nothing, then a familiar, drawled, "Hi."

Every bone in Anne Elise's body melted, just as every bone in Kell's had melted at her soft-spoken hello.

"Hi, there," she said, hoping that she didn't flow off the bed and puddle onto the carpet, which had only recently been cleaned.

"Did you wonder what had happened to me?"

She could have played coy and lied, but it never crossed her mind. "Yes."

"I've been out of the country. Central America."

A pang of concern plucked at her, but she knew better than to express it. She certainly knew better than to ask anything specific about the government job he'd undoubtedly performed. "And how was Central America?"

"Hot." But then, he thought, maybe the heat was coming primarily from memories he couldn't get out of his mind. Like how soft this woman was, how sweet her kiss was, how hot the way she could love was. Kell cleared his throat. "How've you been?"

"Okay," she lied. "And you?"

"Okay," he lied.

Heartbeat . . . heartbeat—his and hers.

"I miss—" they both began.

"I'm sorry," he said. "What were you going to say?"

"No, you go ahead."

"No, you."

She swallowed. "I, uh, I miss you."

Kell closed his eyes, allowing the words to seep into him like the gentle spring rains falling throughout the South. "Funny," he said, in a voice that rumbled like the distant thunder, "that's what I was gonna say."

"Say it," Anne Elise ordered, her breath unraveling into whispers.

"I miss you," he replied simply and from the gut.

In some immeasurable way, they had taken yet another, albeit uncertain, step toward each other.

Each night for the next week, he called her. They laughed together, teased together, spoke of profound and sage things together. He discovered that she liked pearls and poetry and Kenny Rogers. She discovered that he liked spy books and autumn and classical music. Below the surface of their civilized conversations, however, sizzled a sexual tension more primitive than savage drumbeats at midnight. She ached for his touch, he for hers, and both would have killed for a kiss—a slow, wet, curl-your-toes kiss.

"Touch your lips," he said unexpectedly exactly a week later.

"What?"

"Touch your lips." This time his voice sounded like pale moonlight dripping from an ebony sky.

Tentatively, her heart skipping, she pressed one fingertip to her lips.

"Are you?" he asked huskily.

"Yes."

"Are you wearing lipstick?"

"No."

"Are your lips parted?"

"Yes."

"Can you feel your breath?"

"Y-Yes." The last was barely audible.

"Now take the tip of your tongue..." Seconds later, breathless and hard, Kell grumbled, "I think we'd better change the subject."

A series of topics, none as exciting as what they'd abandoned, came and went. Finally Anne Elise posed a question she'd wanted to ask for a long time. "Why did you punch out your commanding officer?"

Kell's silence indicated that her question may have been the last question he'd expected her to ask. "Where did you hear that?"

"The grapevine."

"And why does the grapevine say I punched him out?"

"It doesn't. Only that you did." When it was obvious he wasn't going to respond as to why he'd, in effect, tossed his military career down the tubes, she repeated, "Why, Kell?"

"He deserved it."

"Why?"

"He said something crude and tacky."

"Hey, Chaisson, keep that thing in your pants and out of the bed of that hot little tail. Her husband'll be home soon enough to cool it off himself."

At the memory, Kell's voice tightened, "He made something that wasn't ugly sound ugly."

Intuitively Anne Elise knew that the incident had something to do with the wife of the POW, with the woman Kell had loved. Some sinister emotion—jealousy?—streaked through her, and she wished fervently that she hadn't brought up the subject. She also thought how futile their relationship was. Even if she could have managed to forget the past, it was doubtful Kell could.

"Look, let's drop it. Okay?" he asked.

"Sure," she answered, more than grateful to.

"Have dinner with me tomorrow night." At the surprise he heard in the silence, he added, "I'm leaving for Central America again, and I have a three-hour layover in DFW. I thought maybe we could ask Brooke to join us."

She tried not to focus on the fact that he was again going into some indeterminate danger—after all, he didn't belong to her, and wasn't hers to worry about. Instead, she concentrated on the fact that she was going to see him again. And that he'd cared enough to ask Brooke.

"She'd like that. I'd like that."

"Good. Now, touch your lips . . . and pretend I'm kissing you . . . slowly . . . thoroughly . . . with my tongue curling around yours . . ."

Anne Elise heard the dial tone. She smiled softly at his unique goodbye. But then, the smile disappeared. She didn't really know why. Maybe because he was returning to Central America. Maybe because he'd once loved a woman enough to destroy his career for her. Maybe because she was just tired of goodbyes—unique or otherwise.

The moment her eyes met his across the crowded waiting room of the airport, it felt as if someone had pushed the Start button on life. How odd she hadn't known that life had come to a standstill, but it had. With this sudden, fresh wave of vitality, she saw, felt, that clearly now. In what she assumed was deference to Brooke's presence, he didn't kiss her, although his eyes lowered to her mouth. The world tilted on its axis. It tilted again when she felt his hand at the small of her back, urging her through the parade of passengers and toward the airport's entrance.

She didn't notice when his eyes dropped to her wrist, checking to see if she still wore the silver bracelet. Nor did she feel the dull pain that cut through him when he saw that she did.

"What was Vietnam like?" Brooke asked once they'd been seated at the restaurant.

Anne Elise glanced up at her daughter, then over at Kell.

He was nursing a beer as they waited for their Mexican dinners to be serviced. "It was...frustrating. There was no way to win it, yet we had to keep fighting it."

"Granddad says you're a hero."

Kell shrugged.

How was it possible, Anne Elise thought, for shoulders to grow broader?

"Sometimes anyone left is called a hero," Kell said, negating all the medals he'd won.

"Granddad also said you were a POW?"

"Brooke—" Anne Elise began.

Kell's eyes shifted to the woman who had the most delectable mouth he'd ever seen. "It's all right," he said, wondering if she'd still taste like honeyed velvet, if her kiss could still chase away all his painful nightmares. "Yeah," he answered Brooke, "I was a POW."

"Were you scared?"

"Sure."

"That's what used to worry me about my father," Brooke said, toying with the drops of condensation on her glass of Coke. Anne Elise was once more studying her daughter. "When I was a kid, and they told me he was missing, I thought he was lost, like, you know, in a department store or someplace like that. I'd once gotten lost in a supermarket, and I remembered being scared out of my mind. And I was always afraid that my father had been scared like that, too. But that nobody ever found him like they found me."

Anne Elise listened intently to her daughter. With a heart twisted with emotion. The young woman had never shared this heart secret before. Why had she chosen to share it with this man? Because somehow she knew he'd understand in a way no one else would?

"I'm sure your father was afraid," Kell said candidly. "But I'm also sure he did what he had to do despite his being afraid. And that's what makes a man a real hero. Your father was the hero, Brooke. Not me."

Anne Elise could have argued that point. Heroes came in all sizes, shapes and shades. One, most assuredly, came in the size, shape and shade of Kell Chaisson.

Too short a time later, they were back at the airport, waiting for Kell's flight to be announced. Brooke had wandered off in the direction of a gift shop.

"She's a nice kid," he said about the young woman just disappearing from view. He stood in front of Anne Elise, his thighs occasionally brushing against hers. Each time they did, both bodies tingled with need.

"Yes, she is."

"Her father'd be proud of her."

"Yes, he would."

"They, uh, they just announced my flight."

"Yes, I know that, too."

Neither made the slightest effort, however, to step apart.

"I'll call you when I get back."

"How long—"

"I never know."

She nodded, adding, "Call me."

He nodded, his eyes lowering to her mouth. "I, uh, I don't think it's a good idea if I kiss you."

"Why?" she whispered, disappointment scoring her because his kiss was the only thing in the world she wanted at that moment.

"If I do, I'm gonna be on you like ants on honey."

The image that his words conjured up, the seduction in his voice, swept through her like a surging, hot tide.

"Don't!" he growled.

"Don't what?"

"Don't look at me like that."

"Like what?"

"Like you want exactly what I want!"

He looked away, trying to marshal his control. Finally he looked back. His flight was announced again.

"Be good," he breathed. As though he couldn't stop himself from making some kind of contact, he reached out and brushed an auburn strand of hair from her cheek. His knuckle lingered hungrily at the ivory perfection of her skin.

"You, too," she said, her breath halved by his slight touch.

"Yeah," he said, roughly, pulling his hand away. He grabbed his duffle bag, gave her one last look and started for the line that was forming.

"Kell?"

He turned.

"Be careful."

He grinned. "The good die young. SOB's live forever."

Later, as she watched his plane depart, she hoped to God he was right.

Days bled into days, lonely nights into lonely nights. Ten of each. Anne Elise thought that surely she would go crazy. Crazy with worry. Crazy with a sexual tension that had begun at the airport and seemed to build by the minute. If only he'd kissed her! Perhaps if he'd kissed her, though, her misery would only be that much greater. She went by the cemetery three times. Out of guilt? She didn't know. She just knew that she went and plucked at the blades of grass sprouting around the new marble headstone. She also tried to imagine how Jim would have aged had he lived, but she couldn't. Which made her feel guilty. Especially since she kept seeing a man with dark hair and dark eyes every time she tried to envision blond and blue.

"Do you like him?"

Anne Elise, playing with the food on her plate, looked up at her daughter on the tenth day.

"What?"

"Do you like Kell?"

Her heart fluttering at the very mention of his name, she answered, "Well, of course I like him."

"You know what I mean, Momma."

Yes, she did know. She just didn't know the answer. So she asked a question, instead. "Would it disturb you if I did?"

"The question is, would it disturb you?" Brooke asked with a wisdom far beyond her young years. She laid her hand across her mother's. "You've been to the cemetery three times this week, you know?"

Yes, she knew that, too. She seemed to know everything but the answer to the most important question.

"Well, know what I think?" Brooke said, her blue eyes bubbling. "I think Kell's killer."

Yes, Kell was killer, Anne Elise thought. He was also killing her.

Softly.

Sweetly.

With a song of uncertainty.

For truly she now belonged nowhere—neither in yesterday, nor today.

When the phone rang later that night, at a quarter to ten, Anne Elise's hand hesitated in the act of smoothing moisturizer on her face. The ringing stopped in midpeal, and she could hear Brooke's muted voice speaking to the caller. One of her daughter's many friends, Anne Elise surmised, returning her thoughts to her complexion. She had just recapped the bottle of moisturizer when the young woman appeared at the bedroom door, a smile the size of Texas plastered to her lips.

"It's him," Brooke said with eyebrows that danced.

Anne Elise swiveled on the vanity stool, her stomach suddenly more cavernous than the Grand Canyon. She just stared.

"Momma, did you hear me? It's Kell."

"Yes. Yes, I heard you," she said, rising and moving toward the bedside phone in a cloud of feelings. She'd known that she longed to hear from him; she just hadn't realized how desperate she'd grown until this very moment. As she picked up the receiver, Brooke wriggled her fingers in a sassy goodbye and closed the door behind her. Anne Elise took a deep breath. "Hello?"

The connection wasn't good. She could tell that by the static stumbling through the line. Furthermore, it sounded as if the call were coming from a long way off. Central

America? Regardless of the static, regardless of the distance, Anne Elise heard Kell's opening line clearly.

"I love you," he said, roughly, angrily, as though he'd fought calling her as long as he could, but, in the end, had had to give in to a power stronger than he. "Don't say anything," he threw in before she could even consider speaking. "Don't say you love me; don't say you don't; just listen."

Anne Elise, the strength suddenly sapped from her legs, edged to the side of the bed and tried to find her voice. Her search was only partially successful. "All right."

"Speak louder. I can't hear you. This is a lousy connection."

"All right. I said, all right; I'll listen." Her heart had begun to pound so rapidly, however, that she wasn't certain she could hear anything above its roar.

"I want you to marry me."

"What?"

"Marry me!" he shouted, causing everyone at the Central American airport to glance up—not that they understood what had been said, but the imperious, angry tone demanded attention. Kell glared hotly, then turned his back, trying to affect some privacy.

At the repetition of what Anne Elise had thought she'd heard the first time, the Grand Canyon became more hollowed out, while her heart tripped into a rhythm that defied measurement.

"Can you hear me?" he asked, placing his free hand to his ear to shut out as much of the racket going on around him as he could. For the thousandth time he damned himself for not having the self-discipline to wait to call her until he was in surroundings more conducive to what he had to say. But his self-discipline, or lack thereof, combined with more sleepless nights than a man could handle, had forced him to pick up the first phone after his job was finished.

"Yes. Yes, I hear you."

"I want you to marry me," he said again, "but only under one condition. I want all of you or none of you. I'm through sharing. Do you hear me?"

"Yes. You're through sharing."

"You're damned right!" he barked. "If you can't turn loose of the past, if you can't take that bracelet off..." He didn't finish. It was as though he couldn't make himself say anymore.

"And can you?" she asked, her heart suddenly lodged in her throat at the thought of some faceless woman who'd once lain in Kell's arms. "Can you turn loose of the past? Can you commit all of yourself?"

"Yes."

The reply was singular and simple. But then it didn't have to be anything more. Kell Chaisson was a man of few words.

"I'm flying out of Honduras tonight. I'll be home by noon tomorrow." There was a poignant pause. "Take all the time you need. Just be sure of your answer."

Because of the static, Anne Elise had caught only about every other word. She still understood perfectly that the ball was in her court.

"Kell—"

"Look, I've gotta go. They just called my flight."

"Kell—"

"I'll talk to you stateside."

"Kell?"

He hesitated, as if afraid of what he'd hear. "Yeah?"

"Be careful."

Another hesitation. "Yeah, I will."

Was it disappointment she heard in his voice or relief—disappointment that she hadn't said she loved him or relief that she hadn't said she didn't?

And then there was no more time to ponder the quality of his voice, for the dial tone, chopped with static, was gush-ing into her ear. The man who'd just said he loved her was gone.

She loved him.

Of that Anne Elise had no doubt. But could she give him the all of herself that he so imperiously demanded, that he so unquestionably deserved? Could she, once and for all, turn her back on the past?

These were the questions still roaming her mind three days later as she stood at her husband's grave... or what she hoped was his grave. And therein lay the crux of her problem. Fresh green grass, in seeming defiance of Anne Elise's doubts, was already beginning to grow atop the turned earth, as if it had come to terms with its duty and was already executing it. Anne Elise envied it. She didn't know what her duty was anymore. In fact, she didn't know much of anything anymore. Except that she hadn't had a decent night's sleep since Kell had called. Not that she'd had many before that—they seemed a thing of the past, a thing that belonged only in her pre-Kell days.

She knew, too, because the smiling, heated sun just reminded her of it, that the spring day was one of the most beautiful she'd ever seen. A gentle breeze sighed, tickling the fingers of grass and fluttering the leaves of the nearby tree. The same tree wore tiny pink blossoms as if dressed for a prom, blossoms whose petals were swollen with the sweetest of scents. It was the kind of day in which everything should be perfect. But it wasn't. A feeling of frustration, that dark, prickling feeling that she'd had so often of late, confirmed it. She had no name for the feeling. She had no answers to some of the most important questions in her life. She knew only that she loved Kell... and that, unless she played the game his way, she'd never see him again, for, though he didn't say it, it was clearly written between the lines that it was marriage or nothing.

Could she stand to lose him?

But could she give him what he wanted?

The frustration, the dark, prickling feeling, increased until it seemed painfully incapable of fitting within her skin. She laid her head back, closed her eyes and let the sun bathe her in its cleansing warmth. A thousand thoughts, all conflicting, clamored for her attention.

Turn loose, one said. *You've earned the right to turn loose.*

But you were his wife, another taunted. *That's a forever bond. Shouldn't you try one more time to find out if these remains are really his?*

How, dammit, how? I've done everything I know to do and a thousand things more!

But, maybe just one more something—

I'm tired of trying to find that elusive one more something. I'm tired of living in the past. I'm tired of not living at all. I'm just tired! Tired!

The dark, frustrating, prickling feeling moved closer, closer, closer....

"Oh, God, Jim, I'm just tired," she whispered, choking on a sudden overabundance of emotion.

At first, the moistness on her face startled her. With tentative fingertips, she investigated it. She was crying. Hard and deep and from the soul. The prickling feeling, scalding hot, was also bursting wide within her. It felt like...anger. Simple, old-fashioned anger. And it felt good battering against the walls of her heart. Why had she never known that it could feel so good?

Maybe because she'd never allowed herself to feel it?

In the past, her pragmatism had demanded survival, survival acceptance, and, because anger was nonproductive, she had suppressed it. The truth was that she was angry. Damned angry! At a world that turned to fighting as a solution to its problems, at a foreign Asian war that had torn her world asunder, at a husband who'd had the audacity to get himself killed!

"Damn you, Jim!" she whispered amid tears. "Damn you for leaving me and Brooke!"

Anne Elise cried. She had no idea for how long, but it seemed like the tears would never stop. And when at last they did, in their salty, serene wake, she heard a silence. It was not unlike the tender silence she'd heard day upon day, night upon night, for seventeen years. Yet, even as she listened, the silence filled with sound. She heard the sound of Kell's voice, the sound of his oh-so-rare laughter, the sound of his husky rendering of her name in the heat of passion. And then, like an orchestrated symphony, she heard the quiet voice of her husband.

Turn loose, it said. *Set your sails for tomorrow, and don't look back. Think of me not with sorrow, but with joy. Remember me in the rush of the wind, the glint of the sun, the gentle patter of a spring rain. And know that I, too, Annie, would somehow have found the strength to go on without you.*

Like a toasty hearth in a bone-chilled winter, a peace settled in Anne Elise's heart. She sniffed, sighed, and began, "There's this man I want to tell you about, Jim...."

Chapter Thirteen

Miles away, in the Arkansas hills, Kell, irritated from another in a long line of aborted attempts at meditation,
slammed the refrigerator door, popped the top off of a thin-
necked bottle and guzzled down several swallows of cold
beer. Swiping his hand across his mouth, he stepped from
the kitchen and back into the den. The TV, recounting the
evening news, mumbled in muted tones, while outside the
patio door, opened to emit a breeze, the night buzzed with
mosquitoes and thumped with kamikaze June bugs intent on
hurling themselves at the screen. In the near distance, a
chorus of cicadas sang a cappella. In the far, far distance,
in the blue-gray shadows, a lone whippoorwill chirped its
lonesome song.

Lonesome.

God, he was so lonesome he could die, Kell thought,
standing at the patio door and staring out into the empty
nothing that comprised his life. Why didn't she call? It had

been three whole days. Three unbearably long, eat-at-your-gut days!

You told her to take her time, Chaisson.

Yeah, yeah, I know! What I really wanted, though, was the phone ringing off the wall the moment I walked into the house.

With her proclaiming her undying love?

You got it!

With her saying that her past had been magically forgotten the moment you'd proposed?

You got it!

Well, it seems, Captain, that, as per usual, what you want doesn't matter a rat's ass. You wanted something besides what you got in '73, too.

For a second, Kell's impatience, his irritation, were supplanted by a stronger emotion. He'd experienced the emotion a thousand times before. It was a sense of frustration—he called it that because he knew no other name—so keen, so profound, that it spread over him like a hot, debilitating sickness. He suffered a relapse every time he thought of a sad-eyed woman saying a sad-voiced goodbye. Then and now, even though he'd thought he was going to die at the time, he could find no fault with her farewell. No one had been to blame. Her husband's return, her return to her husband, had been right. He had accepted that rightness because acceptance of it had been the honorable, noble thing to do, but . . .

But what? Kell asked, the frustration building, building, building. He answered his own question. But wouldn't it for once be nice to tell honor to go screw itself? The frustration, spurred on by the impatience that had flowed in his veins for days, erupted in a sulfurous mass of . . .

. . . anger.

The sickness was called anger.

Dammit, right or wrong, he'd been angry that the husband had returned, angry that the woman he'd loved had turned her back on him, forever leaving him the odd man out in an unresolvable triangle! And he was angry now because he hadn't even allowed himself to be angry then! Was it this suppressed anger that had been behind his compulsive need to punch out anything that got in his way? Was he trying to express through violence what he wouldn't allow himself to express naturally? And was this suppressed anger, perhaps on both their parts, the reason that he and Anne Elise were so quick to fling harsh words at each other? Did each remind the other of the past, a past neither had vented his true feelings for—he because how could he be angry with what was so obviously just, she because it was her duty to carry on bravely?

Possibly.

Perhaps even probably.

In the middle of his two-bit analysis, hot anger turned to icy cold fear.

What if Anne Elise walked out of his life, too? What if he once more found himself on the losing end? He was getting old, tired, weary. He no longer had the emotional resilience he'd once had, and the stark truth of the matter was he'd never loved like this before. Like a besotted teenager. Like a foolish fool. Like a man with little pride.

And yet, as much as he loved her, as besotted as he was, as easy as it would be for him to cast all pride aside, he would not, could not, share her. For once in his life, he had to have someone who belonged only to him.

Kell brought the bottle to his lips and drank, closing his eyes as the coolness slid down his throat. His mind immediately filled with images. He saw a smile curling lips that could kiss with wild abandon.

"Only hours ago, it was learned . . ." the TV spoke softly into the silence.

He felt his hands buried deep in the silken skeins of hair the color of fire and passion.

"...that the daughter of the newly appointed under secretary for political affairs..."

He tasted the sweet knowledge that her body fit perfectly beneath his.

"...Anne Elise Terris Butler..."

The images shattered. Kell whirled, his eyes riveted to the television screen.

"...has accepted the chairmanship of the National League of Families of American POWs and MIAs. Ms. Butler herself is the wife of an MIA and, when contacted at her Dallas home today, she had this to say about her acceptance."

Seconds passed in which it was obvious that the camera crew was having trouble with the film. During those same stalled seconds, Kell had trouble with his heart. It refused to beat. Suddenly, unexpectedly, the image of Anne Elise jumped onto the screen. Just as suddenly, Kell's heart ran wild.

She was wearing a turquoise dress, a look that said she was unaccustomed to and uncomfortable with dealing with the press and—Kell lowered his eyes to her wrist—a silver bracelet.

Something died inside him.

"Ms. Butler," the woman reporter, a microphone in her hand, began, "rumor has it that you've been contemplating this chairmanship for several weeks. What finally made you decide to accept it?"

Anne Elise looked at the microphone as though it were an alien, and quite frightful, creature. "I really had little choice," she said in a small voice that bespoke her nervousness. "This organization has meant so much to me—it's been there through the blackest hours of my life—that I simply could not turn my back on it or the countless friends

I've made. In the past, perhaps because I've been so emotionally needy, I've taken more than I've given. I think it's way past time for me to pay the league back in some small way.''

''Do you think your father being under secretary will have any affect on your chairmanship?''

Anne Elise smiled impishly. The action knocked all of the air from Kell's lungs. "I think it already has. If my father were a fireman, a professor or a window washer, I doubt you'd be here interviewing me for the national news." The reporter smiled even as Anne Elise's smile faded. "In answer to the spirit of your question, if any contacts my father makes will mutually benefit the league, I'll be the first to take advantage of them.''

''And what about—''

Kell snapped off the TV, plunging the room into silence. Except for the thudding of his heart. The deep, dark thudding of his heart. Well, he guessed he had her answer. She had just announced before God and country that she was still tied to the past, that she had no intention of severing the bond. If there'd been any lingering doubt, the bracelet would have dispelled it. Kell swore harshly, condemning the bracelet to the hottest corner of hell. He likewise condemned himself for being such a fool.

You just don't get it, do you, Chaisson? You just can't get it through that thick head of yours that you're never going to win! That you're destined to end up alone! That you always manage to fall in love with some other man's wife!

A thick rage spread across his heart, leaving him wanting only one thing. Release. Any release. As long as it was of a violent nature.

The beer bottle crashed against the den wall. Shards of glass splattered onto the carpet, while foamy beer drizzled down the stucco wall. Kell, his hand on his hip, just stood watching as though he got some perverse delight from the sight. He also frankly called a spade a spade. He was angry. Damned angry! With himself. With a woman too beautiful for words. With life in general and love in particular. He clung to that anger as though his very life depended on it. Because it did. For beneath it lay something he couldn't face. Pain. A pain so severe that no man could hope to survive it.

When the phone rang later, Kell made no move to answer it. Instead, leaning against the headboard of the bed, he lazily swigged at another, this his fourth, beer. He wasn't drunk. Simply because he didn't want to be drunk. If he got drunk, his shield of anger might slip.

The phone kept on ringing...five, six, seven...

Whoever it was was persistent!

...eight, nine, ten...

"Hello?" Kell growled, clenching the neck of the bottle in his fist and anchoring it against his bent knee.

There was a pause, then, "Kell?"

Anne Elise's voice cut through him like a piece of the broken glass that still lay scattered on the den floor might have.

"Kell, are you there?"

"Yeah," he said gruffly, "I'm here."

"Hi," she said, the word flowing more smoothly than sunshine-warmed syrup.

Kell said nothing.

When the silence stretched between them, she asked, "Are you all right?"

He drew the bottle to his mouth and took a long, arrogant swallow. "Yeah. Top of the world."

This time the silence was initiated by Anne Elise, as though she were groping to make sense out of his surliness. Finally she asked, "Is something wrong?"

"Now what could possibly be wrong?" he sneered.

"I don't know. You just sound—"

" . . . busy. I'm real busy," he said, tipping his wrist until the bottle rested once more at his lips.

"Oh," she said, trying to keep the hurt from her voice. "Well, I won't keep you, then. I just wondered if you could pick me up at the Little Rock airport tomorrow. I need to talk with you."

Kell grinned wryly. Her sense of duty, the same damned sense of duty that kept her chained to the past, would require her to turn down his proposal in person. "Duty's a bitch, isn't it?" he commented sarcastically.

"What?"

"Never mind. Yeah, I'll be there. Why the hell not?" *I've been run out on before.*

"Kell?"

"Gotta go. I think there's another beer with my name on it."

"Kell, I love—" she heard the click of the phone "—you." The last trailed off.

Anne Elise stared at the dead phone, which she still held in her hand. Confusion flooded her. His reception certainly hadn't been what she'd expected, what she'd needed. To say that he had been aloof was putting it mildly. He was hostile. Angry. Why? Her confusion turned to fear. Had he changed his mind about loving her? About wanting her to marry him? Just as swiftly, fear turned into anger. Well, if he'd changed his mind, he was going to tell her he had!

Quickly, her fingers trembling, she redialed his number. She was formulating a thousand terse things to say when the busy signal beeped in her ear. Four hours and a hundred calls later, it was still beeping. The phone was off the hook. He'd taken the phone off the hook!

Anne Elise tried to sleep, but to little avail. Come morning, at the crack of a weary dawn, she started calling him again. This time the phone repeatedly rang with no answer. With each ring, she grew angrier and angrier.

Damn the man! she thought, hastening to make her early-morning flight. No one, absolutely no one, could make her as angry as he could. Or as happy. Or as miserable.

God, what if he'd changed his mind?

She couldn't even begin to come up with an answer to that question. The process of trying to do so was too painful. She acted simply on the instinct that told her she had to see him. Until she did, she would hide behind her protective anger.

The two wounded warriors spotted each other the moment Anne Elise stepped into the waiting room of the airport. Angry eye met angry eye. Which was to say that hurt—Kell was certain Anne Elise had changed her mind—and fear—Anne Elise feared Kell had changed his—welled deeply in the heart of both.

Kell watched as she walked toward him, the gentle sway of her hips beneath the white skirt reminding him of things that he'd rather not be reminded of. Even under the circumstances, he wanted nothing more than to take her in his arms and lose himself in her softness. God, how he'd missed her! God, how he still wanted her! For just a fraction of a heartbeat, he entertained the notion of taking her under any conditions that she'd allow him to—he'd share her with a dozen men if he had to!—but he forced himself to hold firm to his resolve. He had to have all of her, simply because having less would slowly, surely, kill him. Despite the resolution, he tightened every muscle in his body against physically reaching out for her, anyway.

Anne Elise saw the way one of Kell's shoulders cockily leaned against the wall. On the other shoulder sat a chip the size of Alaska. And the chip was just as cold as that territory's snow and ice. She longed to knock that chip off. The only thing was, she didn't know whether she wanted to do it before or after she threw herself into his arms.

Kell had deliberately refrained from looking at her wrist. He didn't know why. He knew what he'd find there. Which was maybe the reason he'd refrained from looking. Maybe some masochistic part of him was still holding out hope. If so, that hope was dashed when he lowered his eyes and saw the familiar silver bracelet. He had the sudden, harsh urge to smash his fist into something . . . anything.

"Well, well," he drawled, "if it isn't Miss Duty."

Anne Elise had no idea what the insult meant and really didn't care. "Mr. Personality, I presume."

Kell's eyes glittered with a lazy, hostile fire. *Please, God, if you don't help me, I'm gonna reach for her!*

Anne Elise's knees threatened to buckle at his warm nearness. It was a nearness she wanted to be smothered in. *Don't, don't, make a fool of yourself!* she pleaded.

"You want to tell me what this is all about?" she said, cloaking herself once more in anger.

"Me?" he asked incredulously.

"Yes, you. You're the one acting like you've got a major case of PMS!" She could feel her anger building. Even under the strain of the moment, she recognized that this expression of anger was far healthier than the suppression she'd engaged in for seventeen years.

"Hey, if you two want to fight, could you let us by first?" A man spoke from behind Anne Elise. She had stopped at a point that had bottlenecked the flow of disembarking passengers.

Kell gave the man a look that said just where he could go, and that he'd be glad to assist him there. "Come on!" he growled, grabbing Anne Elise by the arm and starting off down the corridor. She went, primarily because she had no choice.

When he hustled her toward a coffee shop, she balked. "We're not going to your house?"

"No," he said, dragging her in, "what you have to say can be said quickly and publicly."

"What *I* have to say?" she asked, plopping down onto the vinyl seat of a booth. Kell plopped down across from her. His knee brushed hers. Both started as though they'd been grazed with fire. "I'm not the one acting like a jerk. I'm not the one who refused to answer his telephone. I'm not the one acting totally uncivilized."

"I hate being civilized."

"Obviously," she said, remembering just how wild and untamed he could be in bed. Under those circumstances, she hated being civilized, too.

"Coffee!" Kell bellowed to the approaching waitress.

"Coffee!" Anne Elise echoed, the previous thought—being in bed with Kell—further igniting her anger.

The waitress, as though blasted by the order, stepped back with a mumbled, "Two coffees."

"I believe you were the one who called me saying that you needed to talk to me," he pointed out, adding sarcastically, "So talk. And fast. I've got things to do." *Like get over you. Or, at least, start trying to.*

Faced with his logic, Anne Elise sighed. "Yes, I did call. Yes, I did want to talk with you. But first I have to find out why you're so angry." *How can I tell you I love you if you no longer want me?*

"Lady, I'm not angry. I'm livid."

"About the three days I took?" It was the only thing that made any sense whatsoever to her. Maybe he'd been hurt by her taking so long. Maybe—please, God!—he was only hurt. Maybe he hadn't changed his mind. "You told me to take as long as I needed. You were adamant I do so. And I did need the time. I had a lot of important decisions to make."

Kell looked stunned at the mention of the three days. "The three days have nothing to do with why I'm angry."

"Then you are angry?"

"You're damned right I am!" he growled, ignoring the coffee the waitress hastily shoved before him.

Anne Elise ignored hers, too. "Why?"

The waitress beat a hasty retreat.

"You really don't know, do you?" he asked.

"No. I really don't."

"Do you think I live so far back in the hills that I don't even have TV?"

The question was so unexpected and seemed so inappropriate to the conversation that for several seconds Anne Elise was dumbfounded. "What has that got to do with your being angry?"

"Everything, *Madame Chairperson*!"

"You saw me on TV?" she asked, as though she could hardly believe the news had traveled so quickly. She'd wanted to be the one to tell him of her decision.

"The nation saw you," he retorted.

"But I still don't see—" Suddenly she stopped. Suddenly she understood. Maybe. A burst of happiness tripped the light fantastic down her frightened senses. "You think—"

"I'll tell you what I think," he interrupted, his face grim with anger. "I think I'm three times a fool for sitting here waiting for you to dump me. I also think you're a bigger fool than I am. If possible. Let me tell you something, lady. Life isn't black or white. You have to live a lot of it in that gray middle. And your gray middle, like it or not, is the fact that you'll never know for certain where your husband's buried. You're never going to have this closure that seems so damned important to you. And even if you had positive proof, I'm still not sure you could walk away. You've been on this merry chase for answers for seventeen years, and, all in all, it's a pretty safe chase. As long as you're on it, you don't have to really get involved with life, with anyone. But let me tell you something else, lady. You've got a helluva lot of cold nights ahead of you.'' He smiled sarcastically. ''But then,'' he said, fingering the silver bracelet, ''you can snuggle up to this.''

On that, he stood and stalked away, sloshing coffee on the table in the process.

''Kell!''

He didn't even acknowledge that she was anywhere in the world. He just kept right on walking...out the coffee-shop door.

''Kell!'' she called scrambling behind him. In scooting from the table, she spilled her coffee, too.

The waitress seemed less upset with the mess than with the fact that the coffee hadn't been paid for. ''Hey, wait! The coffee!'' she cried, starting after her fleeing customers.

Startled onlookers turned to view the strange sight of a man, tall, dark and broody, being pursued by a strikingly attractive woman, both of whom in turn were chased by a gray-haired waitress, the latter's pink apron flapping as the rubber soles of her comfy shoes went splat splat against the tile floor.

''Dammit, Chaisson, will you wait!'' Anne Elise hollered, her hand grasping a fistful of the back of his shirt and pulling it from his jeans.

He whirled. And started to speak. She, however, cut him off at the proverbial pass.

''You are unbelievably, disgustingly, totally obtuse!'' she cried, facing him like a she-tiger, which she was at that moment, a she-tiger fighting for what she wanted. She shoved her hand, the silver bracelet dangling about her wrist, forward. ''Read it.'' When Kell just stared, she repeated, ''Read the name on the bracelet! Or I swear I'll punch you out right here!''

He obeyed the commanding tone of her voice. Possibly because he believed her capable of what she was threatening. Sergeant Major William Dolliver, the bracelet read. And not the familiar name he'd expected to see—not First Lieutenant James Samuel Butler. Kell frowned, his eyes finding Anne Elise's.

She pulled her hand away, using it to thread back her auburn hair, which had gone wild in her haste. Her eyes met his squarely. "I've buried my personal past," she said, thinking how she'd called her lawyer's office that morning to start proceedings to have her husband declared legally dead, "but I can't bury the cause. I can't turn my back on the league. And the reason I can't is simple. Not everyone was lucky enough to have a pigheaded SOB named Kell Chaisson walk into her life."

Kell, not daring to believe what he was hearing, nonetheless felt a wave of pure exhilaration. "What are you saying?" he asked, his voice gnarled with emotion.

"What do you think I'm saying, Chaisson?"

"Say it."

"I'm saying that I love you—" her voice and her eyes had hazed "—I'm saying that I want to be your wife; I'm saying that I want you to make my cause yours and that I'll make yours mine; I'm saying—"

She never got the chance to say what else she was saying, for Kell, with the power of impatience, roughly pulled her into his arms and buried her in his embrace.

The amused onlookers burst into spontaneous applause.

Someone shouted, "Way to go!"

The waitress sighed a heartfelt, "Ah."

Kell pushed Anne Elise from him just far enough to see her face. Quiet tears welled in her emerald eyes; his own brown eyes were none too clear. He lowered his head, his mouth quickly, fiercely taking hers. As he did so, he whispered, "I love you." Followed by, "Let's get the hell outta here."

"Wait!" Anne Elise said. "Give me a dollar."

Kell didn't ask why—at that moment he'd have given her the world without a single question. Fishing a dollar from his pocket, he handed it to her. She, in turn, handed it to the waitress.

"Be happy," the gray-haired woman said.

"You can bet on it," Anne Elise replied. She then slipped into the crook of Kell's waiting arm, looked up into his face and said, "Let's get the heck outta here, Captain."

Epilogue

Life is not an exercise in black and white," Anne Elise said, her voice coming through the sophisticated P.A. system of the Washington, D.C., hotel ballroom. "Most people, certainly those of us assembled here, have of necessity lived much of our lives in a vague gray area. We've struggled to make it through dark nights; we've fought to keep body and soul together; we've prayed to know what to tell our children...and ourselves. Let us be comforted tonight by the knowledge that there were no right or wrong decisions for us to make. There were only decisions. And that each of us made them, and continues to make them, to the best of our abilities."

The ballroom, dotted with tables around which sat league members and their families, was so quiet that one could have heard a pin drop. Everyone there clung to the speaker's every word. For the six months that she'd led the organization, what Anne Elise Terris Butler Chaisson lacked in refined speaking skills, she'd made up for with heart-warming sincerity. Audiences worshipped her, the press adored her, and the man in the back of the room—the man who could always be found in the back of whatever room she was speaking in, cockily leaning against the wall as if he owned it and the world—loved her. To distraction.

"Someone once said that sometimes anyone left is called a hero. That definition, to be sure, is simple, perhaps even glib, for the man who said it—" Anne Elise's gaze brushed that of the man who stood at the back of the room "—was negating the medals of valor this country had awarded him for bravery, all more than earned, all more than deserved, but the truth is he may have spoken with a sageness he did not intend. For the simple truth is that each one of us is a hero, a heroine, by dint of the fact that we were left behind...and that we chose to move forward with our lives in positive ways."

A woman at the front table dabbed at her eyes. A member of the press snapped a picture of the action, then took a quick shot of the inspirational speaker. The man in the back of the room still had reservations about his hero status; he had none about the speaker's. Nor did he have any about how dynamite she looked in the simple-lined, spice-colored suit that enhanced the auburn of her hair. The string of pearls he'd given her as a wedding gift was the perfect addition to her classy look. In fact, she looked so dynamite, so classy, that he was counting the minutes until he could remove both the suit and the pearls.

"As you know, I, and my husband, leave for Vietnam in two weeks to talk to officials there about our missing men." Anne Elise smiled. "It helps to have a father in high places." Laughter skipped about the room, accompanied by a smattering of applause. "Perhaps for some of you," she said, the smile now gone, "I can bring back the news you've long waited for. I can think of nothing I'd like more. But for those of us left, we will continue to live life in that vague gray area; we will continue to make the choices we must; we will continue to go forward with our lives ... with the sure and certain knowledge that our loved ones would want no less. I close tonight with a heartfelt thank-you for all your letters of support. Good night, and God bless.''

Anne Elise moved back from the microphone. She watched as the audience, almost in one motion, rose to its feet. As always, when such an ovation occurred, and it was often, she felt humbled. As she stepped from the platform onto the floor, a swarm of people surrounded her. Cameras flashed; chatter erupted. Dividing her attention, she searched for the man who'd stood at the back of the room. Within minutes, she saw his hand, strong and bronzed, reach out to her. When she placed her hand in his, he tightened his hold.

Encircling the man's wrist was a silver bracelet. The name on it was First Lieutenant James Samuel Butler. It was worn as a personal pledge to a man Kell had never met, a pledge that he would always take care of the woman this man had been forced to leave behind. Had the tables been turned, Kell hoped James Samuel Butler would have done the same for him. Right now, Kell hoped he could tactfully, and quickly, get his wife out of the crowd and back to their room.

His wife.

He could never quite believe the simplicity of those words. *His wife.* He hadn't truly believed the minister who'd pronounced her so in the small ceremony in which both the general and his wife had cried, the stern soldier not even bothering to hide his emotion. Nor had he truly believed it all during their honeymoon, which they'd spent in Bangkok at the Hilton International Hotel, the bridal suite of which still overlooked the inspirational Nai Lert Shrine. He still found it hard to believe when he'd moved into her Dallas condo and harder to believe on the frequent weekends when they returned to the Arkansas hills, for the hills had always been a lonely retreat at best. It came closest to sinking in when they'd moved Brooke onto the Southern Methodist University campus for the fall semester. They'd looked like every other family there. A family. For the first time in his life, he'd been part of an honest-to-God family!

As pleasant as the intrusive thoughts were, he turned his mind back to the mission at hand. It took some doing, some diplomatic doing, but finally he was leading Anne Elise toward the elevator—his silver-braceleted hand holding her silver-braceleted hand. The elevator filled quickly and to capacity. Wordlessly Kell pulled his wife to him until her back was flush with his chest. He slipped an arm around her waist. Discreetly, she edged her hips intimately into him. It was a game they played on elevators. Anne Elise called it claustrophobia therapy. A psychologist would have called it behavior modification. Whatever it was called, it worked. It was hard to be afraid of a cubicle that had become one of the sexiest places in the world.

One by one, two by two, the passengers exited. Kell and Anne Elise worked their way to the back of the elevator, she still nudged seductively against him. The last couple departed on the sixteenth floor. As the elevator doors slid closed, Anne Elise turned in her husband's arms, sliding hers around his neck.

"Scared?" she asked, moving her hips provocatively.

"Yeah," he growled. "That we're not gonna make it back to the room before I start ripping off your clothes."

She laughed. He lowered his head and brushed those laughing lips with his. "Have I told you how incredibly proud I am of you?" he asked seriously.

She hesitated, as if considering. "Not today. Yesterday, the day before, but not today."

"I'm incredibly proud of you."

"I'm incredibly glad you're proud of me. And I'm incredibly proud of you," she said, her mouth grazing his. Her tongue teased like a sensual dancer.

"You're also incredibly sassy tonight, aren't you?"

She looked at him, her eyes wide and bright. "Possibly, maybe, could be."

"I'd say definitely, without a doubt, and—" the elevator door opened "—here's our floor, Miss Sass." This last he said as he threw her over his shoulder like a sack of flour and started off down the hall.

"Kell Chaisson! Put me down this minute!" she squealed, her imperative punctuated with giggles.

"Are you gonna behave?"

"Yes . . . yes . . . I promise I'll be good!"

"Wrong answer."

Anne Elise giggled again. "Then I'll be bad!"

Kell, balancing his precious cargo, fitted the key into the lock and turned the knob. "How bad?" he asked, stepping into the room and closing the door. He drew her from his shoulder and slowly—so slowly every inch of her body slid along his, breast to chest, belly to belly, femininity to masculinity—lowered her to the floor.

"Very . . . very . . . bad," she purred on the deliciously decadent descent.

"That's better," he said around a groan.

Anne Elise was seeing his grin so often she was beginning to think it normal. His new attitude was even reflected in his work. When sent on a troubleshooting assignment, he tried to diplomatically talk through to a solution before resorting to force. Of course, he never backed down from what had to be done—Kell Chaisson had forgotten more about fighting than most men would ever know about it. He just seemed to have little need for violent release these days.

As Anne Elise watched, the grin faded. Kell, his face a sudden study in raw need, claimed her lips in one swift second. She met his need in kind, her mouth consuming even as it was consumed. His tongue, nimble and sure, thrust deep inside, sipping, savoring, out-and-out seducing.

Abruptly, as though overpowered with emotion, he wrenched his mouth from hers and crushed her tightly to him.

"God, I love you!" he groaned.

"I love you, too," she whispered into his shoulder. He wore a golden-yellow sport coat, which, combined with his dark good looks, had turned more than one woman's head that evening. Anne Elise had noticed and had felt a keen sense of pride and ownership. She felt both again as she rested her cheek against the soft wool and the hard man.

"I've never loved like this before," he said, as though suddenly feeling it important that she know this.

"Neither have I."

Both knew they were speaking the truth. Each had loved before—softly, gently, in never-to-be-forgotten ways. Their love for each other, however, was different. It possessed an intensity that made each tremble, a strength that awed, a power that defied description and logic. And it grew—by the day, by the hour, by the minute.

Eager for a taste of him, Anne Elise lifted her head, her lips brushing his neck and the curve of his square jaw. Her lips nipping first at his mustache, they then eased onto his. This kiss was slow and wet.

Kell moaned. And, cupping her hips, pulled her into the thick heat of him. Shamelessly, sassily, she rubbed against him.

"See how bad you make me?" she whispered.

He ground himself against her. "Feel how badly you make me want you? Good Lord, Anne Elise, stop that!"

"When?"

"In a year or so!"

She laughed...throatily,...like a siren. Suddenly her laughter stopped. Drawing a crooked finger across his cheek, she whispered, "Make love to me."

No matter how many times she made the request—and she wasn't shy about making it—Kell couldn't believe he'd heard correctly. But then, there were a lot of things he couldn't believe. Principally he couldn't believe that he was no longer alone.

Threading his fingers in her hair, he kissed her—slowly, deeply. Her mouth, her senses, stung with his arousing play. She felt as hot as a Texas July, though the cool winds of an Eastern autumn stirred outside the hotel window.

"You taste good," she breathed.

"You taste sexy."

Scooping her in his arms, his mouth still on hers, he carried her to the bed and laid her atop it. Wordlessly, he followed her down. In the rustle of fabric, in the whisper of lace, in the sigh of satin, Kell undressed them both. When they were bare, he sinuously, sensuously, slid his body over hers. Without preamble, Anne Elise pulled him to her. Without preamble, he entered her—forcefully, powerfully.

She called his name.

He worshiped the feel of her.

"Oh, God, baby, take all of me!" he growled, pushing even deeper. And then he began to make love to her, in every way he knew...until her body sang and her breath ceased to be. Then, when she doubted she could stand any more, he loved her again. At that moment when heaven and earth met, each cried the other's name.

And then there was silence.

A silence into which fell a long while later, "Kell?"

"Hmm?"

"We broke the bed."

"I know. You're just gonna have to learn to curb your passion."

"Me?"

"Certainly you."

"It wasn't me who—"

"It certainly was."

"*Au contraire,* Chaisson."

"*Au, au contraire,* Mrs. Chaisson."

"Are we gonna fight over this?"

"I hope so. I like the making up part."

"There! That's exactly the move that broke the bed."

"Shut up."

A giggle, a sigh, a moan. And then there was silence. A sweet silence. A contented silence. A love-filled silence to last the love-filled years.

* * * * *

Silhouette Special Edition

presents

LOVE AND GLORY

from
Lindsay McKenna

Introducing a gripping new series celebrating our men—and
women—in uniform. Meet the Trayherns, a military family as proud
and colorful as the American flag, a family fighting the shadow of
dishonor, a family determined to triumph—with
LOVE AND GLORY!

June: **A QUESTION OF HONOR** (SE #529) leads the fast-paced
excitement. When Coast Guard officer Noah Trayhern offers
Kit Anderson a safe house, he unwittingly endangers his own
guarded emotions.

July: **NO SURRENDER** (SE #535) Navy pilot Alyssa Trayhern's
assignment with arrogant jet jockey Clay Cantrell threatens her
career—and her heart—with a crash landing!

August: **RETURN OF A HERO** (SE #541) Strike up the band to
welcome home a man whose top-secret reappearance will make
headline news . . . with a delicate, daring woman by his side.

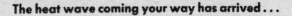